*"Shh,"* Caliga                                                                    *t."*

The silvery notes enfolded her, soothed her, eased

she had found.

*"Yes."*

"Wait," she said, fighting against it, fighting . . . why was she fighting?

*Because I am a fighter. That's what I am.*

Because something here was not right.

Buffy blinked at the silver door.

But it wasn't a door. She was standing in the mirror maze, staring at herself in one of the panels. Alone. Her reflection stared back at her.

"Mom?" she called.

The calliope music played.

*"A-hunting we will go, a hunting we will go . . .*

*"Come to me. Be with me. Your pride will be your greatest pleasure. And you should be proud. You are one of a kind. The only one in all your generation."*

"Come to you," Buffy said, reaching out a hand toward the mirror.

Something reached back.

And grabbed hold.

Hard.

# Buffy the Vampire Slayer™

Buffy the Vampire Slayer
(movie tie-in)
The Harvest
Halloween Rain
Coyote Moon
Night of the Living Rerun
Blooded
Visitors
Unnatural Selection
The Power of Persuasion
Deep Water
Here Be Monsters
Ghoul Trouble
Doomsday Deck
Sweet Sixteen
Crossings
Little Things

The Angel Chronicles, Vol. 1
The Angel Chronicles, Vol. 2
The Angel Chronicles, Vol. 3
The Xander Years, Vol. 1
The Xander Years, Vol. 2
The Willow Files, Vol. 1
The Willow Files, Vol. 2
How I Survived My Summer Vacation,
Vol. 1
The Cordelia Collection, Vol. 1
The Faith Trials, Vol. 1
The Journals of Rupert Giles, Vol. 1
Tales of the Slayer, Vol. 1
Tales of the Slayer, Vol. 2
Tales of the Slayer, Vol. 3
Tales of the Slayer, Vol. 4

The Postcards
The Essential Angel Posterbook
The Sunnydale High Yearbook
Pop Quiz: Buffy the Vampire Slayer
The Monster Book
The Script Book, Season One, Vol. 1
The Script Book, Season One, Vol. 2
The Script Book, Season Two, Vol. 1
The Script Book, Season Two, Vol. 2
The Script Book, Season Two, Vol. 3
The Script Book, Season Two, Vol. 4
The Script Book, Season Three, Vol. 1
The Script Book, Season Three, Vol. 2
The Musical Script Book: Once More, With Feeling
The Watcher's Guide, Vol. 1: The Official Companion to the Hit Show
The Watcher's Guide, Vol. 2: The Official Companion to the Hit Show
The Watcher's Guide, Vol. 3: The Official Companion to the Hit Show

The Lost Slayer serial novel
Part 1: Prophecies
Part 2: Dark Times
Part 3: King of the Dead
Part 4: Original Sins
Omnibus Edition

Child of the Hunt
Return to Chaos
The Gatekeeper Trilogy
Book 1: Out of the Madhouse
Book 2: Ghost Roads
Book 3: Sons of Entropy
Obsidian Fate
Immortal
Sins of the Father
Resurrecting Ravana
Prime Evil
The Evil That Men Do
Paleo
Spike and Dru: Pretty Maids
All in a Row
Revenant
The Book of Fours
Tempted Champions

Oz: Into the Wild
The Wisdom of War
These Our Actors
Blood and Fog
Chosen
Chaos Bleeds
Mortal Fear
Apocalypse Memories
Wicked Willow Trilogy
The Darkening
Shattered Twilight
Broken Sunrise
Stake Your Destiny
The Suicide King
Keep Me in Mind
Colony
Night Terrors
Queen of the Slayers
Spark and Burn
Afterimage
Carnival of Souls

**Available from SIMON & SCHUSTER**

# Carnival of Souls

## Nancy Holder

**An original novel based on the hit television series
created by Joss Whedon**

## SIMON SPOTLIGHT ENTERTAINMENT

New York   London   Toronto   Sydney

This book is a work of fiction. Any references to historical events, real people, or real locales are used fictitiously. Other names, characters, places, and incidents are the product of the author's imagination, and any resemblance to actual events or locales or persons, living or dead, is entirely coincidental.

**S|S|E**

SIMON SPOTLIGHT ENTERTAINMENT

An imprint of Simon & Schuster Children's Publishing Division

1230 Avenue of the Americas, New York, New York 10020

TM & © 2006 Twentieth Century Fox Film Corporation. All rights reserved.

All rights reserved, including the right of reproduction in whole or in part in any form.

SIMON SPOTLIGHT ENTERTAINMENT and related logo are trademarks of Simon & Schuster, Inc.

Manufactured in the United States of America

First Edition 10 9 8 7 6 5 4 3 2 1

Library of Congress Control Number 2005933337

ISBN-13: 978-1-4169-1182-1

ISBN-10: 1-4169-1182-0

In memory of Belle's beloved grandfather,
George Wayne Holder.
*We miss you, Papa Wayne.*

# Acknowledgments

As always, my thanks first and foremost to Joss Whedon; and to Sarah Michelle Gellar, David Boreanaz, David Greenwalt, Tim Minear, Marti Noxon, David Fury, and the many other producers, actors, and staffs of both *Angel* and *Buffy*. My deepest gratitude to my agent and dear friend, Howard Morhaim, and to his assistant, Allison Keiley. Thank you to Patrick Price, who has been such a wonderful editor and a writer's true friend in the publishing loop; and to Debbie Olshan at Fox, whose insights have kept me out of more trouble. Thanks to the *Buffy* and *Angel* fan clubs, Abbie Bernstein, Tara DeLullo, Kristy Bratton; Titan/Dreamwatch; Inkworks; cityofangel.com; litvamp, saveangel.com, IAMTW, novelscribes, SF-FFWs, Persephone, and Buffy Studies gurus David Lavery and Rhonda Wilcox;

Ashley McConnell, Monica Elrod, Terri Grazer Yates, Linda Wilcox, Karen Hackett, Barbara Nierman, Elisa Jimenez-Steiger, Ellen Greenfield, Wayne Holder, Amy Shricker, Jennifer and Janice Kayler; and Christie and Richard Holt; to Steve Perry; Del and Sue Howison, Lydia Marano and Art Cover, the YaYa's— Lucy Walker, Anny Caya, Leslie Ackel Jones, Elise Jones, Kerri Ingle, and Belle Holder; to Sandra Morehouse and Richard Wilkinson; to Bob Vardeman, and Jeff Mariotte and Maryelizabeth Hart. Thanks to Andy Thompson at Family Karate for teaching us to live the black belt way. Lisa Clancy, you are my Termie. Belle Holder, you're my daughter, and I love you. Courtesy, integrity, perseverance, self-control, indominitable spirit.

# Carnival of Souls

# Prologue

It was Tuesday.

After nightfall.

In Sunnydale.

And Buffy Summers the Vampire Slayer was out on patrol instead of at the Bronze with Willow and Xander (and hopefully Angel) because Giles had figured out that tonight was the Rising.

The Rising of what, Buffy's watcher did not know, but it was easy to guess that it probably meant vampires. Maybe zombies. Something that rose from graves, anyway.

Something that kept her from the fun other sixteen-year-olds were having.

Sighing, Buffy trailed her fingers over the lowered head of a weeping cherub statue and waved her flashlight in an arc.

"Here, rising guys," she called plaintively. "Ready to play when you are."

She had on her black knitted cap and Angel's black leather jacket, but she was still a little chilly. Maybe it was just because she was walking through Blessed Memories, the graveyard that contained the du Lac tomb, famed in the annals of Buffy's diary as the graveyard out of which Spike and Dru had stolen a fancy decoding cross called, amazingly enough, the du Lac Cross. They had used it to nearly kill Angel. Since then, it was not her favorite cemetery ever.

Blessed Memories also contained a pet cemetery, a little square of plots with miniature headstones that tugged at Buffy's heart. TOBY MY PUP RIP 1898. R KITTIE LUCY 1931. She had no time for pets, not even zombie cats freshly risen from the grave. She had hardly any time for anything, what with the slayage and the studying, okay, not the studying; but still and all, it was Sunnydale that was the problem, with all its death and monsters and standard normal-teenage-girl pressures, like having friends and not getting kicked out of school. . . .

*If my best buds and I could be anywhere but here, that would be . . .* She thought for a moment. She and Willow were really good at that game. Anywhere But Here was created for high school kids, especially those who had to live in Sunnydale.

*. . . in Maui, with Angel. . . . Okay, not. Too much sun for a boyfriend who would burst into flames if he stepped into the tropical rays. So . . .*

*. . . in Paris, with Angel . . . and Willow could be with James Spader—I officially give him to her*

*because I'm with Angel now—and we're so not eating snails, but oh, I know! French pastries. And we are shopping . . .*

*. . . for rings . . .*

Buffy stopped and cocked her head. Did she just hear something? Snap of a twig, maybe? A cough?

She listened eagerly for a replay so she could head toward it. She waited. Waited yet more. Heard nothing. Turned off her flashlight. More waiting.

Behold the sounds of silence.

She tried to pick up the Paris thread again. French pastries, okay, maybe too early in the relationship to shop for rings, then for shoes. . . . Truth was, she really *would* be happy to be just about anywhere but here. If only she could just run away, join in the fun-having of other kids her age. Join the circus, even.

Except she didn't like circuses. Never had. What was with those clowns, anyway? She shivered. She was with Xander on that one: They gave her a wiggins.

*Send in the clowns.*

Six miles away, just past the outbuildings of Crest College, the trees shivered. The clouds fled and the moon trailed after them, desperate to hide.

Sunnydale, loaded with souls ripe for the plucking . . .

Five miles away.

The clowns materialized first, big feet flapping, overstuffed bottoms wiggling, in polka dots and rainbow stripes, and white gloves hiding fingers that no one should ever see.

A jag of lightning:

A parade of trucks, wagons, lorries. A maroon wagon, its panels festooned with golden Harlequins and bird women plucking lyres, shimmered and stayed solid. Behind it, a Gypsy cart with a Conestoga-style bonnet jangled with painted cowbells, and beneath the overhanging roof, black-and-silver ribbons swayed. Behind the wagon, a forties-era freight truck blew diesel exhaust into the velvet layers of moonlight. A jagged line, creaking back into shadows, disappearing. Maybe the entire apparition was just a dream.

Thunder rolled, and they reappeared.

Maybe they were just a nightmare.

Spectral horses whinnied and chuffed; it began to rain, and through the murky veil of downpour and fog, the horses' heads were skulls; their heads were . . . heads. They breathed fire; they didn't breathe at all.

They began to rot in slow motion.

The clowns ran up and down the advancing line, applauding and laughing at the flicker-show, the black magic lantern extravaganza.

Skeletons and corpses hunkered inside truck and wagon cabs and buckboard seats. Whipcracks sparked. Eyes lolled. Mouths hung open, snapped shut. Teeth fell out. Eyes bobbed from optic nerves.

Things . . . reassembled.

A creak, and then nothing.

Two ebony steeds pulled the last vehicle—the thirteenth wagon in the cortege. It was an old Victorian traveling-medicine-show wagon, maybe something that had crisscrossed the prairies and the badlands, promising remedies for rheumatism and the gout when the only ingredients in the jug were castor oil, a dead rattlesnake, and wood alcohol.

Where their hooves touched, the earth smoked. Black feathers bobbing in their harnesses, black feathers waving from the four corners of the ornate, ebony wagon, the horses were skeletons were horse flesh were demon stallions ridden by misshapen, leathery creatures with sagging shoulder blades, flared ears, and pencil-stub fingers. And as the moon shied away from the grotesquerie, the angle of light revealed words emblazoned on each of the thirteen vehicles that snuck toward Sunnydale, home to hundreds of thousands of souls determined to ignore the peril they were in:

*PROFESSOR CALIGARI'S TRAVELING CARNIVAL*

The wind howled through the trees—or was it the ghostly dirge of a calliope?

Too soon to tell.

Too late to do anything about it.

# Chapter One

*What the heck is that?* Buffy wondered as she stepped from beneath the shelter of a tomb in Shady Rest, cemetery number eight on her hit parade of twelve. The repeated hollow sounds, which maybe were musical notes, had coincided with the stopping of the rain. They were even stranger than the Hindi songfest she had watched with Willow and Xander, the one about the podiatrist and the water buffalo.

She listened hard. Was it a distant boom box? Did it have anything—*please*—to do with the Rising? It would be so nice if something actually happened before she packed it in, aside from ripping her black leather pants on the chain-link fence she'd hopped to get in there. Plus dropping her big black flashlight, which now no longer worked.

There it was again, kind of a sinister tootling or something. . . . She was already trying to figure out how to describe it to Giles. It was nothing she had ever heard before.

A terrified shriek pierced the darkness.

Ah! But *that* was!

The Slayer brightened. No, no, not brightened— because that would be wrong—so much as erupted into action, racing toward the plea for help. She put on the turbo as the shriek was joined by a cry, this one lower in pitch. A guy and a girl, then.

Without her flashlight, Buffy scrutinized the passing shadows: grave, grave, crypt, tree draped with moss, grave, stone vase of dead flowers, darkness. Naturally whatever was going down, would go down in darkness. It was the way of evil.

From the sleeve of Angel's leather jacket, she pulled out a stake. Well-whittled death, that was the way of the Slayer.

She ran into the black gloom, her gorgeous and, unfortunately, suede boots crunching wet leaves and twigs, and a plastic drink cup—wishing now for Angel's help, because he could see in the dark—and then she stepped on, or rather in, something slippery and gross—okay, maybe it was okay that he wasn't here to witness that.

"Oh my God! Help!" screamed a girl. She was maybe twenty yards to Buffy's left . . . and she was being pursued by something big—make that a lot of something bigs, judging by the rhythmic thudding of many footfalls.

"Stephanie!" yelled a guy. From the somewhat familiar sound of his voice, Buffy figured him for David Hahn; and that would mean these were the Hahn twins. Sophomores, kind of geeky, definitely not part of the socially acceptable crowd. They both had scraggly teeth, which couldn't really be laid at the door of fault; but no one was forcing them to appear in public with monumentally bad hair, unless they were under a curse or something.

"David!!" Stephanie shouted.

"The Hahns it is," Buffy crowed under her breath as she homed in on their voices.

She did a huge leap across an open grave—*hmm, the Rising, as in finally rising from a grave?*—and landed hard in a pile of leaves.

There they were, two freaked-out figures dashing through a patch of moonlight. They were wearing baggy jeans and badly fitting sweaters with matching diamond patterns. The Hahns were as unfashionable, and therefore conspicuous, as vampires that had stayed underground too long, then tried to pass as regular kids.

The moonlight also revealed that the things after them *were* vampires, with elongated faces, mouths full of fangs, and glowing gold eyes. Not such good outfits on them, either, all dressed in black and thick, heavy boots—the total vamp fashion trend Spike seemed to have started. Maybe it would eventually die along with him.

"Vampires, *so* not a problem," Buffy muttered, gripping the stake in her fist as she ran toward the terrified twins. Stephanie and David were zigzagging, in an effort to dodge the monsters. Good strategy.

But the tallest of the vampires gained on them. He was scary-bad with tattoos—maybe brands—on his bald head and a motorcycle patch on his jacket that featured a skull wearing a pirate hat. The insignia read DEAD MEN TELL NO TALES, but Buffy knew that was wrong. In Sunnydale, the dead had lots to say.

Sure enough, the vampire caught David's sweater and gave it a good, hard yank. The fabric of the sweater ripped down the back, and the two sides flapped like wings.

"Hey! Stop that!" Buffy yelled, although truth be told, the vamp had done David a favor.

In response, one of the other vampires whirled around and hunched forward in a hulking stance with outstretched arms and slashing nails. Its hair was yellow-white, like Spike's, and it had piercings all over its face. The pose was meant to be menacing, and it would have been if Buffy weren't the Slayer and had therefore seen the same stance a bazillion times before.

"Didn't anyone tell you guys not to play with your food?" she asked the monster. It was a lame quip and she'd used it before, but she doubted the life of a stand-up comedian awaited her.

"The Slayer!" it shouted, maybe hoping to warn the others. Although, frankly, vampires were not usually known for their thoughtfulness.

"*C'est moi,*" she said, in a pretty good French accent if she did say so herself. Then she sprang forward so fast that it didn't have time to dart out of her way. It had a second to stare in shock at the thick end of Mr. Pointy's cousin sticking out of the dead-center heart area of its black T-shirt; and then—*whoosh!*—it exploded into a shower of dust.

One down, and she counted five more as she ran through the vampire dust, waving her hands in front of her face to keep it out of her eyes. It looked like none of the others were stupid enough—at least so far—to take up where this guy had left off. The remaining five were all busy dogging David and Stephanie.

Then one of the vamps began to lose ground. It was a female wearing a Sunnydale High School letter jacket, and as it turned to glance over its shoulder at the Slayer, Buffy recognized it. *Her.* Her name was Mariann Palmer, and they both had had Dr. Gregory for science before Miss French the giant praying mantis had decapitated him. Buffy felt a pang that she had not been able to save Mariann from becoming a vampire any more than she had been able to save Dr. Gregory from getting beheaded. But this was not the time for sentimental reunions or regrets. This was time to deal more vamp destruction.

Buffy used a flat gravestone in her path as a springboard to vault high into the air, and landed piggyback-style on Mariann's back.

Mariann—or, more correctly, the demon now

inhabiting her body—stumbled forward as Buffy shouted, "Ride 'em, cowgirl!"

Mariann whirled in a circle, her arms flailing, trying to grab Buffy's legs and/or throw Buffy off. It was like riding a mechanical bull—or so Buffy imagined.

Although Buffy's thighs were clamped against Mariann's sides and her ankles were locked across the vamp's stomach, Mariann kept trying to grab her arms, which was an indication that this particular evil undead was really stupid. If their positions had been reversed, Buffy would have (a) gone for her feet, which were dangling right in front of her; or (b) tucked into a forward roll, which might have resulted in her rider doing a face plant as she went over and down.

However, Mariann had yet to learn some strategic moves.

"And time is up!" Buffy exulted. "I win a silver buckle, and *you* win a trip to hell!"

Arcing both arms over the vampire's shoulders, she jabbed the stake toward Mariann's dead, unbeating heart, hard.

The stake hit the mark, and the demon inhabiting Mariann screamed. That's how Buffy had to think of it as the face and body of a girl Buffy had known exploded into dust.

As Buffy landed, the ground beneath her left heel gave way—a little sinkhole, a common problem with Sunnydale cemeteries, on account of all the tunnels and empty graves—and she swayed left and right, straining to maintain her balance.

Vamp number three, a big burly guy in a sleeveless denim vest, with closely shaven black hair and a goatee to match, took advantage of the moment to turn and charge her like a bull, head-butting her just beneath her rib cage.

With an "ooph!" Buffy tumbled backward, landing on her butt, then slamming her lower back against the edge of a low stone border outlining a grave. Her head smacked the gravestone proper. She saw stars and little birdies, but she ignored them as she scrabbled back up. No lying down on the job, especially if she didn't want to die on the job.

Rather than follow through with his attack, the vampire whirled around and caught up with the other three. She wondered why the forces of darkness stopped to take her on under any circumstances. If she were one of these vampires, she would take off as soon as she realized the Slayer had spotted her. Of course, if she were a vampire, she wouldn't be Buffy, who thought like that. She'd be a demon inhabiting a human body, with a whole new set of operating instructions: *Bite, rip, suck, maim, kill.*

The little birdies blurred into a gray haze, and Buffy steadied herself by grabbing on to the monument at the head of the plot—an obelisk topped with a cross—and realized she had let go of her stake. The world took shape again, pretty much; she glanced down and scanned the plot, her eyesight smeary. The dim, watery moonlight didn't help. If only she had some light.

It was *le grand boo-boo*—hey, she was thinking in French!—to have carried only one flashlight. There was so much to keep track of in the exciting world of slayage. Problem was, while she was still learning on the job, other people sometimes paid the price for her ignorance.

If she didn't get a move on, the other people might be David and Stephanie.

She reached up and broke off an overhanging tree branch, tapping her fingertips along the break to make sure it was good and sharp.

Ouch. It so was.

She broke off another one and slid it inside the sleeve of Angel's jacket.

Buffy resumed her pursuit, down a small hill and into a shallow stream sloshing over smooth, round pebbles. It was artificial, part of the landscaping of the cemetery. Her mom, Joyce, had once said it might be nice to be buried beside the little brook, which gave Buffy a wiggins, because who on earth wanted to think about their mom dying?

Speaking of dying, the twins had stopped screaming, but she was relieved to see that they were still running. That happened; people ran out of breath if they tried to do both. For most people there were usually two reactions to being attacked by vampires: fright—freezing in one's tracks, unable to move; or flight—running faster than you had ever dreamed was possible, usually without any plan for survival beyond putting as much distance between you and the thing that was after you.

For the Slayer there was another option: fight. That was what a slayer was born to do, lived to do—well, besides shopping and smoochies with Angel—and Buffy knew she was in full kick-ass mode as she burst into a record-breaking sprint after the vampire quartet. She wished Giles could see her. Maybe then he would let up on the training.

"Go to your right! There's a hole in the fence!" she shouted to David and Stephanie. "Go right!"

She had no idea if they could hear her, or if they *would* hear her. Blind panic could turn "Go right!" into "Smarfhsufl!" or make someone completely forget the difference between right and left. It was the adrenaline. It told you to forget everything except being afraid. She knew how that worked. Panic made you do the wacky.

"Go right!" she yelled again. Of course the *vampires* were listening to her, so they started cutting to the right, in anticipation of David and Stephanie's doing the same.

But the twins kept running forward. In fact, they were flying full speed ahead, not seeming to compute that they were about to run straight into the chain-link fence that bounded the perimeter of the graveyard. She grimaced, her mind fast-fowarding to the inevitable collision with the fence, the collapse to the ground, and the vampires either trying to tear out the twins' throats right there or carrying them off like so much delectable takeout.

"Stop going straight!" she ordered them, legs and arms pumping. She wasn't even sure they could put on the brakes in time, even if they could make sense of what she was saying.

Then she heard the weird music again, the weird tootling or organ or whatever—oh, it was a calliope.

*A calliope?*

And it was closer this time. Or maybe just louder.

She filed that away for a time when she could think about it, and kept running forward. The vampires had figured out that David and Stephanie weren't going to go toward the hole in the fence, and had veered back to the left, hot on their heels.

"Help!" Stephanie screamed.

That told Buffy that Stephanie wasn't completely out of her mind with fear, so she shouted, "Go to the left! Left! Left, left, left!"

But it was too late. Stephanie and David slammed into the fence at the same time, really crashing into it; and Buffy grimaced as she put on a burst of speed in hopes of getting to them before the vamps did.

Then, to Buffy's utter amazement, that section of the fence gave way. Clanging and rattling, it dropped forward just like a drawbridge on a castle. David and Stephanie ran right over it.

And so did the vampires.

Shrieking and clinging to each other—which was slowing them down—the twins disappeared into the dense forest just behind the graveyard. The vampires followed after, and Buffy brought up the rear.

The treetops sucked up the moonlight, and within seconds Buffy was running through pitch-black woods. Tree branches whipped her face and neck as the vampires pushed through them, then let them *fwap* backward. She smelled pine and tree resin.

"Stephanie! David! Where are you?" she shouted into the blackness as she raised her hands to shield her face and kept running.

That was when vampire number three tackled her *again* and the two sailed backward. Buffy kept hold of the vamp as her back slammed hard against a tree trunk. Straightening her arms, she immediately slid downward, hauling the vamp's face against the trunk. It roared in pain as it fell, and Buffy executed a totally righteous snapkick into its groin for good measure.

Then she rolled to the right, extricating herself before the vampire landed on top of her. Twigs snapped beneath its weight. Before it could react, Buffy flipped it over, straddled it, raised her arms above her head, and staked it.

Dustorama!

Three down, three to go.

Then it started to rain again.

"Great," she muttered, getting to her feet as big, ploppy drops tapped her on the head. She *had* to go and buy the suede boots, didn't she. Even after her mother reminded her that they weren't very practical. Joyce didn't know the half of it. But for a few brief weeks, they had been Buffy's pride and joy.

You'd think the Watchers Council would at least give her a clothing allowance, but no. Here she was saving the world and she could actually make more baby-sitting. No pay, no tips, no rewards, nothing. That was the definition of a sacred duty, she supposed: no gain, all pain.

Oh, well, nothing to be done about it now.

The rain muffled sound as she crashed through the dense stands of trees. There were fifty percent fewer vampires to deal with than when she had first given chase, but she figured they had been the slower, stupider ones. The vamps that were left were probably going to be able to run the twins to ground unless she got to them first.

Problem was, she couldn't tell where David and Stephanie had gone. She ran blindly into a thick tree limb and then very nearly got tripped by a root.

She looked upward and squinted into the rain, hoping for a slice of the moon to steer by, but the tree coverage was thick. A burst of helpful lightning, then? Or even the winking lights of a plane bound for Anywhere But Here?

Nada.

She exhaled, trying to come up with a plan B. But all her plan B's included flashlights.

She listened hard, hoping one of the Hahns would scream. Or not. Not screaming might mean they successfully got away. But few humans managed to outrun vampires. Which was why no one in Sunnydale seemed to know there *were* vampires. City Hall called them gangs on PCP, and everybody bought that, just another example of how hard people around here just didn't want to know.

She couldn't just stand here. She was all about moving and getting it done. Buffy tried to remember if she had ever seen a map of the forest. It was so hard to pay attention during Giles's stuffy, scone-y lectures. She had been startled to realize that what he called "training sessions"—air quotes there—were occasionally more like study hall, with quizzes on crystals and all kinds of stuff. Instead of whacking at Giles with a quarterstaff, she was forced to *sit in a chair* and memorize useless facts—

—useless facts such as the layouts of the graveyards, the school, and the rest of Sunnydale, including the forest.

*Not using air quotes now, are you, Buffy?*

She started running. Her boots squished in mud and tufts of grass. Her knitted cap grew sodden and heavy and she whipped it off as she galloped along, wondering if her eye makeup was running. She had gotten smart; she always wore waterproof mascara against just such an occasion as this. A *girl* watcher would have tips like that for a slayer. Whoever got to have a female watcher was lucky.

A bolt of lightning lit up the forest perimeter and she took note of the locations of the trees. Buffy saw a colorful flash of movement just before the shadows swallowed up the light. Purple splotches? Yellowish gray polka dots? She wasn't sure. But neither twin had been wearing busy patterns like that. None of the vamps, either, from what she had seen. But what she had seen *was* a pattern, or something mottled by the play of light and shadow.

That could only mean that someone *else* was in the forest. She approached cautiously, rain sluicing down her head to drip off the tip of her nose as she kept herself pointed in the direction of the flash. Thunder rumbled and she crossed her fingers for another crash of lightning. She wondered if he or she of the nonconformist outfit had spotted her and was just waiting for her to walk straight into his or her clutches—or his or her tentacles, or his or her huge, gaping maw.

*Before I moved to Sunnydale, I thought "maw" was Southernspeak for "mom." And I didn't realize that "exsanguinated" meant "completely drained of blood." Being the Slayer has certainly improved my vocabulary. There's a plus.*

She reached a hand forward, grabbing a hunk of pine branch and bending it out of her way.

A few more steps forward, and she realized she was at the same impasse as before. Options, options, who's got the options? Maybe she could climb a tree and—

Then she felt warm breath against the back of her neck, and a low, gravelly voice whispered, *"Boo!"*

Buffy whirled around with her arms outstretched.

There was nothing there, accompanied by a loud flapping of wings, and noisy cawing, like from a crow. Several. Birds were fluttering out of their sentry stations and flying away.

From . . . what?

"Okay, you got me. Very funny. Tag, I'm it," she said, raising a hand. Was it a ghost? Didn't matter, though. The Slayer motto was "Feel the wig and kill it anyway."

"You have my attention," Buffy said. "What do you want?"

As if in response, there was that weird music again. Yes, it was a calliope. The notes sounded off, very . . . very . . . She didn't have a good word for it, like exsanguinated or maw.

Just . . . *weird.*

Cascades of notes, barrels of them, rolled through the trees. The music sounded as if it were coming from the other side of the forest. Maybe whoever was playing it was trying to make some kind of statement. Maybe it was the supersized version of "Boo!" Or David or Stephanie had found the calliope and were sending out a distress call. Or the vamps were having a dinner show bizarro-world style. Someone was playing the hits of Zombie Broadway while the others sucked the Hahn twins dry.

The calliope music rose like a scream. The forest quaked as if every living thing was screaming right along with it.

Lacking any other plan, Buffy kicked it up a notch and ran like a bat out of hell, toward the music.

And voila! She heard the Hahns screaming again, and they were close. She followed, veering around some large bushes.

*Whoa. Where on earth did this come from?*

An illuminated white-painted wooden archway stretched about fifteen feet across a clearing. Baseball-size lightbulbs spelled out words: PROFESSOR CALIGARI'S TRAVELING CARNIVAL. Two columns formed an entryway decorated with painted clowns holding balloons.

*Brrr. Clowns.*

Behind the entrance, wind whipped the canvas flaps of a trio of two-story, multistriped tents. A darkened Ferris wheel cut a sharp silhouette in the night sky. Where did the twins go?

Inside the carnival, Buffy flew past a silent Tilt-A-Whirl and other rides, surrounded wooden buildings in crazy cartoon colors with garish, hand-painted signs proclaiming DOGS ON A STICK! CONES! COTTON CANDY!

And then she heard Stephanie scream.

Buffy followed the sound, shouting, "I'm right behind you!"

A calliope began to play, slowly, eerily. Up the scale, down the scale, warbling and trembling. The volume made the bones in Buffy's head vibrate.

There was another scream, barely audible above the playing. She followed it toward a large oblong tent. Above the tent flap door, which was popping in the wind, a curlicue sign read FUN HOUSE.

Buffy ran inside and found herself in a narrow, dark tunnel made of wood. Fake cobwebs draped overhead.

As Buffy took a step forward, a green light winked on about two feet above her head, revealing a realistic-looking skull and crossbones. The jawbone dropped open and the skull cried, "Arrr!" Crazy laughter bounced off the walls.

The skull was at the top of a T-intersection. She took advantage of the light to consider whether she should go right or left. The light went out. The cackling stopped.

She glanced quickly in both directions, and still had no clue which way to go. On the right: darkness. On the left: darkness, too.

She thought she heard another scream, but it was hard to be sure. Still, her Slayer reflexes responded to it the way mothers jump at the cry of a baby, and she resumed her dashing in the dark, hands outstretched. She hated running blind.

"Gah!" she shouted as a light flashed on and a clown hopped from the darkness on long, flappy shoes. Its lifeless eyes widened and its mouth opened in a wicked, spooky grin.

*Just a statue,* Buffy told herself, and ran on by. A chill ran down her spine. *Stupid clown statue.*

More lights flicked on overhead, dim-colored lightbulbs of blue, green, and red. Buffy spared a thought for the high-school boys who would traipse through here and take breaking those bulbs as a personal challenge.

Then she encountered another clown statue, this one with black Rasta braids and an evil, leering grimace that reminded her of Spike. It stood at the end of the next corner, light bearing straight down on it, concealing its eyes while highlighting its mouth.

Just for good measure, she said to it, "Stay."

It stayed where it was, and she jogged on, safe from her childhood fears.

But as for her sixteen-year-old fears, those were alive and kicking.

Another corner—she was in a maze that folded back upon itself, and back again—and then the lights got brighter, although no less colorful, and she put on the brakes when she realized she was running full tilt toward a mirror reflection of herself.

*Stop!* she told her entire body, but she couldn't slow down fast enough.

Shutting her eyes, she slammed into the mirror with horrendous impact. The breath was knocked out of her and she braced herself for the surface to shatter. But it didn't. She bounced off of it as if it were made of rubber, not glass.

She staggered backward, hitting the wall on the opposite side of the tunnel. It was also a mirror.

In front of her, Mirror Buffy frowned and rubbed her right shoulder.

She realized she had just begun to navigate a mirror maze, which would slow her down, so no joy there.

"Stephanie? David?" she shouted, but the calliope and the crazy laughter drowned her out.

Buffy thought about the kind of life one would have to have to think this fun house was fun.

She tentatively started moving forward and smacked into a mirror. Muttered, "O-kay," and tried turning to the right.

Bingo. She advanced one whole step.

Then she smacked into another mirror. She leaped back through one panel's worth of space and found another empty section to her left. Then to her left again. Then to her right.

In the next reflection, the clown with the black braids appeared behind her.

*Oh, God, it* is *alive!* she thought, whirring around in a fists-up fighter stance.

It had vanished.

Buffy looked back at her reflection.

The clown was there.

She darted to the left, to look at it in a different mirror.

It disappeared again. Trick?

She didn't have time to find out. She kept one eye on the mirrors as she found a space, and moved forward.

And reflected a thousand times in a galaxy far away, Stephanie Hahn's face opened its mouth and shrieked.

*Über-bingo!*

Buffy darted forward and touched the next mirror. It was solid. The next one, solid.

Her hand reached across the threshold of the next one. Empty space. *Yes!* Buffy jumped through it.

The next one, solid.

But forty-five degrees to the right, empty space.

Buffy stepped through.

Stepped through.

Solid.

Solid.

Solid.

She moved in a circle, touching a mirrored surface every time.

She groaned. Dead end.

She leaped back through one panel's worth of space and found another empty section to her left. Then to her left again. Then to her right.

The calliope stopped playing.

"Oh my God!" Stephanie cried somewhere off-stage. "Help us, someone! Help!"

"I'm here!" Buffy shouted. "Keep making noise!"

"Oh my God! Something's wrong with their faces. Their faces are . . . their faces . . ."

She trailed off. Buffy went super-alert, fearing the worst.

"Stephanie?"

"*My* face," Stephanie said slowly.

*Uh-oh, sounds like she's going into shock.*

The Slayer knew she had to pick up the pace. She flailed her arms as she began to run, crashing into another mirror. She tried to jump straight up, but the mirror reached down from the ceiling.

"Stephanie?"

She heard nothing.

"David?"

Nothing, squared.

Then she whipped around a corner and flew down a straightaway.

*Stephanie!*

"Okay, you're all right," Buffy told her, coming up behind her and putting her hands on her shoulders.

"Oh my God," Stephanie whispered without turning around.

"I know. It's okay now. Let's go save your brother."

Buffy wrapped her hand around Stephanie's and turned to go.

Stephanie stumbled, but she otherwise didn't move. She was staring at herself in the mirror.

"I'm so beautiful," she said. "I am the most beautiful thing I've ever seen."

Wow, she had gone completely catatonic or something. "You are a thing of beauty," Buffy humored her. "Now, come on."

Stephanie turned her head and studied her profile. "I never realized how *perfect* my nose is."

"We have got to go. Now," Buffy said, putting her hands on Stephanie's shoulders and looking hard into her myopic, very ordinary hazel eyes.

"But I'm-I'm so beautiful." Stephanie gazed back at the mirror.

Buffy hoisted Stephanie off her feet and slung her over her shoulder, firefighter style.

"Wait, no, I want to see myself!" Stephanie pleaded, reaching out with both her hands. "Am I still hot? I need to see if I'm still hot!"

"You so do not," Buffy muttered, and picked up the pace. Lucky thing about being the Slayer: Carrying a squirming body didn't slow her down terribly much.

She hustled on, stretching out her right hand as she held onto Stephanie with her left.

And then she found David. One vamp was holding his limp body; the other was diving in for a good chomp . . .

"Hel-*lo*," one of the vamps said as it turned and

spotted Buffy, with Stephanie still over her shoulder.

"Hel-*lo*," Stephanie cooed at it. Oh, God, she was flirting with a vampire.

"Shut up," Buffy said sternly. She set Stephanie down. "Stay here."

"My eyes," Stephanie sighed happily. "Do you see all the gold flecks in them?"

"Glad you're listening," Buffy said. Then she launched herself at the vamp that was holding David, rushing it as she extracted the extra tree branch from the sleeve of Angel's jacket.

The vamp tried shielding himself with David. Buffy reached down and slipped her arm behind David's knees. Then she lifted him up like a curtain, ducked underneath him, and rammed the tree branch through the vampire's heart.

It shrieked as it dusted. Number five came at her, and all she had to do was take another lunge forward and dust that one too.

The other one took off. Buffy let it go as she caught David and set him down. He was only semi-conscious, which was a good thing because it would keep the cost of his therapy down once this was all over and he started acting out. There were puncture holes, but the bleeding had already stopped, which was a good sign unless it meant that he was dead. Which he was not.

The dead don't drool.

She tore off a section of his god-awful sweater, breaking the ends, and wrapped it around his neck like a scarf. He was wearing a green-and-brown plaid button-down shirt beneath the sweater. It was hideous. He looked even nerdier than before, and she honestly had not thought that would be possible.

"David, wake up. We have to go," Buffy said to him, giving him an experimental shake.

"Hey, what?" David murmured, half-opening his eyes. "You're not Stephanie."

"Shh," Buffy urged him. "Can you stand?"

He nodded. She helped him to his feet, but he drooped over her shoulder and she picked him up. Then she turned to Stephanie, who was staring at herself again and said, "Earth to Stephanie Hahn. Your brother is wounded and we need to get out of here."

"Wh-what?" Stephanie blinked as if someone had slapped her. She was coming out of it, whatever "it" was. "Who—Buffy Summers? From school?" She looked around. "Where are we?"

"Somewhere we shouldn't be," Buffy replied. "Come on."

Clearly perplexed, Stephanie took Buffy's offered hand. Her brow wrinkled as she gazed at her brother.

"Where are we? What happened?" Stephanie asked again, stumbling along behind Buffy. Buffy didn't like having her there. It was a vulnerable position. But Buffy had to remain on point, which was even more vulnerable.

No time to worry about it; she hustled along as fast as she could, bumping into mirrors, finding the path. There was a flash of red in the corner of one mirror; of green in another.

"What are you doing here?" a voice demanded. It was low and deep, and from a darkened doorway about ten feet to the Slayer's right.

Moonlight silhouetted the figure of a man. Tall, thin, and hunched, and wearing a dress? There was some kind of hat on his head.

A harsh fluorescent light flicked on.

His face was thin, and long, and etched with lines like muddy ruts in a road. Long white hair tumbled down over his shoulders. He wasn't wearing a dress, but a black satin bathrobe covered with stars embroidered in black. His red hat was the kind of hat an organ-grinder monkey wore, with a tassel and all that. Not that she had ever actually seen an organ-grinder monkey. But she had read about them during her *Curious George* period.

His bony hand was on a light switch. Dark, purple veins bulged through the white skin. His fingernails were way too long. This was not a person who was going to stare into a mirror and tell himself he was hot.

"Ah," Buffy said. "Hi."

"Hey," Stephanie added, letting go of Buffy. She sidled toward him. "New in town?"

"Yes, I'm new in town. This is my carnival, and you kids are trespassing," he snapped at her. He crossed his arms over his chest. He had hair on his ears and the pupils in his eyes were a little too big.

Buffy's jangle vibes were off the charts.

"Sneaking around, destroying my property . . ."

The scrap of sweater had loosened around David's neck, revealing the vampire bite. Moving fast, Buffy covered it with her palm and said, "No destroying—just wacky teen pranks. We came here on a dare and we kind of got lost and now it's time to say good night, and we are *so* sorry."

"This is your carnival?" Stephanie said, drifting closer. "Wow. That's so cool." She actually fluttered her lashes. "I'm Stephanie. Most of my friends call me . . . Stephanie."

*You* have *no friends,* Buffy wanted to say. Was she actually coming on to this weird guy?

The man swept his gaze up and down Stephanie, grinning with dark brown teeth. "You are very lovely," he said.

"I know," she cooed, smiling at him like smiling at him was doing him a favor.

He seemed charmed, which increased his skank factor. He tore his attention from Stephanie to David and said, "Is he all right?"

"Just too much fun," Buffy said. "He, ah, he goes to bed early because he's a jock. . . ." She winced. There was no way David Hahn could be mistaken for a person who exercised. He was thin and skinny and on the destined-to-be-picked-on size.

"I see." He ticked his glance from David to Buffy. "And how are *you* feeling?"

It sounded like a trick question. She kept her eyes wide and innocent as she answered, "Great! Never better. I'm all about staying up late and . . . leaving." She nodded at him. "So, we'll just do that."

At that moment David raised his head and blinked a couple of times. He looked at Buffy, then at Stephanie, and said, "Hey."

Buffy took that as her cue. "And I am feeling so very much all right that I can walk my friends home now. So."

"I was practicing my calliope," the man said, his voice shifting. He was changing the subject. "I would have heard you sneaking around if I hadn't been so devoted to my instrument." He pulled back his lips, which would technically be termed a smile. Lots of dark brown dental problems. "Would you like to stay and listen for a while?"

"Oh, no. No, we're late as it is. We got kind of lost and . . . good fun house," Buffy assured him. She recalled the one vamp getting away. "You might want to lock it up for the night. And maybe go into your . . . where you sleep, because there's other, ah, kids out, you know, mischief-making." *And hang some garlic and crosses on the doors.*

"Your concern is touching," he said. He slid his fingers into the pocket of his robe and fished around. Buffy tensed.

Then he pulled out a handful of colorful cardboard rectangles.

"Here are some tickets. Bring your friends. Tell them they can get in free *legitimately* during our operating hours."

"Oh, you are so nice." Stephanie put her hand on his shoulder. He smiled at her.

Concealing a grimace, Buffy took the passes,

glancing down at them and reading aloud, "'Professor Copernicus Caligari's Traveling Carnival.'"

He unpeeled Stephanie's fingers from his shoulder and enfolded them between his hands as he bowed from the waist. "At your service. And you are? . . ."

"Buffy. Summers," she said. She didn't like telling him. She wished she had told him her name was Cordelia Chase.

"What a lovely name," he said. "It has a certain . . . ring to it." His voice was breathy, fake. She really didn't like him.

"That's nice," Buffy replied. "So now, good-bye." She reached out an arm and grabbed Stephanie's elbow. Then she took a couple of steps forward, making it clear that it was time for him to move away from the door and let them leave.

"Good night, young Buffy. Dear Stephanie. And friend." He indicated David with a nod.

"He's my brother David," Stephanie announced. David bobbed his head. He still wasn't a hundred percent back in the game.

Professor Caligari made a big deal out of moving aside to let them pass. "Shall I walk you off the grounds?"

"Oh!" Stephanie trilled.

"No," Buffy said quickly. "We are going. So, thank you," Buffy said. "And seriously, there are some . . . gang members lurking around, and it might be better if you locked up for the night."

He raised his brows and cocked his head. His

hair was so thin that she could see his ears through it. "Such concern. See you soon," he said, waving his fingers at her, one at a time. He was very creepy.

Buffy hustled Stephanie and David out of there as fast as she could without dragging them. Stephanie smiled at Caligari until she was walking backward.

"Come on," Buffy gritted.

They walked back through the silent carnival, which Buffy found no less sinister on the return trip. The lightbulbs over the entrance had been turned off, and Buffy had only dim moonlight to navigate back toward the forest.

"Where do you guys live?" she asked Stephanie.

Stephanie gave an address that was surprisingly only two streets over from Buffy's.

Back onto the main drag, a car whizzed by, and Stephanie waved at it. Buffy figured she was trying to flag down a ride.

A few vehicles later, a truck flashed its brights, slowed, and pulled up beside them. There were three guys in the back in Sunnydale High School letter jackets, and they started hooting and whistling.

"Hi, guys," Stephanie called, waving at them. She wiggled her hips and the guys burst into guffaws. "Can I have a ride?"

"Oh, *yeah*, baby," one of them shot back. "On the rear bumper!"

"Hey," Buffy said.

But Stephanie didn't seem to understand that she'd

been dissed. She just laughed and waved as the truck took off.

"What is your deal?" Buffy said under her breath.

Stephanie's body language did not alter as she said to Buffy, "Try not to be jealous. It's not my fault I was born this way."

"But it is *your* good fortune," David piped up, sliding his arm around Buffy. "I can have any chick I want, and you're the one."

Buffy blinked at him. David had sort of activated— maybe it was the night air—and he had the goofiest smile plastered on his face. He was actually posing, his nose lifted into the air, his lids half-closed, his chest puffed out. It would have been pathetic if it had not been so out of character for him.

He winked at her. "Don't hate us because we're beautiful."

"Okay," Buffy said. "I am walking you both home right now."

She got them home; how, she did not know, because they put on a show for every car that drove past, waving and blowing kisses. Once she had pushed David into the house so he couldn't try to do her another favor and kiss her good night, she realized it was nearly 2 a.m.

If her mom had happened to look in on her in her bedroom only to find her missing, she would be grounded until she was as old and spindly as Professor Caligari. She'd talk to Giles first thing tomorrow morning about the weirdness of Caligari. And of his carnival.

Buffy climbed up the duodera pine tree outside her house and flattened her hand on the sill. Climbed into the open window.

A handwritten note rested on her bed. *His* handwriting.

*Hey, Buffy,*
*Stopped by Bronze, then here. Maybe you're out*
*patrolling.*

*A.*

Dejected, she quickly undressed and got into her pajamas—spaghetti-strap T-shirt and long pink pants with navy blue Japanese writing on them. She climbed under the covers and sank her head back on her pillow, sighing as her sore, tired body began to relax.

Her mind returned to its regularly scheduled dozing: Anywhere But Here. Disneyland. Paris. Bakersfield.

Okay, not Bakersfield . . .

Her eyes grew heavy. She sighed and settled in . . . and she dreamed: of the Eiffel Tower, and Angel smiling; and flower fields spreading across acres and acres of land; and a river, and a valley, and a man with a long, lined face . . . and white hair . . . reflected in a mirror of red-flecked gold and glittering jewels. Caligari, his eyes glowing a deep blood-red.

The calliope played, sinister and strange, the notes rising and falling . . .

And the mirror filled with faces. Men, women, children, stretching in ways that bones could not stretch; eyes pulled wide, narrow, contorted with agony; screaming, writhing, begging . . .

. . . and the calliope wail became their shrieks of terror and despair.

As the Slayer groaned and dreamed on.

# Chapter Two

Giles sat by himself at a black lacquer table in the Lucky Pint and drank a black and tan. The Lucky Pint was the closest thing Sunnydale had to a pub, although it more resembled a Chinese opium den than, say, the Plough. The Plough was his favorite pub, all shiny brass and hunter green, located in the Bloomsbury section of London, near the British Museum. Just thinking of it made him homesick. By contrast, the Pint was garish in the extreme, decorated in the scarlet-and-jade-green color scheme Americans seemed to associate with things of the Orient—primarily, Bruce Lee movies and fortune cookies.

He sighed and tapped the table to the rhythm of the song they were playing. "Piece of My Heart" by Janis Joplin. He used to listen to this very song in London, after he'd gone down from Oxford. That was where he,

Ethan Rayne, and the others in their black-magick circle had raised the dread demon, Eyghon. They were all dead now, except Ethan; and if Giles had his way, Ethan would be dead one day soon. The sorcerer had tried to kill Buffy, offering her to Eyghon in his place. And Eyghon had possessed Jenny, who still hadn't gotten over the ordeal, and was only now beginning to thaw toward him.

If Ethan's death came tomorrow, it would not be soon enough.

Buffy had not checked in and Giles was a trifle worried. He still hadn't figured out what the Rising was, and he wondered, not for the first time, if both of them were on a fool's errand tonight: his Slayer, out looking for the Rising, and he, here to get information about it. Better to be near a phone, in case Buffy rang him up, than sitting here waiting for an unreliable informant who might or might not show.

He moved his neck in a slow circle. He had a headache, and he was tired. He looked at himself in the mirrored wall beside his table. God, he looked old. Where had that angry young man gone? The one who had worn working-class clothes and an accent to match, and played the guitar like a very demon?

That stuffy and proper man in the mirror had swallowed him up, forced him to be someone else, to *grow* up.

*Ripper, you're not Peter Pan,* he reminded himself. *You have a slayer to guide. You have responsibilities. So get over it, as Buffy would say.*

"Giles," said a voice, although there was no reflection of its owner in the mirror.

"Angel," Giles replied, swiveling his head toward Buffy's vampire boyfriend. He was tall, handsome, and unsmiling. Precisely the sort of bad boy Giles had been in his day. However, when one was over 240 years old, one hardly qualified as a "boy." And bad men were something else entirely.

"Did you bring Clem with you?" Clem was the name of a demon Angel had located at Willy's Alibi. This Clem had offered to tell Giles about the Rising— for a small price, of course. In this case, it was not too high, although it was rather off-putting: It seemed he was part of a floating demonic poker game that placed bets using kittens.

Angel shook his head. "Said he couldn't make it." He glanced down at the table. "Black and tan. The black is Guinness. That's from my part of the world."

"Have a seat," Giles said, gesturing to the banquette across from him. "We'll order up a round."

Giles gestured the perky, heavily tanned waitress over and ordered two more.

As she left to place their order, Angel leaned forward. "Clem did tell me a few things over the phone."

"About the Rising?"

Angel nodded. "It has something to do with a carnival."

Giles raised his brows. "Indeed? I haven't heard anything at all about a carnival."

"Clem says that's all they're talking about at Willy's Alibi." Although Willy was a human—technically speaking; personally, Giles thought him a bit less than that—his bar was a favorite haunt for demons. More than once, he had provided valuable information that had helped Buffy immeasurably in her slaying duties—not because he was a good man, but because either he got paid for it, or to avoid the beating Buffy threatened him with.

Also for money or to avoid physical pain, he had just as handily betrayed Buffy or her friends.

"What are they saying?" Giles asked Angel.

Their drinks came. Angel hesitated, took a tentative sip, and looked disappointed. Giles surmised that despite knowing he couldn't taste it, Angel had hoped.

"They're excited about it," Angel replied. "They say it'll tear Sunnydale apart. Bring the Slayer down."

"Oh, well, they say things like that all the time. Bit of false bravado, to deny how much Buffy intimidates them."

Angel wrapped his hands around his beer glass as he leaned forward. "It's real enough to keep Clem from being seen with me. Or you. Not that I'm real popular with demons to start with."

Giles considered. "So, are you saying the Rising refers to the arrival of this carnival?"

"From the sound of it," Angel replied.

"So . . . Buffy needs to stop this carnival from coming here."

Angel nodded.

Giles leaned forward, his Watcher brain going into overdrive. "How?"

Angel shook his head. "That's all I got. He didn't even want to tell me that much. He's scared."

Giles slid out of the booth, gathering his jacket from beside himself on the leatherette.

"Where are you going?" Angel asked.

"To the library. To my books. To look stuff up."

Angel drained his black and tan and set down the empty glass. Then he rose, as steadily as he sat down.

"Where are you going?" Giles asked him.

"Back to Willy's. See if I can get more information to take to Buffy." He cocked his head. "Did you bring kittens?"

Giles looked mildly shocked. "I didn't realize you were a gambling man."

"I'm not. I was just going to suggest that you give them back, if you can."

They walked out of the Lucky Pint, into cool, but not cold, air. It had rained earlier that evening, but as was usually the case with this accursed land, it had not lasted long.

Angel stopped. He lifted his chin slightly, concentrating; when Giles began to speak, the vampire held up his hand for silence, and Giles complied.

After a few seconds, Angel asked, "Did you hear that?"

Giles cocked his head. "I don't hear anything except the music in the bar." Which was something far more current than "Piece of My Heart" and far less melodious.

"It's a calliope," Angel said.

"I can't hear it," Giles repeated, concentrating. He shook his head.

"I can. It's playing circus music."

"As in a carnival," Giles replied. "So it's already on its way here. Perhaps already setting up."

"I'll skip Willy's and take a look."

"I'll go with you," Giles said.

There was no answer.

He looked to his right, where Angel had been standing. There was no one there.

"I wonder how he does that," Giles muttered.

He decided to take a two-pronged approach to the developments at hand. Angel could look for the carnival. Giles would begin the research.

He walked to his Citroën and drove back to the school library, to do what he did best.

In the backseat his two new pets mewed.

From the backseat of her car with the license plate QUEEN C, Cordelia raised her head and said, "Wait. Stop. You're distracting me."

"*Distracting* you?" Xander asked, peeved.

"Listen." She unleashed her patented you're-existing-when-you-shouldn't scowl. "That is *music*. Meaning that someone else is out here!" She put her hand on the armrest, about to wrench open the door and sail out into the night. "This is *my* place to park! If someone else is trespassing—"

"There is no one out there," Xander said, urging her back to the make-out zone.

She wouldn't go. She stayed as she was, lifting the tail of Xander's dark blue plaid shirt to wipe the steam off the window. "There is, too. I can hear music."

"We're fine in here," Xander argued. "The windows are all steamed up. No one can see a thing."

She gazed at him as if he were the king of cretins. "Hel-*lo*? How many cars with personalized license plates that read QUEEN C are there in Sunnydale? *One.* And do I lend my car to my friends? *No.* So who would be in here? *Me.*"

He reached for her hand. "Okay, but since no one knows we're, um, seeing each other—"

Her glare could have melted him, except she was one superpower short. "We are *not* seeing each other. Okay? There is no seeing each other going on. This, this insanity is not seeing each other!"

"Okay! I get it! I'm only saying—"

She batted his hand away, hard. "Look, I told you there would be no making out within two hundred yards of anywhere anyone could catch us doing . . . this." She shuddered. "Except somewhere hidden, like a closet. That music means there's someone nearby, and I, for one, have much to lose if anybody sees me with you." She smiled at him without smiling. Back to the melting of his manly self.

"Got it?" she asked.

"Oh, I got it," he said angrily. "I'm just not keeping it. *I'm* not the one who said, 'Oh, what the heck,' and drove up here. I was perfectly happy to wait until we could sneak into your gazebo and go for it there."

"Excuse me?" Now she pulled herself up to a fully upright position and tucked in her shirt. "The gazebo is being painted, remember?"

"Oh, sorry, Veronica Lodge," he bit off. "It's very difficult for me to keep track of all the many home repairs you invent so I won't end up at your house."

She flared. "The only place you're going to end up is in my trunk—"

They stared at each other. There was that crazy moment that happened between them where their blood pressure skyrocketed and their eyes glazed and it was like . . . wow, talk about *lust*. . . .

And then they both shook their heads at the exact same time and said, "No. Too small."

"Besides, we might suffocate," Cordelia offered.

"Great minds think alike," Xander said.

"Our minds have nothing to do with this," Cordelia retorted. "It's just physical, pure and simple. Although when I think about it, when I'm not around you . . ." She looked away and muttered, "I just want to throw up."

"Hey, I feel the same way," Xander said. "It puts me off my snack foods." He reached down and held up a bag of Cheetos. Then he made as if to unroll the window—which he couldn't do, because the windows were electric—and cast the bag out.

"Oh, *please*." Cordelia grabbed the bag from him and tossed it to the floor.

"Ask me again," he urged her.

"What?"

"Say please." He grinned at her.

"I loathe myself," Cordelia said, moaning.

Then she resumed smooching Xander for all she was worth.

Which was, actually—especially if you counted all the money her father had set aside for college—quite a lot.

Angel walked alone.

As he followed the sound of the calliope, he strode down Main Street, past the Sun Cinema and the Espresso Pump. He thought about Buffy, aware that as he passed each storefront he cast no reflection—and equally aware that no one on Main Street noticed.

Even Buffy had stopped noticing.

Ever since the day he had taken her skating, he couldn't stop replaying what had happened. It had shaken his world. The Master had sent assassins to kill her, and one of the Three had attacked her at the rink. Angel had vamped, and in the ensuing fight he had been injured. She had tenderly touched his cut, and kissed him with such sweetness . . .

Kissed him while he still wore the true face of his demonic nature: fangs, glowing eyes, nothing there for her to love. He'd been overwhelmed with shame. But Buffy didn't care.

He paused.

The feelings raised in him—hope, for himself; and intense fear, for her—had been almost more than he could handle. They still were. It was classic Beauty and the Beast. He had been at his most repulsive—the antithesis of everything she stood for—and she had loved him anyway.

Was it weakness, to have a relationship with Buffy? She was only sixteen years old, a young girl.

*But she's the Slayer. She's not just sixteen years old. Her life moves faster; her life is different. Every night she stares death down. Every night she conquers it.*

*I've conquered death.*

*She moves in the darkness.*

*Like I do.*

And she loved him.

*And I love her. I'm not leaving her alone in the shadows. She tries so hard to have a normal life, but it isn't normal. Her friends think they understand, but they don't.*

*I do.*

*So . . . would it be moral to abandon her because of what I am, or what I was?*

He didn't know.

He just didn't know. She was still so young and unformed; she moved in a world that revolved around crushes and fashions that changed at lightning speed. Whereas for him, time dragged . . . or *had* dragged, until Buffy had come into his life.

She was the sunshine that he had not been permitted to walk in for nearly two hundred fifty years. And to bask in her love, even when he was at his worst . . . it was a gift he had never dreamed he would ever receive.

*I have to put this out of my mind,* he told himself. *I have other things to do tonight.*

So Angel glided through downtown Sunnydale, brooding, ignoring the occasional smile that flickered over the mouth of a female pedestrian, or two, or three.

A kid on a skateboard barreled past. A woman walked a toy poodle on a pink leather leash studded with rhinestones. The poodle growled at Angel.

He walked on.

Then he heard a scream from the alley to his left.

Putting on a burst of speed, he ran into the alley.

He saw a kid, possibly eighteen, and in the military, as evident by his camouflage uniform and cap. Marine Corps. His black lace-up boots were dangling off the pavement as two vampires in game face toyed with him. One of them had its hands around the soldier's neck, squeezing the life out of him, while the other dove in for a bite—

Angel vamped and rushed them, grabbing the one who was choking the marine, and throwing him against the alley wall. The soldier fell to his knees, coughing and gasping. His cap fell off, and his—*her*—hair tumbled over her shoulders. She was a girl.

The other vamp growled and attacked Angel with a sharp snapkick to the face. Angel staggered backward from the impact, and took advantage of his own momentum to deal the vamp a roundhouse kick. Then he planted his palms on the ground and added a back kick for good measure.

Next he executed a three-sixty backflip and landed on his feet. The soldier, who had recovered, was pummeling the vamp in the face with her fists.

Angel grinned. *Semper fi.*

Then the vamp Angel had thrown across the alley picked himself up and launched at the marine. She saw it coming and thrust the pummeled vampire in front of herself, like a shield. The other vampire couldn't stop in time, and crashed into its partner.

At the same time, Angel bodyslammed them both, sending the two flying. While the marine attacked the nearest one again, Angel grabbed a piece of wood off the ground and snapped it in two. Result: two sharp, if jagged, stakes.

He rejoined the fight, to discover that the marine's vampire had gotten the upper hand. The soldier was flat on her back and the vamps were bending over her, fangs glistening as they got ready to tear out her throat. He could smell her fear. Her heart was pounding into overdrive.

Angel grabbed the first vamp around the neck, pulling it to an upright position, and staked it. It dusted.

The second one lunged for him—*what a moron*—and Angel shot his hand through the dust to take it out as well.

Then he turned his face into the shadows and said, "Are you all right?"

"Yessir," the soldier said in a deep Southern accent. She gathered her hair up, feeling around among the curls as if she might be looking for a barrette. "Thank you. What *were* those things?" the young woman asked as she walked across the alley to retrieve her hat.

Angel said nothing. Apparently she hadn't seen his face in vamp mode.

"What's the Rising?" she continued.

"Where did you hear about that?" he asked her.

"Those two. They said this town was going to bleed." She found her cap and popped it back on her head. "Because of the Rising."

"Anything else?"

"No, sir. That was it. What was wrong with their *faces*?"

"Gang," he said. It was what everybody in Sunnydale said to explain away the reality of vampires.

"I thought as much," she drawled. "I've seen the same gang in Virginia. Where I'm from."

Angel hesitated, wondering if she was trying to send him a code. If she *knew* about vampires. He asked, "Are you stationed at the Sunnydale Armory?"

"No, sir. I'm here on R and R." Her answer came so fast, he wondered if she had practiced saying it.

"In Sunnydale?" he asked.

"It's got a beach," she responded casually. "And a nice mall. My cousin lives here. She goes to high school. Melody Nierman. I'm her cousin Claire. Maybe you know her?"

"No."

"I guess it's not *that* small of a town."

"No, it's not." He started walking down the alley, back toward Main Street.

"Thanks again, sir," she said. And then, "Do *you* know what the Rising is?"

"No."

But he sure as hell was going to find out.


Willow Rosenberg was having a hideous nightmare. Others might simply call it a dream, but to Willow it signified much that was very bad. For in it Xander was explaining to her that the reason Miss Jenny Calendar never taught her any spells was because the pretty computer science teacher at Sunnydale High was afraid of competition.

"See, the only places where she comes out ahead of you are spellcasting, and hotness," Xander explained. "And also fashion. But then, she has a lot of money to spend on her appearance because she has a job. Face it, Will, you are job-free."

"I have no job," Willow sadly concurred.

"When it comes to job-having, you're not there."

"Maybe someday I could have Ms. Calendar's job," she said wistfully.

He wagged his finger at her. "Then it wouldn't be her job anymore, would it? Envy's not a pretty color on you, *chica*."

"I'm not envious. I just want . . . her clothes and her job and her . . . hotness," Willow told him.

"All quite understandable," he said, talking through a mouthful of Doritos. He was carrying a bag the size of a Miata, and stuffing his mouth so fast that sometimes she couldn't actually see his hand.

They were walking together through a multistriped tent, just Willow and Xander and his enormous bag of Doritos, like in the old days of elementary school when they had been best buds. Now they weren't such best buds because Xander liked Buffy and not Willow. Not in the bud-liking way, but in the way of sweeties. It put a space between them, only Xander didn't know it.

Now Xander was gorging on Twinkies, cramming

them uneaten into his mouth until his cheeks stuck out like a chipmunk's. There were several enormous packages of them cradled in his arms and it kind of irritated her how he just kept eating. Pigging out. He was such a glutton.

"Buffy also has it over you in the clothing arena," Xander continued, talking with his mouth full; now he was eating a giant glazed Krispy Kreme donut. "Of course, Buffy's mom has more going on than your mom, so that makes sense."

Bits of glaze sprinkled the front of his oversized plaid shirt. Talk about lack of fashion statement. Only on him, it looked so *cute*. . . .

She sighed. Xander was right, of course. She was such a loser. If only she could be more like Ms. Calendar. Or Buffy. . . .

"I'm all about the envy," Willow murmured, as she turned over in her sleep.

From the window, calliope music drifted.

# Chapter Three

**B**uffy was the luckiest slayer ever.

About an hour after she had snuck into her room, she had jerked awake from a deep sleep—nightmare? she couldn't remember now—and gone downstairs in search of a comforting bowl of Cherry Garcia ice cream. There she had discovered that Joyce Summers had fallen asleep on the couch.

Her mother sighed in her sleep, and Buffy got a blanket, covered Joyce up to her shoulders, and kissed her forehead.

In the morning Joyce—who had no clue how late Buffy had come in—was so touched by Buffy's thoughtful gesture that she decided to make an example of it. There was to be a reward involved—a mother-daughter shopping trip to the mall.

Still glowing from the good Buffy behavior, Joyce

pulled to the curb in front of the very nice exterior of Sunnydale High and beamed at her little bundle of former juvenile delinquency.

"Have a good day, honey," she said, and Buffy didn't mind the kiss good-bye.

Buffy was halfway up the steps leading to the main entrance of the gulag when Harmony Kendall, one of Cordelia's so-very Cordettes, stepped in her way with a shake of her blond hair and said, "Hi, um, Buffy, right?" As if she didn't spend half of every lunch period gossiping with Cordelia about Buffy, Xander, and Willow. Or maybe that was an exaggeration. Maybe they didn't even warrant that much gossip time.

"Hi, Harmony," Buffy said uncertainly. Cordelia's friends were not famous for being nice to anybody, not even to one another.

Harmony had on a pretty royal blue jacket, black jazz pants piped in navy, and a pair of black boots. She was holding a silver clipboard and a pen with a silver unicorn charm dangling from the eraser end.

"I have to do this thing," Harmony said, sighing, "for extra credit. So I can pass Life Studies." She looked skyward, as if the angels were surely weeping over her fate. "I'm supposed to help the losers on the Student Council with their stupid fund-raising survey."

"I'm all for it," Buffy assured her. "The raising of funds."

Harmony shook her head. "No, I have to ask you what kind of school-wide fund-raiser we should have. I said blood drive, but apparently we can't charge for that. I don't see why not. After all, this *is* a free country."

"But we should," Buffy shot back. "We give enough." Seeing Harmony's confused look, she added, "Um, seeing as how they bleed us dry of the fun with too much homework and pointless surveys."

"Exactly!" Harmony pointed her pen at her. "You are so right. See? Blood drive is the best idea." She looked down at her clipboard. "Some people are so lame. Willow wants to have a book fair. Who would spend money on books? I mean, really. They have them for free in the library. And besides, how many books can one person seriously have?"

Buffy pressed her lips together and gave Harmony a very thoughtful look. "Exactly. I mean, why buy books when you can buy shoes?"

"Yes," Harmony said, her voice rising. "That's what I told Willow."

"You have to have a different heel height for every pair of pants," Buffy continued. "That is not the case with books."

Harmony's face was wide with wonder. "Gee, Buffy, you're really not as hopelessly out of it as Cordelia says you are."

"Oh. Thanks." Buffy knew Harmony wouldn't catch the sarcasm in her voice.

"Oh, sure, no problem," she said, with total sincerity. "So, shall I put you down for shoe sale?"

Buffy started reading the list upside down. *Bake sale, car wash, book fair, blood drive, raffle, play, dance* . . . When one got in trouble at school as often as she did, one got very good at reading upside down.

*. . . carnival.*

"Oh." Buffy glanced from the list to Harmony. She kept her voice deliberately casual as she asked, "Who suggested a carnival?"

"Some lame-o freshman named Jonathan." Harmony flashed Buffy a *what-a-dork* expression. Then she grew more thoughtful. "But Cordelia said that might have possibilities, if we made sure there was a carnival queen and her royal court."

*Yeah, I bet.*

Buffy was about to ask Harmony if she knew Jonathan very well when Stephanie and David Hahn strolled up the stairs.

*Oh my God.*

She had no idea where they had gotten their outfits—as far as she knew, Sluts R Us was closed at night—but they had gone shopping somewhere. Stephanie was wearing a black denim miniskirt that would surely get her sent home and a black baby tee decorated with a large pair of red rhinestone lips. And David . . .

He hadn't shaved his head, exactly, but call what was left mere stubble. His jeans were tight and he had on a white wifebeater beneath an unbuttoned clinging black silk shirt that outlined his scrawny rib cage. And was that an *earring* poking through his upper lip?

On a TV show they would be walking in slow motion as they sashayed up the stairs—someone should clue David in that hot guys did not move their hips like that when they walked—and preening as heads turned in their direction. But the heads that were turning were not heads of admiration and lust; they were heads that were cracking up at the two of them.

But neither Hahn seemed to notice.

Then they were swallowed up by the crush of morning at school, and Buffy was left to blink in their wake, rendered speechless by what she had seen.

"So, Buffy?" Harmony prodded. She had been focused on her list, and so had missed the grand entrance. "Do you think we should sell just any kind of shoes, or only fashionable ones? Boots included?"

"Um." Buffy turned her attention back to Harmony and tried to care anymore. "Definitely boots." Harmony began to write that down. "No, wait. A shoe sale at school, I don't know."

"It would put us on the map," Harmony assured her.

*We're already on the map,* Buffy thought. *We have more deaths per graduating class than any other high school in California.*

Then Cordelia's voice rose above the dull roar. *"Excuse me? Who gave you permission to ask me to move?"*

Both Buffy and Harmony turned to see what was happening.

At the top of the stairs Cordelia and Stephanie Hahn were facing off. Stephanie, who was taller than Cordelia, was at that moment raising her chin and looking down her nose with derision at the one and only girl at Sunnydale High School to hold dual black belts in popular and mean. They were glaring at each other at twenty paces, and other students, sensing a girl fight, were beginning to form a ring around them. Not that Cordelia Chase would ever stoop to physical blows. Why exert yourself when you had a tongue like a complete Ginsu kitchen knife collection plus the blade sharpener *and* the shrimp deveiner?

"Just admit it, Cordelia," Stephanie said, thrusting out her left hip. "You're pissed off because *I* am the school's hottest hottie, and everything about you is so very over."

There was scattered applause around the ring of onlookers, which ended as soon as Cordelia scrutinized the crowd to see who was doing it.

"Oh my God," Harmony said, covering her mouth with her hand. "Has that girl lost her mind?"

"Sounds right," Buffy murmured.

"If you know what's good for you, you'll apologize right now," Cordelia said. "If you don't . . ."—she narrowed her eyes—". . . you'll be so very, very sorry."

"I *am* sorry," Stephanie said. Cordelia visibly relaxed. "Sorry that anyone has to look at *you* first thing in the morning."

The crowd gasped. Cordelia's answering look could have set off a car alarm.

"Buffy, who *is* that?" Harmony demanded.

But before Buffy had a chance to answer, Harmony was fighting her way up the stairs through the crowd. Not to come to Cordelia's defense, it appeared. Just to get a better view.

No one gave ground as Buffy tried to follow Harmony up the increasingly populated steps. There was blood in the water, and the sharks wanted a taste.

Rather than add to the chaos, Buffy left the stairway and jogged up the grassy hill beside it—only to take note of something even more distressing than the impending smackdown between Cordelia and Stephanie:

On the other side of the main building, Glenn Wilcox and Mark Morel, two of the defensive linemen for the Sunnydale Razorbacks, were wailing the tar out of David Hahn. Correction: Glenn was holding him by the arms while Mark was wailing the tar out of him. Gut-punching him, in fact.

"Not the face!" David yelled.

"Stop it!" Buffy cried.

"Hit him harder, Mark," Glenn urged him.

Mark obliged with another punch, and David's knees buckled as he gasped, "Don't touch my face."

"*I'll* touch your face," Glenn said, letting go of one of David's arms and wheeling him around. He showed him his fist. "I'll show it to you after I've ripped it off your head. Who the *hell* do you think you are, loser?"

He was just about to smash in David's mouth when Buffy wedged herself between David and him, grabbing Glenn's fist and using it to force him backward.

Mark started pointing and laughing, and Glenn got that furious, astounded look bullies got when Buffy interrupted their reindeer games. She had humiliated a bully not only in front of a fellow bully, but also in front of his target, which meant that Glenn Wilcox was now her enemy for life.

What with her habit of defending the weak from jerks like these two, it was getting to be a pretty big club.

"What, is he your boyfriend, *freak*?" Glenn asked, trying to cut her down to size by humiliating her in return. "The only loser you can get?"

"Just leave him alone," Buffy said. She grabbed David by the forearm. "Come on. Let's get out of here."

"No way," Mark said, taking a quick step in front of her to block her exit. "He's ours. He came on to our girlfriends and he's going to pay."

"You're just jealous," David said, sneering over Buffy's head at Mark. "Because your chicks think I'm hotter than you are."

*Could you be any more self-destructive?* Buffy thought.

She said to Mark, "Let me get him out of here. You can see that something's wrong with him."

"Yeah. He's alive," Mark said, shaking his head. "That's what's wrong with him. And he's going to be very sorry about that."

"Sorry is good," she said. "How about if he apologizes?" She blinked at David and tugged on his shirt.

"Hey, watch the outfit," he admonished her.

*Oh my God. You are so whacked.* Buffy turned back to Mark. "See? *Seriously* wrong." *Because no one on Earth should be seen in that outfit, much less defend its right to exist.*

As an answer, Mark made a fist and slammed it into his open palm.

"Listen," Buffy said, "I really don't want to hurt you."

He snorted and looked her up and down, the big sneer on his face instantly changing into the huge sneer on his face.

Then he took a swing at David, over her head, so technically, not at her—*give him points for chivalry, not*—and Buffy blocked him by raising her arm to block, then extending her arm in a downward arc, using the force of Mark's punch to throw him off balance. It worked: He fell on his butt.

Mark yelled something at Buffy that was not appropriate for family viewing. Then he lunged forward, grabbing for her.

She drew her leg up to a modified stork position and was just about to connect with his chin—

—when Principal Snyder stomped around the corner, froze, and shouted, "Summers! When they told me there was a fight, I should have known."

Without missing a beat, he walked up to David, glared at him, and added, "Visitors are required to check in at the office, and we are a zero-tolerance campus. No weapons, no drugs, and no motorcycle gangs." Obviously he didn't recognize David. Or maybe he had never noticed him before. In their normal state the Hahns were overlookable to the max.

David tentatively pressed his fingertips over his cheekbones. "Are there any bruises?" he asked anxiously.

"As if," Mark said. "Nice going, hiding behind a girl."

"I had to protect my face," David said. "It's my passport out of here."

"Are you on drugs?" Snyder demanded.

"That guy was hitting on our girlfriends," Mark said.

"Is that true? Were you harassing our coeds?" Snyder asked David. Then, frowning at him, "Are you even a student here?"

"I'm a sophomore," David said. "And I wasn't bothering their girlfriends. I was only asking them out."

"And they started beating him up," Buffy interjected. "Those two, not the girlfriends."

"The only hitting I saw was you," Snyder told her.

"You . . . didn't," she argued.

Snyder grinned. "I think I smell an expulsion in the air. Possibly two—one for brawling and one for sexual harassment. What a wonderful way to end a long, exhausting week of school."

He was practically rubbing his hands. "Do you have parents?" he asked David. "Because they should be called."

Buffy wasn't finished. "*They* were the brawlers. He was the . . . brawlee."

Snyder crossed his arms over his chest. "Well, you're the expert on violence on campus, *and*, may I add, these are two of the finest first-string ball players we have. Because of them, we may actually have a shot at the championship this year—if nobody on the football team dies before the end of the season. So you can see that I have every reason in the world to believe you when you accuse them of something that could get them benched." His voice dripped sarcasm.

"What?" Mark said anxiously.

"Relax, brain trust, he's on our side," Glenn told him.

"Yes. I am. And in case *you* have trouble following me, Miss Summers, follow me. To my office. *Now*."

She held out her hands. "But . . ." Dropped them, because really, what was the point? "Fine."

He cricked his finger at David. "We're walking."

"But I look all right. Right?" David asked Buffy anxiously.

*You look like you've lost your mind.*

"Sure," she said, "you look great."

"You want me," he said. His voice dripped lounge lizard.

Buffy couldn't help the dull flush that traveled up her neck and fanned across her face. She also couldn't help the fact that as soon as her mother heard about this—and Snyder would make sure she did—there would be no mother-daughter shopping trip to the mall. Joyce would ground her faster than one could say "single moms overcompensate."

As she and David trailed after Snyder, Mark and Glenn burst into fresh, rollicking laughter.

"See you, gorgeous!" Glenn yelled. "You too, Summers!"

• • •

"Oh my God, things are seriously weird," Buffy said as she sailed through the double doors of Slayer Central—i.e., the school library—as soon as the after-school detention bell rang and she was set free.

Willow was already seated at the study table, a two-foot-tall stack of big, dusty, leather-bound tomes beside her. She had on a standard-issue Willow ensemble—jumper, tights, and running shoes—and her straight red hair hung loosely over her shoulders.

Xander had been pacing, and he stopped when he saw Buffy; he was wearing cords and an oversized plaid shirt topping a dark blue T-shirt. His dark bangs hung in his eyes; he raked them back a little self consciously and said, "Hey, Buffy."

"Ah. Good." A beat. "You're late." Giles bustled out of his office with a cup of tea and another big thick book, his personal version of Brit nirvana. In tweed, of course. No vest. After all, it was southern California, where the teachers could wear casual clothes like regular people. Except for Giles, who still dressed like Sherlock Holmes.

"That's always good," Buffy ventured, confused. "Being late."

Giles said, "Did you encounter some difficulty getting here on time?"

"No, she's been right here all along, only we didn't notice it," Xander supplied, giving Giles a quick grin.

Giles sighed and sipped his tea, waiting for Buffy's response.

"I did," Buffy told Giles. "Encounter some difficulty. There was a fight this morning. Two football players attacked David Hahn. Who is a sophomore."

"Who has a twin sister named Stephanie Hahn," Willow supplied, eyes wide as she earnestly nodded. "Who Cordelia has declared war on. Actually, that should be 'whom,'" she said thoughtfully.

"I saw the beginning of that fight, but I also saw what led to it. Last night."

"Oh?" Giles took a sip of his tea.

"I was patrolling last night," Buffy began. "Looking for the Rising."

Giles raised his teacup. "Which has been found. It's a carnival. Angel came by and told me," Giles said. "At the Lucky Pint."

"He was everywhere last night," Buffy muttered. "How come *I* never saw him?" She moved on. "Okay, evil carnival. And?"

"Angel's informant didn't give us much. Neither of his informants, actually. Seems he saved a soldier in an alley who had also heard about the Rising. He called me about it later."

"So you both saw him and spoke to him on the phone," Buffy said. Humph.

Giles took another sip of tea. "Which reminds me. Willow, can you see if you can find out anything about possible covert governmental activities here in Sunnydale? Perhaps in the Marine Corps?"

Willow pondered that. "Well, sometimes even asking sends up a red flag, you know? I'll probably hit a jillion fire walls. I should probably use a computer in the lab so it'll be harder to trace the search to me."

"Governmental activities?" Buffy asked. "You

mean, like making the enemy go crazy by playing the calliope?"

"The army I was in would so do that," Xander informed her. He had become a soldier last Halloween, when a sorcerer named Ethan Rayne had rented the gang enchanted costumes.

"So now we're worrying about the government," Buffy said.

"Not necessarily," Giles said. "Please, continue, Buffy. What did *you* discover?"

"Well, I was in Blessed Memories, near the du Lac tomb, and the twins came screaming past me," Buffy said. "Half a dozen vampires were chasing them. So I went after them."

"Of course," Giles said approvingly.

"And were the Hahns totally into themselves at that time? Maybe trying to date the vampires?" Xander asked.

Buffy pondered. "Hard to say. They were so busy screaming and running for their lives."

Xander nodded. "I've been on dates like that. Several, in fact."

"I think the vampires were only in it for the usual vampire thing," Buffy said.

"Only in it for the necking. I've been on dates like that, too." Xander's voice had an unusual edge to it.

"Go on, please," Giles said, sounding a little weary.

She told the whole story, including the "boo" part in the forest and the entire adventure in the fun house, complete with the wicked-scary clown.

"Brrr," Xander said, shuddering.

"I double that," Willow said.

"And this Professor Caligari . . . ," Giles said, then set down his tea as Buffy fished the passes out of her purse and held them out to him.

"He was weird, Giles. Woo-woo weird," Buffy assured him. "And Stephanie was flirting with him." Buffy closed her eyes and shook her head at the grossness of that. "She couldn't stop staring at herself in the mirrors. She kept talking about how beautiful she was."

Xander snorted. At the stereo glares from Buffy and Willow, he said, "Sorry. All women are beautiful."

"Then this morning, she picked that fight," Buffy said, ignoring Xander. "She told Cordelia that she was the new school hottie and Cordelia was over."

Willow's eyes got huge. "You're kidding! I missed all that?" She caught herself and lowered her voice, sounding more serious. "I mean, I missed all that. Oh my God, no wonder Cordelia's declared war on her."

"I dunno," Xander said. "That's a little overly, don't you think?" He held out both hands as if he were weighing things. "Why not just laugh in that snotty, spoiled rich-girl way she has and flounce off, making Stephanie feel like a worm beneath her stiletto heel?"

"It was actually kind of a compliment for her to bother being mean to Stephanie," Willow countered. "It does take some effort."

"Guys, hello, we *are* talking about Cordelia, right?" Buffy asked pointedly. "Missing a chance like that to slaughter someone in public? I don't think so."

Willow shrugged. "All I'm saying is, it's obvious that Cordelia is light-years more gorgeous. I mean, right, Xander?

Xander flushed and rocked back in his chair. "Hah, I guess. If you're into superficial prom queens with bad breath who make people feel like punctured worms."

"Back to the Rising," Buffy said.

"Yes." Giles activated, picking up a big, dusty book and kind of waving it at her. "I've been researching carnivals. Specifically, Caligari's Traveling Carnival."

"That would be the one," Buffy said. "What'd you find?" She took a seat beside Willow. Willow smiled faintly and turned her attention back to Giles.

"Nothing."

"Well, then it's certainly worth mentioning," Buffy drawled.

Giles scratched his forehead with his thumb. "But that's not to say there isn't anything. Merely that we haven't found it yet." He waved a hand at the leaning tower of knowledge. "We have quite a few books to peruse."

"And also to look through," Xander added.

"What did Angel find last night?" Buffy asked. *Since he didn't find me?*

"The carnival was locked up tight. There was a gate across the entrance that you ran through. He hopped the fence and looked around, but found nothing out of the ordinary before it was getting close to dawn and he had to leave. Then he phoned me."

"Did Angel find my missing vampire?"

"He didn't mention it. However, as you know, he can be quite laconic."

"He can?" Buffy asked, having had no idea there were going to be hard words in the conversation.

"Taciturn," Giles explained.

*I gotta read more.*

"Right," she said brightly.

As Willow took a dusty book off the stack and passed it to Buffy, she said, "My father used to talk about running away to join the circus."

"As have I," Giles muttered.

Buffy raised a brow as she traced the picture of a demon on the front cover of the book. It seemed to her that a lot of people talked about running away to join the circus. It was the universal Anywhere But Here destination.

"I would rather be electrocuted," Xander said. As the others stared at him, he said, "What? Clowns."

"The clowns were wicked scary," Buffy agreed, shivering all over again.

"But they weren't real," Willow ventured. "Were they?"

"I don't know. They seemed to be following me in the fun house. And there was that moment in the forest."

"Computerized robots?" Xander asked. "Like in *The Terminator*?"

"Or like in Ted, that robot my mom was dating?" Buffy added.

"Or demonic minions of some sort," Giles said. He set down the book he was holding and pondered the large stack beside Willow. He picked up the first, muttered to himself, and set it down. He went through about half the stack.

"Ah, perhaps this one," he said, hefting a book bound in black. He began flipping through thick pages covered with large, heavily decorated lettering.

"This is a diary from the Rhine Valley in the mid-1500s," Giles announced. "Look here."

He pointed at a page. "Did your Professor Caligari look like this?"

She looked down at a tall, thin man wearing an eye patch and a robe with a hood.

"Two eyes," she said. "The resemblance isn't so much. But it's just a drawing."

"A woodcut, actually," Giles said. "This is reputed to be Hans Von Der Sieben. Hans of the Seven. Seven what, I have no idea. He held some kind of occult gatherings for noblemen. No peasants allowed. No one spoke of what happened there, on pain of death."

"I'm guessing they weren't quilting bees," Xander ventured.

Giles continued. "This diary was written by a Germanic princeling named Jakob Wilhelm, who claimed to have witnessed one of the gatherings. It was he who made the woodcut. I vaguely recalled it as you began to describe your Professor Caligari."

"Not my professor," Buffy protested. "I flunked out of fun house."

"What does Jakob Wilhelm say?" Willow asked.

"About Hans of the Shriners?" Xander riffed.

Giles said, "I'll translate as I go."

"'What transpired at the gathering was a terrible abomination. I pray God I may forget the rending of souls from their bodies. It was unspeakable.'"

Giles stopped reading.

"And? . . ." Buffy prodded.

Giles shook his head. "He says nothing more."

"He unspeaks," Xander said.

"Nonspeaks," Buffy shot back.

They both smiled at Giles, whose head was bent over the book as he studied the page.

"There are no more entries after this one. I researched Jakob Wilhelm. As far as I can ascertain, he disappeared right after having written it and was never heard from again."

"So unspeakable that he didn't speak of it," Xander said.

"Or was prevented," Giles replied.

"Gulp," Willow murmured.

Giles whapped the book shut, making Buffy jump. Dust powdered the air. "However, so many of these old texts are gross exaggerations. People twisted the truth to obtain an end result. For example, during the Spanish Inquisition, several noble families were accused of heresy so that the church could take their lands."

"Maybe we could get someone to accuse Snyder of heresy so they could seize the school," Xander said.

"We'll have to continue researching. However, I suggest we go to the carnival," Giles said, setting the book down. There was more dust. He brushed it off his jacket lapel without even looking. "As a group. We stick close together, and see what we can find out."

"I'm probably being grounded tonight," Buffy informed him, "for the same reason that I was late."

Giles thought a moment. "Perhaps I can help with that. Give your mother a call and explain that Principal Snyder misrepresented what occurred."

"And you can tell her that he lied about it," Xander added helpfully.

"My mom told me she'd be in a meeting until five," Buffy said. "Something about a bank loan. She said not to call her unless it was an emergency."

"Very well. We'll wait until five," Giles said.

Buffy sat next to Willow, who smiled and scooted her chair over. Across the table Xander drummed his fingers and hunkered forward. "Okay. Gimme some books. I'm in."

Buffy was impressed. Xander was not big on the research, but he always did his share. Even though she had turned down his invitation to go to the Spring Fling together, he had her back. A better friend was never born . . . unless her name was Willow.

At five on the dot, Giles made the call. Buffy's mom was amazed, as always, at how much Sunnydale High looked out for its students. She liked Principal Snyder a lot less since "that gang on PCP" (i.e., Spike and his lackeys) had ruined Back-to-School Night, so it was easy for her to believe that the rodent-eyed jerk had totally busted Buffy for something she didn't do. She asked to speak to Buffy on the phone. Joyce told her thoughtful child that their shopping trip was still a go, scheduled for Saturday morning, and Buffy could hang with her friends this evening.

Much joy.

*Plus* . . .

Giles got a second call.

"Angel's going to meet us at the carnival," he announced as he set the phone in its cradle. "At the Tunnel of Love."

Buffy beamed with happiness. Her guy, carnival. It was almost like she was a normal girl.

# Chapter Four

Elsewhere, in Sunnydale . . .

In the lavish hotel suite he currently occupied under the name C. Haos, the tall, dark-haired sorcerer smiled rather unpleasantly at the even taller, darker warlock he had just defeated in a game referred to in America as "twenty-one." Sunnydale was quite the hot spot for gambling. The humans gambled. The demons gambled. One assumed that was because gambling was a vice, and vices were little bits of evil. The Hell-mouth's vibrations drew and increased evil of all sorts. The forces of darkness loved Sunnydale.

Witness the newest arrival. Who would have expected it? What a treat, the actual carnival of Professor Copernicus Caligari, legendary in the history of planetary and dimensional evil.

"Malfaiteur, old . . . man, you know how it goes,"

the sorcerer said, as he gathered up the playing cards. "I won. And to the victor go the spoils. So, until I release you, you're bound to me."

Le Malfaiteur scowled. His black eyes narrowed and he clenched his teeth together hard. "You 'ave cheated," he said in a French accent. "There's no way you could 'ave gotten that last hand."

"The twenty-one with the ace and the queen of hearts?" Mr. Haos asked, snapping his fingers. The very card materialized between his fingers, and he grinned as he flicked it toward Le Malfaiteur. "Because you had hidden the queen underneath your chair?"

Le Malfaiteur's purplish eyelids flickered, but he remained silent.

"So, it's true," Haos gloated. "You *did* cheat. You French, you never played fair. It's because you're lazy. Your entire nation is a testament to the perils of laziness. You once ruled vast colonies. Now they've all gone their merry ways, and you've become a nation of dressmakers."

Le Malfaiteur twisted his mouth in an ugly smile. "As you are English, I could point out that the sun 'as set on your empire as well. But it does you no good to insult my native land," he informed his foe. "I 'ave no loyalty to France. My only loyalty is to the black arts."

As Haos applauded, the queen of hearts vanished, to reappear as dozens of copies on the table. Gleefully, he made a show of scratching his chin as he regarded his vanquished opponent. "Nevertheless, you did cheat. Let me see. What shall I do with you? Darling," he said over his shoulder, "do you have any ideas?"

Modeling the floor-length Italian leather coat C. Haos had just given her, Claire Nierman glided forward like a vampire—although she was all-too-deliciously human—and put her arms around his neck. She leaned over him in a tantalizing mist of perfume, brushing her lips across his cheek.

"Whatever you do to him, do it fast," she said. "You're due at the carnival."

Her lover tilted his head so that her lips could slide to his earlobe. "Thank you for that reminder, darling," he said. "You're always so careful of me."

"I wish you wouldn't go there alone," she whispered in his ear. "That place frightens me. It's dangerous."

"It is indeed," he said. "You're quite right. I oughtn't go there alone." He grinned across the table at his defeated opponent. "And I won't."

With a wave of his hands, he began to recite a very powerful spell.

Le Malfaiteur recognized it at once. *"Attends!"* he protested, scooting back his chair and jumping to his feet with feral sleekness. "I am a fellow sorcerer! You cannot debase so! You cannot do this to me!"

"Oh yes, I can," his enemy informed him. "And I will."

He continued to chant.

The transformation took place.

"All right," the victor said cheerfully. "We're off, then." He rose from his chair. "I suppose I ought to chain him up."

"Y-yes," Claire whispered in a strangled voice, backing away from what C. Haos had wrought. "Good idea."

• • •

"Now, about this attraction," Giles said as they putted along in the Giles-mobile at about two inches per hour. Buffy wondered if he would ever buy a grown-up car. She kind of doubted it. He loved this bucket of bolts.

But who cared? She was moments away from seeing Angel.

Or maybe hours, at the rate they were going. . . .

"Buffy," Giles said, looking across at her. "I was discussing the attraction."

"Um, I know he's a vampire," she began, feeling guilty. Clearly she had not been paying attention to something he thought was important. "But y'know, he has a soul, and—"

"Whatever are you talking about?" he asked, blinking at her.

"'Attraction' being another term for 'ride,'" Willow said loudly—and nick-of-timey—from the backseat. "A *ride* such as the Tunnel of Love."

"Oh." Buffy closed her eyes and leaned back against the seat. "Right."

"Angel said that he noticed people acting strangely after they'd been on the . . . ride. They're highly charged, sexually, that is, to the extent that they're, ah, extremely inappropriate," Giles continued.

"Well, it *is* called the Tunnel of Love," Xander said, sitting next to Willow. "People ride it so they can make out and stuff. Some people get tired of closets . . . of closeness in other places."

"Yes, well, I dare say *we* will all keep a level head at this carnival tonight," Giles said.

"On guard we shall be," Xander said. "Like sentries." He flashed a snappy military salute.

"Hey. Listen," Buffy said. She cracked open her window.

It was the calliope.

The tune was jaunty, but beneath it was a coldness that ran down Buffy's spine.

"Angel heard it as well, when we were at the Lucky Pint," Giles said.

"Calliope music, the new music of the bar set," Xander said. "It's got a certain zest."

It was like putting makeup on a corpse before a funeral. Like someone smiling at you with a knife hidden behind their back . . .

"It's wiggy," Buffy said.

"Ya think?" Xander asked. "What's not to like, Buff?"

"*I* don't like it either," Willow said. "It makes my skin crawl."

"Indeed," Giles said slowly. "Mine as well. But not yours, Xander?"

"Well, it may be creepy to some, but actually, it summons images of tasty treats such as peanuts, popcorn, and Cracker Jacks, thus making me hungry."

"Everything makes you hungry," Willow teased him.

"Except food." Xander leaned forward and said to Buffy, "You said they had hot dogs on a stick?"

"We probably shouldn't eat anything there," Giles reminded him.

"Then we should have stopped at the Double Meat Palace for dinner," he retorted. "I'm starving."

"Xander, it's not even dinnertime," Willow said. "I *told* you to eat more mystery surprise at lunch."

"Yeah, well, I was too busy gawking at all the drama," he said. "Plus, mystery surprise . . ." He trailed off. "Even *I* have standards when it comes to my federally funded school lunch program."

Buffy thought to ask about the drama—part of the fun of detention was being forced to eat lunch with the other prisoners, so she had spent most of her time fending off David Hahn—but she was too lost in the anticipation of what lay ahead in her immediate future:

*I am meeting Angel in the Tunnel of Love.*

Then they were there. The section of the clearing in front of the carnival had been transformed into a grassy parking lot.

"Hey, that's Carl Palmer, Mariann Palmer's brother," Willow said, pointing to a guy sliding a piece of paper beneath the windshield wiper of a nearby Volvo station wagon. "I saw him coming out of the copy store yesterday. He had just gotten another batch of missing-person flyers. You know, for Mariann." She leaned forward. "Didn't you say you staked her last night?"

Buffy sighed, watching Carl as Giles rolled down his window and handed a parking attendant some money. There were dark circles under Carl's eyes. He looked like an old man, not a kid one year younger than Buffy.

"Yeah," she said softly. "God, I wish I could tell him to stop looking for her."

"I know," Giles murmured, pausing a moment to watch Carl too. Then he convinced the car to move forward toward an empty space. "But you do understand why you can't, yes?" His voice was kind, gentle.

"I do." Occupational hazard, keeping uncomfortable secrets like this one.

"I wonder what it would be like, to wonder your entire life what happened to someone you care about," Willow said. "I so don't envy him."

"Agreed. He is to be pitied," Giles murmured, turning off the engine.

*Because I didn't save her,* Buffy thought. *I failed. So many times, I don't get it done. . . .*

Giles turned to her. "Are you all right?"

She pressed her lips into a little smile and bobbed her head. "I'm good," she said, but her voice was scratchy. She cleared her throat and reached for the door handle.

They joined the masses of Sunnydale citizens moving toward the entrance.

"So far, typical carnival," Xander said, "not that we usually have carnivals in Sunnydale. Except for our own lame school carnival."

"It's fun," Willow protested. "I always win a cake at the cakewalk."

"And I don't. So where's the fun?" Xander argued, smiling to show he was goofing with her.

"Hurry, hurry, hurry, step right up!" cried a man dressed like Uncle Sam in a blue jacket and yards-long red satin pants covering a pair of stilts. He stood in the center of the entrance gate, and he looked a little bit like Professor Caligari.

"Come see the wonders of Professor Caligari's Traveling Carnival! The Chamber of Horrors! The freak show! The fortune-teller! One price for all the attractions! A bargain at twice the price!"

Two ticket booths were backed up against the sides of the entrance gate. Giles handed the ticket-taker four of the free passes Caligari had given Buffy.

Securing a map of the grounds, Giles studied it as they walked beneath the entrance arch. Unlike Buffy's first visit, the carnival was now wall-to-wall people. The smells of popcorn and hot dogs mingled with body odor, perfume, piney evergreens, and sawdust, which had been strewn everywhere.

"I smell nachos," Xander said dreamily.

"We need to go to the left to reach the Tunnel of Love," Giles said.

"Yikes, nightmare merry-go-round at three o'clock," Xander announced.

They all stopped to stare.

The central core of the merry-go-round was an elaborate automated diorama. Men dressed in drooping hats, puffy shirts, and colored tights rode horses whose backs were covered with fancy blankets. Some of the men wore leather gloves decorated with tassels. Large black birds topped with brown leather hoods perched on the gloves.

Other men, less richly dressed, stood beside the

riders, banging drums attached to leather belts and clashing cymbals strapped to their hands.

As the carousel began to rotate, more calliope music could be heard.

"What is that, a happy funeral march?" Willow asked.

"Check out the animals," Xander added. "Maybe this thing is the freak show."

On the rotating platform of the carousel, eager kids and indulgent parents rode brightly painted dragons, unicorns, and what looked like a hippopotamus with a fish tail.

Giles nodded to himself. "These are all figures from medieval folklore. "That's a gryphon. Over there, a hippocampus. That would fit with the Hans Von Der Sieben time period. The scene in the middle is a great hunt. The lord of the manor would gather all his friends. Those drummers are called threshers. They would frighten the wildlife out of their hiding places so the hunters could slaughter them."

"Hey, check out that moon," Xander said as he pointed toward the carousel's ceiling. "It's so clean I can see myself in it."

Above the hunting scene a silvery sphere hung from a cord covered with silver stars. The carousel's patrons were reflected in it as they rode past. Though in real life the parents and kids were laughing and smiling, their reflections appeared to be screaming as the images elongated.

Buffy stared at the mirror ball and frowned to herself. Her spider sense was tingling. The images reminded her of something, but she couldn't remember what. Something she had seen in another mirror. Something she had dreamed. . . .

A woman in a down vest and a pair of jeans laughed and waved at someone on the carousel. She wasn't riding the merry-go-round; she was standing in front of it, watching other people having a good time.

Buffy knew how that worked.

The people on the merry-go-round were so lucky. Look at that kid; he was maybe three, had no cares in the world. He had no idea that when the sun went down, the world changed. He was free of the knowledge that she carried: Every night might be her last. It made it hard to get out of bed some days.

Maybe she'd just ride the carousel for a while; round and round she goes, where she'll stop nobody knows. Just around and around, relaxing, taking a load off.

As she took a step, the music changed. She could name that tune: *"A-hunting we will go, a-hunting we will go!"*

"Buffy?" Giles called.

The Slayer blinked and looked around. The others had moved on ahead. About twenty feet away Willow was peering at the map and Xander was tucking in his shirt and smoothing back his hair—decidedly un-Xander-like behavior.

With an impatient expression, Giles gestured for Buffy to catch up.

Buffy gave the carousel one more glance, then hurried to rejoin the others.

"We agreed to stick together," Giles reminded her.

"Like glue," Buffy promised.

"Or a half-melted candy cane stuck to a couch cushion," Xander offered; then, off everyone's looks, "What? I can't come up with analogies?"

"Not gross ones," Buffy said.

"Gross? Candy canes are sweet and nutritious," Xander argued. "Even when fuzzy."

Eww, yet speaking of sweet:

There he was: tall, dark, and Angel, standing beside a wooden heart-shaped sign on a post that said TUNNEL OF LOVE THIS WAY. A painted cupid had notched an arrow in his bow that pointed to the left.

Buffy's boyfriend was wearing his long, black coat. She felt her stomach go up and down just like the carousel horses as she and the others walked toward him.

"Good evening," Giles said.

Angel nodded at him, and at Willow and Xander. Then he said, "Buffy."

Just hearing her name on his lips made her evening, but she forced herself to stay cool and composed.

"Oh my God, Xander, it's the drama!" Willow cried.

A young couple sauntered toward them from the direction of the ride. They were clinging to each other as if they had just survived the sinking of the *Titanic*, and they were kissing so hard that Buffy was afraid one of them would, like, deflate.

They shuffled past Buffy and Company, still locked in eternal make-out.

"Okay, I'm on board. That is weird," Xander announced. "The ride's possessed."

"I missed the drama," Buffy said, looking from Willow and Xander to the couple and back again. "What's going on?"

Willow pointed at the pair as they smooched on into oblivion. "That's Melody Nierman and Chris Holt," she said, probably for Giles's benefit. "Today at lunch she told her whole table that she found out he's on antidepressants. She made fun of him for it. Called him a 'psycho looney.'"

"How perfectly hideous," Giles said.

Buffy's cheeks burned. She wondered if they knew that Cordelia once had used that trademark term to refer to *her*.

Willow continued, "He left the cafeteria humiliated."

"Perhaps they had a change of heart," Giles said. "As happens in your age group. Quite often, I might add."

"Yeah, some people are into drama like that," Xander ventured. "The making-up smoochies make it worth it for them. 'Cause sometimes those smoochies are *hot*."

"Passion," Angel said. "It's what drives some people." He cocked his head. "You said her name is Melody Nierman? Her cousin Claire was the marine I told you about."

Giles took that in. "Possible covert government operation," he mused.

"Hi, Buffy! Hi, um, her friends!" It was Harmony, she of the blood-drive fund-raiser. Bursting through the crowd, she skipped over to the gang with both sets of French-manicured nails curled around the biceps of none other than Marc Greenfield, who had been dating Ellen Hubermann ever since freshman year. "Guess what! We're a thing!"

Marc nuzzled her temple. Harmony reached up on tiptoe and kissed his chin.

"Let's go back through again," Marc stage-whispered.

"Okay!" Harmony giggled at the others and said, "Catch ya later!" She and Marc hung a U-turn and trotted off together like they were in a road-show production of *The Wizard of Oz*.

"What the *hell* was that all about?" said a sharp voice behind Buffy. It was none other than Cordelia. She was exquisitely dressed in a black cashmere sweater, dark pants, boots, and a black-and-white-checked jacket. Her hair was pulled back and Buffy hated to admit it, but she looked very pretty.

Cordelia's perfectly sculpted brows lowered as she narrowed her eyes. "I can't believe Harmony was actually speaking to you guys in *public*. And what is she thinking, stealing such a B-list guy?"

"Hey, Cordelia," Xander said. "How nice of you to greet us all."

She rolled her eyes and exhaled loudly. "Oh,

please. I see you, you see me. What are you people doing here?" She lowered her voice and said conspiratorially, "Did some evil vampires sneak in without paying?"

"Cordelia, please, keep your voice down," Giles admonished her. "As we've discussed, there are certain secrets . . ."

"Yes, sorry." She pressed her hand to her forehead. "I'm just so *shocked* to see those two together." She whipped out her cell phone. "I have to call everyone I know."

"I definitely think we should investigate," Buffy said to Angel. "Don't you?"

"Where are you going? What *are* you investigating?" Cordelia asked Xander. "Yes, hi, Emily! I have dish! Call me back!"

"The Tunnel of Luuuv," Xander replied with a silky tone.

Cordelia's hand was poised over the keypad of her cell phone. "I didn't know that was even a real ride. I thought it was just some made-up thing for those stupid sixties beach movies."

"Actually, not," Giles said. "Made up. Although they are from a gentler era."

"Yeah, the *Psycho Beach Party* years," Xander put in.

"Everyone who rides it comes out smooching," Buffy explained.

"That's just terrible," Cordelia deadpanned. She punched in a number. "Samantha! You will never guess!"

Giles ignored them. "I'm reconsidering our plan,"

he announced. "If the Tunnel of Love adversely affects the judgment of those who ride it, perhaps we should attempt an alternate course of action."

"Oh, what could it hurt," Xander said. "Especially if you go with someone you *know* you would never be tempted to kiss."

"There's a thought," Giles mused. Buffy could practically see the gears in his brain whirling as they all resumed walking.

"Maybe you should ride with Giles," Willow said to Xander.

"You want me to be seen riding in the Tunnel of Love with a male librarian," Xander said flatly.

"Or Xander could ride with me," Cordelia said. "Because there's no way I would ever be interested in a *loser* like him."

"There's a plan. Because also no way would I ever be interested in a *vapid gold digger* like her," Xander shot back.

Buffy was very impressed that he knew the word "vapid."

Unphased and unimpressed, Cordelia snorted. "As if."

"I can ride with you, Buffy," Willow said.

"Wil-low," Buffy muttered through clenched teeth. Willow raised her eyebrows. Buffy cleared her throat and jerked her head the merest inch in the direction of Angel.

"But what if you-know-who gets, like, *too* smoochie?" Willow whispered. "And he goes all, 'Grr'?"

"I'm the Slayer. I'll handle it," Buffy whispered back.

Giles shook his head. "But you two are on record as being attracted to each other. You're hardly good candidates to resist possible enchantment."

"Ah, but we're Slayer and vampire," Buffy replied. "We can fight the unknown better than any of you if it attacks us, say, with fists or a claw hammer." She tried not to look too eager.

"All right, then," said Giles. "I must say this goes against my better judgment, but as in other matters, I—"

"Yay," Buffy said.

Giles gave her a look. "Willow and I will serve as the control group, as it were. We'll sit out the ride. At least *we* will be safe and unaffected."

"Good idea," Willow murmured. "Sitting it out."

"I'm only doing this for the good of humanity," Cordelia said.

"I'm willing to bet that's what you always say," Xander shot back.

"Well, here we are." Giles put his hands on his hips as they came in sight of the potentially evil Tunnel of Love.

Laughing and teasing, guys and girls Buffy's age waited their turn to climb up onto a platform and then sit in a scuffed white fiberglass rectangle—call them actual boats only if you were feeling generous—with a triangular orange beak and beady, raised eyes extending from the front.

The procession of swan boats drifted in shallow water toward a dark gray fiberglass cave that was maybe fifteen feet high. A section on the right side of the cave had worn away, revealing some tar paper and a two-by-four. Fog billowed from inside the cave, enveloping each boat as it entered.

"Where's the exit?" Willow asked, her gaze traveling from the line of waiting riders to the boats disappearing inside. Empty boats drifted past a tattooed man in a red T-shirt at the control panel, but there were no people getting out of them.

"The ride must end on the opposite side of the tunnel," Angel said. "I'm with Giles. I've got a bad feeling about this. I'm not sure any of us should ride it."

"Look," Buffy said, walking over to Angel. "We're here to see what's going on. How are we going to do that if we don't, you know, *do* things? I vote for riding the ride. Let's just all make a pledge that no one deliriously hooks up tonight. Deal?"

Everyone nodded.

"Come on, dork. Get in line," Cordelia grumped at Xander, grabbing his sweater sleeve and edging behind Angel and Buffy as they joined the queue.

It was a bit of a wait, but Buffy and Angel finally reached their swan. Buffy climbed in first, sitting on a very uncomfortable wooden seat with an inch-thick layer of vinyl padding, which suddenly became more comfortable once Angel's hip brushed hers.

"Well, this is cozy," Buffy said. She was pretty jazzed.

"Am I crowding you?" Angel asked with a sexy smile.

"What do you think?" she answered coyly, while her heart treated her rib cage like a mosh pit.

She looked over her shoulder at Xander and Cordelia. They were arguing. What about, Buffy had no clue. Buffy was sorry that Willow wasn't going to be in the swan with Xander. Maybe one day Xander would finally wake up and smell the hottie.

"Here we go," Angel said as the boat began to move.

They drifted toward the cavern entrance, fog wafting toward them. It was scented, and it smelled like bathroom deodorizer. Okay, not quite as romantic as she had hoped but, darkness, boyfriend . . . what was not to love?

Angel put his arm around her shoulders and rockets blasted off inside her stomach. She leaned her head on his shoulder and closed her eyes, feeling the joy.

"Let's go this way," Giles said to Willow as he began to move through the crowds. "We'll wait for them at the exit."

She nodded, feeling dejected and rejected. Xander and Cordelia Chase were in the Tunnel of Love together. It seemed so weird. And also wrong.

But to be honest, she was also a little relieved. If there was something to the theory that the Tunnel magically made people get together, she didn't want Xander to finally finish that end-of-summer-beginning-of-fall kiss that that stupid vampire had interrupted, just because he was under a spell.

"You coming, Willow?" Giles asked her.

"Yes," she said softly. "Of course."

Inside the Tunnel of Love, Angel could hear Buffy's heartbeat picking up speed as he put his arm around her shoulders. Accompanied by syrupy elevator music, their boat bobbed along the mist-laden waters past cardboard displays of bordering roses and hearts.

A male figure dressed in dusty Renaissance clothing came within sight. He was stretching out his arms to a girl in an equally dusty dark blue gown about five feet above him on a plywood balcony painted to look like stone. The figures might be wax, or plaster, but they weren't very life-like.

Buffy giggled. "This is pretty dorky," she said. "But it's fun."

The boat drifted past the figures. The next display was on Buffy's side of the boat. It portrayed a beautiful Egyptian princess holding a snake against her chest.

"Cleopatra," Angel filled in. "Her lover, Marc Antony, was killed in battle, so she killed herself."

"Huh," Buffy said, her heartbeat picking up. "That's pretty extreme, you know?"

"Dying for love, yes, that's extreme," Angel replied,

nuzzling her cheek. "Also, not very practical."

"Ooh, that's kind of pretty," she said, pointing upward.

Angel followed her line of sight. About ten feet above them, garlands of silk roses hung from the ceiling. Gold-painted cherubs and spangly hearts were twined into the garland, and a large ruby heart hung from the center. By the way it sparkled, he assumed it was made of glass. Light moved and drifted inside it. . . . There was something about it . . .

He felt dizzy for a moment. Something silvery shimmered in his line of vision. He tried to blink or turn his head but he . . .

*"She's the Slayer. She wants you,"* a voice whispered seductively inside his head. *"Can you imagine what that would be like? All that strength, that stamina, possibly matching your own?"*

His arm around her tightened. He felt her warmth. Her heartbeat quickened. The rhythm of her blood roared in his ears.

"You're so beautiful tonight," he said huskily.

Her eyes widened. "Thank you." Her lips were moist, her eyes shiny.

*"She wants you,"* said the voice. *"Listen to her heartbeat."*

Lub-dub, *take-her*, lub-dub, *take-her* . . .

He turned to her, cupping her chin with his fingertips. Yes, of course she wanted him.

His lips met hers in a long, soulful kiss. There had

been other kisses, of course, but none like this. It was as if all Angel's senses were heightened: touch, smell, sound . . . and taste. He had not been able to taste the pungent bitterness of his black and tan, but he tasted Buffy. And she was sweet.

"Oh, Angel," she breathed, putting her arms around him and drawing him closer. Her strength excited him. "This is nice."

He kissed her again. And again. And again.

"Yes," said the voice inside his head, "Go for it."

"Whoa," she said, catching her breath and laughing a little. "Maybe we should slow down, you know?" She smoothed back her hair. "Are you feeling extra . . . um, are you? . . ."

"I'm just me," he assured her. "Me with you."

Her beautiful blond hair. He caught it up, smelling it, closing his eyes as fresh desire washed over him. He inhaled her scent.

"God, you smell so good," he said.

"Vanilla," she said. "New."

"It's great." He sniffed her neck. Smelled the blood. He caught up her hand in his and kissed her fingertips.

"Wow," she murmured. Her heartbeat was faster. He could hear it so clearly.

"Buffy, I can't get over how beautiful you are."

She was blushy. It was so adorable.

"You're sure you're not, like, enchanted, are you?" she asked.

"You know how I feel about you," he said, smiling.

She put her arms around him. "That's nice," she said.

So innocent. So lovely. So alive.

One swan boat back, Cordelia stared up at the pretty rose garlands accented with the big red glass heart. Its bloodred glow reminded Cordelia of flames. Flames reminded her of passion. Passion reminded her of the names of perfume. Perfume reminded her of shopping. And shopping made her hot.

"Cordy," Xander protested. "Um, hello, we're not in a closet?"

"Shut up," she said, kissing him so that he would.

He kissed her in kind—who would have ever guessed that Xander Harris was a good kisser, truly the best she had ever had? His lips were warm and he didn't smell bad, and he put his hand on the back of her neck and it was better than all the closet groping they had shared.

Then Xander murmured, "You said you didn't want anyone to see us together."

"Well, it's dark," she said reasonably.

"Does this mean we're *seeing* each other?" he panted, breathless after another kiss.

"Whatever," she whispered. Kiss, kiss, kiss-kiss-kiss—

*Wait.*

"No," she informed him. "It does *not* mean we're seeing each other."

A beat, and then Xander said, "Fine."

They each scooted to the opposite side of their swan boat.

And didn't speak for the rest of the long, boring, long, lame ride of boring lameness.

# Chapter Five

All done.

Carl Palmer hoped no one would complain about the missing-person flyers with which he had blanketed the windshields in the carnival parking lot. After all, he was searching for his sister, not trying to sucker people into joining the Sunnydale Athletic Club.

"You there!" said a low, gravelly voice. "What are you doing?"

Carl whirled around.

About ten feet away, a tall, thin man with a mane of white hair stood with his arms folded across his chest. He was wearing some kind of long robe and a little fez. His face was long, his features sharp. And his dark eyes blazed with anger.

"I . . ." Carl held out his stack of flyers. He had at least a hundred left. "My sister's missing."

The man unfolded his arms and gestured for Carl to approach. His fingers were skeletal, his nails like claws. He was a very creepy old guy.

Swallowing, Carl handed him a flyer. The guy smelled . . . kind of moldy. It was gross.

"Mariann Palmer," the man read aloud. He cocked his head. "Haven't seen her." He looked at Carl. "I see the resemblance."

Carl didn't know what to say to that.

"It must be difficult for you," the man said. "Her disappearance."

Carl nodded. "Very," he replied.

The man folded the flyer and put it in the pocket of his robe. Then he swept his arm to the right, gesturing toward the carnival. "Have you been to my playground yet?" At Carl's look of surprise, he said, "I'm Professor Copernicus Caligari. I own this little traveling entertainment."

"Oh." Carl shook his head. "Not really in the mood, you know? No offense."

"Why don't you go on in," the man said kindly. "Take your mind off your troubles for a while. Have a little fun. Indulge yourself."

"No, I . . ." Carl sighed heavily and ran his hand through his hair. "We're a little low on money right now. My mom hired a private detective, but she's been staying home from work. My dad lives in Texas, so . . ."

"Oh, this is too much for such young shoulders," Professor Caligari said kindly. "Here."

He fished in the same pocket and brought out a

small rectangle. "This is a free pass. Go on in. I insist."
He pulled back his lips in a smile, revealing brown,
scraggly teeth. His eyes in the moonlight seemed to be
gleaming. Carl was still freaked.

And yet . . . the calliope music sounded so happy.
The rides were lit up against the sky. He smelled popcorn and hot dogs.

"Go on in," Professor Caligari said again.

"Okay," Carl replied, ducking his head. "Thanks."

"The pleasure is all mine," the man said.

The man gestured for Carl to run along. Carl did
so, scooting around him. Professor Caligari was nice,
but he still smelled weird.

Carl hurried through the entrance arches, waving
his thanks over his shoulder, mostly to get away from
Caligari. There was so much noise and life. He actually
did feel a little better, a little more lighthearted.

He wandered around for a few minutes, until he
saw a large blinking disk that spelled out "Midway" in
lightbulbs. He ambled beneath it, to discover that he
had entered the fun zone: Rows of wooden stalls beckoned with flashing strobes, colorful graphics, and men
and women in red T-shirts just like his, wearing head
mics and shouting, *Come win a prize, four throws for
a dollar, everyone a winner, go home happy!"*

The closest stall was maybe twelve feet on a side,
painted black and decorated with bloodred dollar
signs. Carl's fellow Sunnydalians surrounded it. He
saw some of the super-popular kids from school,
tossing coins at an enormous tower of glass bowls,
dishes, shot glasses, and vases. Everything gleamed

and shined. He figured out the game—if you threw a coin inside one of the objects, you got to keep it.

*Cool.*

*Easy.*

He immediately focused on little purple-tinted glass baskets with frosted handles.

*Mom would like one of those,* he thought. His mother hadn't had a moment of pleasure since Mariann had gone missing. Maybe a little present would cheer her up.

He fished a bill out of his wallet. It was a twenty. He had just cashed his paycheck from his part-time job at the library.

*I'll just get a dollar's worth.*

The girl working the booth ticked her glance his way. He was startled for a moment. Her skin was dead white. Her lips, bloodred. Then he realized she was a Goth. She was wearing a black hooded sweatshirt unzipped to reveal a red Caligari T-shirt, and a canvas apron around her waist, over black pants. He bet her hair was a deep, shiny black, but her hood obscured it.

As she came toward him, a wind ruffled his hair, and for a moment he smelled something foul in the air, like a backed-up toilet. He grimaced, looking for the source.

Then she approached, and all he smelled was strong, heady perfume.

She smiled, raising her dark, painted-on eyebrows, and said, "Try your luck?"

"Yeah, okay. Can you sell me some change?" he asked her, showing her the twenty.

She took his twenty. "Two rolls of quarters okay? It's a quarter a throw."

"I just want a dollar in quarters," he said. "The rest in bills."

She made a little face. Her eyes were very dark. He couldn't see any color in the irises. And there was that *smell* again. It was awful. He looked around, then back at her. *She* smelled great.

"Sorry, I don't have any paper money," she told him. "Bills get instantly dropped in the safe. All I carry are rolls of quarters. I'll give you two rolls and you can just save what you don't use."

They made the exchange. She pushed his twenty into a metal box with a slot in the top.

The glassware glittered and shimmered almost as if it were magical—like fairy gold, pirate treasure. It was so bright it just about blinded him. He became aware of a silver flash just beyond the range of his peripheral vision. The space between his eyelids and his forehead ached for a second. He felt dizzy. Then it passed.

*Stress,* he guessed. *Every since Mariann ran away, I've been maxed out on stress.*

He hefted a quarter in his palm, judging the distance, the trajectory. If he didn't get the basket, he'd get the shot glass sitting next to it for sure. The shot glass was kind of cool, black with a red seven on it. He might like that for himself.

He lowered his arm, took a breath, and held it. Then he tossed the quarter into the air. He watched it catch the garish neon lights—purple, pink, green—

before it landed between the shot glass and the basket, on a section of black wood.

"Oh, too bad." The girl stuck out her lower lip in sympathy. "Want to buy another roll?"

*What?*

He looked down at his hands. They were empty. The two rolls of quarters were nowhere to be seen.

"I . . . I played them *all*?" he asked. He didn't remember that. He didn't remember anything past the first quarter.

She gave him a quizzical look. "You feeling okay?"

"Sure." Whatever.

"You almost had it that one time. I never saw any one get that close and not actually win."

He fished another twenty out and handed it to her. "I'd like two more rolls of quarters."

They made the transaction. He took a quarter and flipped it with his thumb into the air—*heads, you win, tails, you win*—

"Man, that one was even closer," she said, theatrically wincing in a gesture of sympathy. "Want some more?"

He blinked. Felt in his pockets. No quarters. None. No more bills, either.

He fumbled through all his pockets again, doing a visible sweep of the ground, of the top of the black wood barrier. Nothing.

"I-I'm out of money," he told her.

She shrugged. "Better luck next time."

"But . . ." He frowned. "I can't be."

"Well, you are." She raised her brows.

"That's impossible." He rooted around in his pockets one more time. "How much did I give you?"

She paused, mentally totting it up. Then she looked at him and said, "Eighty bucks."

He couldn't believe it. "How long have I been here?"

She shrugged. "Long enough to lose eighty bucks."

He stared at the glass baskets. "I have to have one of those baskets. For my mom. I *have* to."

"I thought you said something about going home and getting some more money," she said, hooking her thumbs into the waistband of her canvas apron. The silver stud in her eyebrow sported a tiny little seven. He hadn't noticed that before.

"I don't have any cash at home," he said.

"You said you would go home and steal whatever you can find out of your mother's purse," she replied.

He felt another strange wave of vertigo. A voice inside his head said, *"More than anything in this world, you want a basket. You will do anything for a basket. A basket will make you rich. You need one. You will die without one."*

"Her purse," the girl repeated.

"Oh, that's right. I did," he replied, nodding eagerly.

"And you said that if she caught you, you'd beat her head in." She reached into her apron and handed him a big, black flashlight. "With this."

"Yes." He took it from her. Hefted it. It could pack quite a wallop. "*Now* I remember."

"Good."

"Miss?" someone called to her. It was Principal Snyder, rolling his eyes and crossing his arms over his chest. "When you're finished *flirting* . . ."

"Be right there," she sang out. She turned back to Carl. His stomach growled and she giggled. "Maybe you should get something to eat. Our hot dogs are to die for. Old family recipe."

"I'd like to, but I have to hurry," he said. His stomach rumbled louder.

She laughed. He hadn't noticed before how shiny and white her teeth were—like little pearls.

"You sound like you're awfully hungry."

"I am," he admitted.

Her smile grew. "So are we."


"Well?" Giles asked Xander as the six of them regrouped at the exit to the Tunnel of Love.

"Nothing," Xander said emphatically. "I am lust free." *And no lie there.*

*Much.*

"Me, too. Very lust free," Cordelia snapped.

"Wasn't it even fun?" Willow asked.

"Completely lame," Xander told his red-haired buddy. "You are so lucky you didn't go on it."

"No unusual feelings?" Giles prompted.

"I feel less than nothing for this loser," Cordelia said. "The thought of kissing Xander? Bleah."

"So, the Tunnel of Love did not affect you?" Giles asked Cordelia.

"It was a bunch of wax statues of famous lovers through history, like Julio and Cleopatra or whatever,"

Cordelia said. She counted off on her fingers. "Hokey statues, bubbles, fog, and it smelled like those little trees people hang in their cars."

"I think it was supposed to be perfume," Angel said, moving toward Buffy. She smiled up at him.

"Well, Angel's the one with the good nose," Xander said. "Oh, wait. That would be for telling blood in live things apart from blood in dead things."

"It definitely had a Motel Six bouquet," Cordelia insisted, perhaps missing the point that Xander was trying to make: Buffy's boyfriend was not normal. "Not that I have ever been to a Motel Six in my entire life."

"Yep, just bad statues," Buffy said. "And as a place to make out, slightly less comfortable than the couch in my hous . . . than one would expect teenagers to put up with," she finished. "If a teenager was going to make out in a ride with room deodor-izer and the statues that have already been men-tioned."

*Ooh, quick save.* Xander silently congratulated her.

Giles was parsing the data. "So, it's your opinion that those rather . . . love-struck pairs we observed pre-viously were simply enjoying their dates?"

"I guess," Xander said. "*We* sure didn't go all romance novel, did we, Cordelia?"

"Yuck."

Buffy smoothed her hair. She was all blushy and rosy. Kissage had obviously occurred, but from what Xander could tell, the sanctity of family hour appeared to have remained intact.

"Then how on earth can we explain Harmony's terrible lapse?" Cordelia murmured, stricken, as she pulled out her cell phone again. "Where was I?"

"Samantha," Willow said.

"Right!" She pressed a key.

"*I* still haven't ridden it," Willow said, raising her eyebrows.

"We're forgetting the Hahn twins," Buffy pointed out. "They went all lookie-loo once they got inside the mirror maze."

"Maybe only certain rides are cursed," Willow suggested.

"Like 'It's a Small World' at Disneyland," Xander agreed. "Everyone knows that thing is the work of the devil."

"Maybe the Hahns were already enchanted or whatever *before* they got into the fun house," Cordelia pointed out. "Maybe they thought they were hot-looking, like, the day before. It's hard to check your appearance when you're running for your life. Believe me, I've tried. But when they had a spare moment . . ." She held out her hands as if to say, *See where I'm going with this?*

Buffy looked at Giles. "Okay, point taken. We don't know if any of the rides are evil. Maybe there's something else lurking around here and *it's* evil. It could be a monster, or a demon that lives inside the fun house."

"Or the prices they charge for admission," Giles grumped. "And parking on top of it."

"Don't you have a Watcher's expense account?" Cordelia asked Giles.

"Hardly." Giles looked affronted.

"Not even a dry-cleaning allowance?" she pushed. "Because I've been meaning to talk to you about that. If I'm going to be running around with you people— well, there's all this *goo* and dirt and stuff. I had no idea demons had green blood, and that it stained!"

"Well, we got in for free, so that's not too bad," Buffy said. She came to a decision. "I think we should split up. We can cover more ground that way."

Xander held up a finger. "Maybe not so much, Buffy. That's the Camp Crystal Lake approach, and that usually results in a machete to the forehead."

"True," Buffy said thoughtfully.

Giles adjusted his glasses. "I beg your pardon?"

"Camp Crystal Lake? Jason? Hockey mask?" Xander prompted. Giles continued to stare at him as if he were speaking Swahili. "Giles, how can you be so up on all things wiggy and not know about this stuff?"

Willow stepped up to the plate. "You see, in slasher movies, when people go off in different directions to search for the killer, that's when they get the axe. Literally." She tapped the crown of her head. She smiled pleasantly at Cordelia. "Brain comes out with Spray 'n Wash."

"Oh my God," Cordelia said, looking ill.

"However, playing devil's advocate here," Xander cut in. "If we observe the *Scooby-Doo* mystery-solving method, we note that all the creepiest things happen to the group when they're together."

"And you do call yourselves the Scoobies," Cordelia put in, cocking her head. "And Xander is kind of like a big, weird, goofy dog."

"All's I'm saying is, either approach has its time-honored plusses and minuses," Xander said. "Splitting up, or hanging together."

"Yeah, because we could die either way," Willow finished helpfully.

"Exactly my point," Xander concluded. They smiled and nodded at each other.

"I still say we should split up," Buffy said. "We can each do one thing and then meet back in, like, half an hour with a report."

"Oh my God," Cordelia blurted, staring at her. "You had a good idea."

"Still," Giles said. "It may be dangerous."

"Good ideas often are," Xander riffed. "They can lead to political upheaval and . . ." His gaze wandered to an extremely, uh, woman wiggling her hips past him. ". . . the invention of Spandex."

He caught himself. "Buffy's right. We should explore in ones and twos. Hey, we're not the Slayerettes for the T-shirts."

"There are T-shirts?" Willow asked, sounding sad.

"The T-shirts are a metaphor," Cordelia informed her. She narrowed her eyes. "Right?"

"Right. You haven't missed out, Cordelia. There is nothing to get that you don't have," Xander replied.

"*That's* for sure," she said.

"We'll split up, then," Giles said.

"With you there," Xander bit off.

"Me, too," Cordelia shot back. "Splitting up forever."

"What are you going to investigate?" Giles asked Buffy.

"Maybe we should go back through the Tunnel of Love," Angel said.

Buffy looked interested. Then she gave her head a little shake. "I'm thinking the Ferris wheel," she said. "We'll be able to see a lot from up there."

"Good thinking." Giles looked at Willow. "What about you?"

"I think I'll go to the fortune-teller's tent," she said.

"I'll go to the freak show," Cordelia volunteered. "Since I've had a lot of experience hanging around freaks."

"Very well." Giles looked to Xander.

"Carousel," he decided. "I'll whirl around in lazy circles and take in my surroundings."

"Gee, that's just like your life," Cordelia sniped.

"Then I'll investigate the Chamber of Horrors," Giles said, "since I've already had so much experience with that."

"A watcher's existence," Willow murmured sympathetically.

"I was thinking of having to live here, in southern California," Giles informed her.

"Good." Buffy beamed at Angel. "We have a plan. Let's go."

"Gone," Angel said. He laced his fingers through Buffy's.

"Remember, we'll regroup in thirty minutes," Giles said.

"We will," Buffy promised.

"Half an hour," Giles said.

"Aye, aye, captain," Xander replied.

They turned their backs and scooted off.

The carousel.

Xander found a cozy little bench on the carousel, behind a trio of angry-looking black stallions with red flames painted on their faces and hooves. His bench was decorated to look like a chariot, and not only could you sit down in it, but you could plop down length-wise, rest your head, and prop your feet up like you were in a hammock.

*Round and round and round I go, when I'll get up, no one knows,* Xander thought, settling in.

Feeling very relaxed, he watched the first load of riders trot to their creatures of choice, and climb on. Funky dolphin things, unicorns, weird metamorph-style combo creatures.

*I might be more impressed if I hadn't already seen a lot of this in real life.*

The music started, and the drums banged and the cymbals clanged as everyone went up and down, up and down, like on slow-motion pogo sticks.

He wished he could tell Carl Palmer about his sister. Or at least stake the vamp that had chomped her and changed her into one of the living undead. That was pretty much Buffy's job, but he wished he could do more than he did.

He kept a sharp lookout—with one eye open—all the while inhaling the multilayered, tantalizing scents of nacho cheese, chocolate, and hot dogs. All was laced with the sweet odor of hydrolyzed vegetable oil.

*Churros,* he thought, with the love he had always thought he would reserve for a woman. *Ooh, I'll bet they have kettle corn, too. Giles said we shouldn't eat anything, but hey, other people are doing the munch thing, and they're not keeling over and dying.*

The little boy on the black stallion in front of Xander's chariot was licking an ice-cream cone, and he was just fine.

Xander shifted his weight, watching the silvery moon-ball glow as the cymbals clanged and the drums crashed and thundered.

Around and around and around. Xander watched and listened, and yawned.

*Nothing's happening. This is boring. Also nice. I move around too much, as a rule. Except for all the TV watching. And dozing off in class. But there's the walking, and the skateboarding, and the dancing . . . no wonder I'm so tired.*

He opened his eyes, realizing that he had dozed off. The carousel had stopped, and the little ice-cream-cone boy was gone.

He looked up at the bright mirror-moon. The silver glanced and darted across his field of vision, and for a moment, he felt a little dizzy. Probably from hunger.

*"You deserve something tasty and sweet. Something delicious to fill your stomach. It's so empty. You're aching with hunger, aren't you?"*

Xander's stomach growled.

A little redheaded girl about *Teletubbies* age and her equally redheaded mother were visible. Mom and Mini-Mom were each snacking on an enormous chocolate chip cookie, the tantalizing disks so large that the little girl's resembled a Frisbee in her grasp.

The cookies were loaded with chocolate chips and . . . merciful Zeus, were those M&Ms as well? Chocolate chips *and* M&Ms? Did it get any better than that?

Xander's mouth watered.

The mom handed her cookie to her daughter as she picked her up to set her on the fierce-looking ebony steed. Xander scrutinized the two cookies now in the little girl's possession.

It *did* get better. There were chunks of white chocolate too. Three kinds of chocolate in one delectable cookie.

His stomach growled.

As the little girl settled on her horsie's wooden back, both cookies slipped from her grasp and tumbled to the wooden floor. They broke into large, crumbly chunks. The M&Ms poked out from the crumbs like jewels in buried treasure.

Xander thought briefly about reaching out and scooping up a handful.

"All gone, Mommy," the little girl said mournfully.

"That's okay, Boo-boo," the woman soothed. "We'll get some more."

"Yeah, for five bucks each," Xander said under his breath.

The woman heard him. She looked at him and said, "Oh, no, they're free tonight."

Xander blinked. "What?"

She pointed. "They're right over there."

Xander followed her line of vision.

And shuddered.

Sure enough, there were heaps and heaps of cookies

on two red trays. The trays were labeled FREE!

Each tray held by two hands.

Each pair of hands belonging to a clown—a fully made-up, dressed-up, wicked-scary clown, grinning and bowing as people grabbed themselves a little bit of heaven.

Xander wasn't at all sure that he could make himself walk up close enough to one of those guys to snag a cookie no matter how hungry he was. Those big weird grins, those blank eyes of doom . . . nope.

He stayed safely prone.

"They're giving away little bags of toffee, too," the woman added. "And kettle corn."

Xander sat up. "*And* kettle corn?"

# Chapter Six

The crush inside the Chamber of Horrors was so oppressive that Giles wondered why the tacky wax figures didn't melt. He was hot, and hemmed in on all sides by noisy boys with terrible body odor. There were so many of them that Giles couldn't have left if he wanted to.

And he very much did want to.

The Chamber of Horrors was a series of tableaux, each a ghastly display of the sort of things one expected to find in a Chamber of Horrors—a poor fellow being stretched on the rack by hooded priests of the Spanish Inquisition; a statue of Jack the Ripper and one of his prostitute victims. Everything very crudely done— badly proportioned bodies, amateurishly arranged displays of skulls and bats. Compared to Madame Tussauds, the legendary wax museum back in London, it was farcical. Had he paid a separate entrance fee, he would have demanded it back.

*As it is, all I've lost is*—he checked his watch—*fifteen minutes of my life.*

He sighed as he was pushed by the crowd along to the next dreary scene. Ah, the French Revolution, of course. A scaffold, and upon it, a guillotine. An unmoving body was posed kneeling in position, with its head thrust through the restraining wooden-stocks portion of the execution device.

From a speaker a voice crackled, "No! I'm innocent!" It was a terrible French accent.

"Guilty!" another voice shouted.

The blade slid down two guy wires, and lopped off the head. A wax stump of a neck was revealed. It was painted red. The head tumbled into a basket.

"Dude, this is so lame," said the pale, foul-smelling boy closest to Giles.

His friend, a shorter, tanner, but no-less-foul-smelling boy, yawned and said, "We are totally wasting our time."

Giles had to agree.

All twenty or so of the onlookers moved on. Giles exhaled and snaked his left hand up his side, to dab his forehead with the paper napkin he'd found in his pocket.

Ahead, something glittered, catching his eye. Giles wearily craned his neck over the heads of the two boys, wondering what less-than-stellar monument lay in store.

"Vampires, cool," the pale boy announced.

It was a scene from *Dracula*. Van Helsing, the vampire hunter, was holding a mirror pointed at a fanged man who was shielding himself from a wooden cross, held by a man in a cowboy hat. Ah, in the original novel that would be Quincy Morris, the Texan.

From the chest of the Quincy Morris statue, a man's voice twanged, "Stake him, professor!"

The vampire hissed. His reflection could not be seen in the mirror. It was probably not a mirror at all, but something sprayed with nonreflective silver paint.

"Lame," another boy opined.

Or the angle of the mirror was deliberately off. The trick worked either way. The trick, because . . . Giles felt a wave of vertigo. Something flashed silver.

*It's so hot in here,* he thought. *I think I'm going to faint.*

It was so hot that summer, that summer of black magicks and free love and chicks who wanted to be with powerful young sorcerers. Rupert Giles and Ethan Rayne cut such a swath! The black arts belonged to them.

"We're going to rule the night," Ethan told him.

It was midsummer, a powerful time in the lunar year. They were drunk on Guinness and potions and magicks. "We have done the impossible, Ripper-Rupert. That makes us mighty."

*"We are the champions,"* Giles sang. But deep beneath his euphoria, he seethed. Double, double toil and trouble, his anger was rising to the top.

*This is not my life,* he thought through the haze. *This is not for me.*

*I am a watcher.*

His grandmother, also a watcher, had written him a terrible letter, a death sentence, and he received it in the post that morning:

*Rupert,*

*I know this is so hard for you, but you must accept your destiny. The Watchers Council have asked me repeatedly what they are to do about you. I tell them to be patient. You're young. But I fear you, my boy. I sense that you're playing with fire. There may be a girl who will need you, and you cannot fail her. I'm old, Rupert, and I . . . I suppose that I must tell you, dear, that I don't anticipate being here much longer. Before I depart this world, I need to know that you have joined the good fight. Come home.*

*Your devoted*
*Gran*

God, how he hated her in that moment. Hated her and all she stood for: that damnable Watchers Council, relic of a bygone age, when the only person who could go up against the forces of evil was some young chit. He and Ethan had proven that wrong a hundred times. Called up viler evil than those old watchers could imagine, then shot it back down. Raised demons, and destroyed them. The world didn't need a slayer. It needed more men like Ethan, and him.

*I won't do it. I won't go back,* he thought. Fury rose inside him like a Roman candle.

Shocked out of his reverie by a blast of cold water, Giles opened his eyes. He was seated on the floor of the Chamber of Horrors with his back against the wall. Two of the several boys were bent over him, and the freckle-faced one was pouring a sports bottle on his head.

"Stop that!" Giles cried.

"You okay, dude?" the boy asked Giles as he obeyed him. He cradled the water bottle against his chest. "Are you, like, having a heart attack or something?"

"Dude, he didn't have a heart attack," the older boy snapped. He looked anxiously at Giles. "Did you?"

Giles touched his forehead. "It must have been the heat. No, that's all right. I'm fine."

"Do you want us to get help?" the older boy said.

"No, thank you. That's not necessary." Calling attention to himself was the last thing he needed. Carefully, he got to his feet. His surroundings swirled.

"You look bad," the freckle-faced boy informed him. "Maybe you should just wait a minute."

Giles felt a sudden rush of anger. He said through his teeth, *"Damn your eyes, I am leaving."*

Goggle-eyed, both boys took a step away from him. "Whoa. No problem," the older boy assured him.

Giles was shocked. *What the devil is wrong with me?* He wanted to apologize to them both, but he didn't trust himself to speak. Because he was very afraid he might give voice to the words that were flashing through his mind:

*Dare to question me, will you? I ought to bash your heads in.*

Silently, he inclined his head.

And hurried out of the Chamber of Horrors as fast as he could possibly go.

He stood in the rush and glitter, listening to the chatter and the noise and the calliope. Looked up, and saw the Uncle Sam person on stilts.

Looked around . . . at the smiling faces.

And the clown, staring right at him from a little platform across the breezeway. It was holding a seltzer bottle, which it pantomimed spraying at him.

*Yes, someone ought to cool me off a trifle more,* he thought. *I am out of sorts. I am . . .*

The calliope played. The clown dipped a low bow and began to dance in a circle. Then it pulled three glass balls from its sleeves and began to juggle them with remarkable skill.

Giles watched, his practiced eye following the path of the third ball as the fellow went through the motions. The glass caught the colored lights of the fair—red, blue, pink, green—or perhaps the balls themselves were tinted. They seemed to retain their hues against the white of the clown's gloves.

The clown looked at Giles with its silly, happy face. Giles found himself smiling back.

Then he glanced down at his watch and thought, *Oh, damn! I'm late!*

He was furious with himself.

The kissing was great. It was wonderful.

But they hadn't ridden the Ferris wheel yet, and . . .

"Angel, we're late!" Buffy said, glancing at the large illuminated clock face on a pedestal behind him. "We have to go!"

"But you're so beautiful tonight," he said, covering

her face with kisses. It was beyond nice. It was the best.

But they were *so late*.

"Okay." Angel kissed her again.

They stumbled out of their secret hideaway, Buffy walking backward as Angel bent down and kissed her, kissed her, kissed her. She smacked into something— one of those cutout figures you can stick your face in and then take a picture with.

This one was a clown. The back of her head filled the hole for the face.

"Buffy," he murmured, "why can't we just get out of here?"

Someone shouted. "Get a room!"

"We have to stop," she said. She put her hands against his chest and pushed him gently away.

"God, I love it when you do that," he moaned.

*I think we've taken it to the next level,* Buffy thought. It was not an unwelcome move. However.

"Smoochies later," she promised. "Work now."

"You drive a hard bargain," Angel breathed.


The sign read WELCOME TO MADAME LAZABRA'S.

Willow stepped through a black curtain and into the darkly lit tent. Glow-in-the-dark objects were suspended in the air—a green drill-team baton, a yellow skull, and a purplish letter with the words FROM BEYOND in red where the address should be.

Exotic scents of the Arabian Nights wafted on the night air. Bells tinkled. A gong sounded, vibrating through Willow's feet.

Across the room the black curtain divided in two

as a tall, dark-haired guy about Willow's age emerged from between two black hangings. As he did so, the suspended objects raised up about two feet in the air. She saw now that they were attached to a rod and pulley.

The guy had on a white shirt and an embroidered black vest, and tight black leather pants and black boots that came up to his knees. A red-and-black sash was tied around his waist.

On his cheek . . . was that a birthmark?

He silently stared at Willow.

"Vaclav!" a woman's voice shouted.

"Welcome to the tent of the Gypsy fortune-teller," the guy said in a loud, showy voice. He sounded like the Count on *Sesame Street*. "Madame Lazabra knows all, sees all."

He gestured for Willow to come with him beyond the curtain.

She followed.

Inside were two black, overstuffed chairs and a circular brass table. A petite, olive-skinned woman sat in the chair opposite Willow; she was very beautiful, maybe twenty-five, and she wore a dark scarf with scarlet markings that looked like claw marks. Her two enormous hoop earrings caught the light from a black candle burning on top of what Willow hoped was a prop human skull.

Willow noted the rings on the woman's fingers, including her thumbs; some had two or three. Most of them were silver; one had a little skull on the front. Another was a large seven studded in rubies.

The backs of her hands were tattooed with swirly henna designs, and her hands were cupped around something as if she were warming them.

As Willow glanced down, the woman slid her hands away, revealing a crystal ball.

It gleamed, throwing off white light.

It was . . . beautiful.

"Madame Lazabra knows the wishes of your heart," the woman said in the same horror movie wha-haha accent. "You have occult gifts. Your red hair promises that. But occult means hidden. Others over-look you. They don't see you as you are."

*That'd be nice if that were true,* Willow thought. *But I have a feeling I'm just plain old regular me.*

"Sit down. I will show you."

A black cat perched on the back of the chair, looking curiously at Willow with its golden almond eyes.

"Look," the woman invited, gesturing to her crystal ball.

Willow looked.

And she saw:

She saw . . .

*Oh, God, inside the crystal ball . . .*

Her lids drooped. She heard a buzzing in her ears, and something silvery sort of grew inside her mind, expanding outward, firing neurons and setting up new pathways.

It felt like she was getting *different*.

And different was good.

The interior of the crystal ball blazed with a fiery

scarlet. The scarlet became pink, and then silver. It was a mirror. And the face of an elderly man smiled straight at her. His hair was long and white, and his nose and chin were very sharp. He said to her, *"No wonder you're so envious."*

His smile was gentle. *"You are being completely overlooked, aren't you? It's hard to be so young, and so aware of your limitations."*

*Yes,* she thought, although she couldn't speak. *Oh yes, I'm so glad someone understands. . . .*

Then the ball swirled again; the red fire returned and Willow saw faces, stretched and pulled out of shape.

"Oh!" Sounding surprised, the woman draped a black velvet cloth over the crystal ball as if to hide it from Willow. "That's enough."

Willow's lids drooped again. She saw silver again; the neurons fired like cannons.

Drifting, moving, shifting . . .

She woke herself up with a snore.

"Oh, wow," she murmured, licking her lips. "Did I just fall asleep?"

She opened her eyes, to see a tarot reading spread before her. Madame Lazabra sat across from her, holding a glass of water.

"Are you all right?" she asked.

Willow frowned. "Am I? . . ."

"I went to get you some water and you dozed off." She wrinkled her nose. "It's stuffy in here, isn't it?"

"It's . . ." Willow nodded. "*Very* stuffy."

"I need to tell the management." She shook her

head. "The last place we were, it was even warmer than this." She chuckled. "So, what do you think?" She gestured to the cards. "Look at them, each in turn. Each in turn."

The woman's voice was soothing. Calming.

"I . . ." Willow scanned the layout. She didn't remember . . . wait, now it was coming. Now she remembered sitting down, and having a reading.

She had asked about Xander, and the tarot had delivered bad news. She remembered it all now. He was in love with another.

That would be Buffy, obviously.

"I can help you with this problem," Madame Lazabra said.

"Thank you," Willow murmured. Then she inhaled sharply and said, "What time is it?"

"Vaclav!" Madame Lazabra cried, clapping her hands.

The young man who had led Willow in reappeared, holding an ebony clock.

Yikes! She was nearly half an hour late for the rendezvous.

"I'm so sorry. Thank you so much. Is there a charge?" Willow asked anxiously.

Madame Lazabra waved her hand.

"Payment will be made," she assured Willow. Then her mouth practically split open, her smile was so wide. "Soon."

Giles was pissed off.

"The thing of it is, you're all late," he admonished

Buffy and her friends. And Cordy, who, of course, was not friends with any of them.

"You were late too," Cordy said. She was *so* not taking his crap. "I saw you walking up at the same time as me."

Giles opened and closed his mouth like a fish. His eyes practically spun. God, what was his deal?

"Okay, look," Xander said. He burped, and a shot of bad breath misted in Cordy's air space. "Sorry."

"Oh my God, you are disgusting," Cordy said. She waved a hand in front of her face to make it go away. "What have you been eating?"

"Eating? Did you eat anything? I specifically told you not to." Giles wiped his forehead. He was all sweaty. He reminded Cordy of some mangy creature about to chew off its own foot.

"I didn't eat anything," Xander assured him. "The only food I could get near was being served by clowns."

"And?" Giles prompted.

"*Clowns?*" Xander said again.

While Giles was busy scowling at Xander, Angel bent down and kissed Buffy on the earlobe. Flushing, Buffy gently batted him away.

Just then, Willow trudged up, and Giles's wrath was directed at the mousy little Slayerette. Tonight she was screaming street urchin even more than usual, because instead of her usual humble, self-effacing attitude, she looked completely and totally defeated.

"You are very, very late," Giles flung at her. "Where have you been?"

"I'm sorry," Willow said. "I lost track of time." Willow was her usual kick-me self. "I wouldn't have been so late if . . . if I had had a beautiful, expensive watch like Cordelia's," she said.

Surprised, Cordy glanced down at the one-of-a-kind watch her father had purchased for her in Gstaad. She didn't even realize Willow paid the slightest bit of attention to accessorizing. Because it sure didn't show in the way she dressed.

"This thing? Please," Cordy said, adding silently, *Touch it and die.*

"Well, we're all here now," Xander said. "No machetes in our foreheads either."

"All right, then let's debrief. Everyone, check in," Giles said impatiently. "Did anything unusual happen to any of you? Cordelia, how was the freak show?"

"Freak . . . *oh*. I didn't go," she confessed, so very much wishing she had just lied.

Giles blinked at her as if she had just told him she bought off the rack.

"Okay," she rushed on, holding out her hands. "I was headed for it, but I had to go down the midway to get to it. And there were all these games with prizes. These adorable purple baskets made out of glass, and teddy bears dressed like Elvis and . . . I didn't win any of them!"

Giles said calmly, "You played games."

"Yes. Okay, I said I was sorry!"

"No. You didn't." Giles crossed his arms over his chest.

"Well, I meant to!"

"Giles," Buffy said. "It's no big, okay? Right?" she persisted.

*Wow, Buffy is defending me,* Cordelia thought. *Maybe I'm in bigger trouble than I know.*

Giles jabbed a finger at Cordy like it was a butcher knife and he was a serial killer. "You specifically said you would go to the freak show! And you didn't, and now we don't know a thing about it!"

"It's okay," Cordelia pleaded. "We can still go to the freak show. It's still there. It's not like it's, um, any big deal."

"That's right," Xander jumped in. "Like Buffy said. No big."

"Yeah," Cordelia said. "No big."

*"No big?"* Giles asked icily. "Lives are at stake! In fact, *I* have sacrificed *my* entire life, and for what? Selfish girls like you who don't do what they're told!"

"Hey, hold on," Cordelia said. Now *she* was pissed. "I am *not* one of . . . of you guys, and I know you people have saved my life a few times, but that does not mean you can tell me what to do!"

His eyes bugged out. His face went purple. For a second, Cordy thought he might be having a heart attack.

"Giles, hey, dude," Xander began. "May I use the word 'overly' here? Because—"

"You stay out of this!" Giles shouted at him.

*"Giles,"* Buffy said. "Are you feeling all right."

"I'm fine," he said. He looked at Cordelia.

"Okay. I'm sorry, okay?" Cordy said, trying to put an end to the discussion. If it could be called a discussion. She was all whiny. She hated whiny, but he was freaking her out. "It's on my list. Freak show."

That seemed to satisfy him. But Cordy wasn't sure it satisfied her. She hadn't signed on for this ghostbusting stuff the way Buffy, Xander, and Willow had. She was still her own person.

"Angel? Buffy? Ferris wheel?" Was Giles actually snapping his fingers at them? God, if she were Buffy, she'd just break them right off and shove them up his—

"Ferris wheel." Buffy cleared her throat. "It . . . the line was so long . . ."

"Long line," Angel chimed in, wrapping his arm around her waist. He was all white-knight protector, and it was a good look for him.

"But we *wanted* to," Buffy said, snuggling up. "We were just worried w-we wouldn't be able to get back to the group in time."

Angel nodded.

"As it was, we were still a little late, because the carnival is so crowded and . . . and we wanted to be *polite*."

"Indeed," Giles sniffed.

"Yes!" Buffy said. "Because I was totally listening to you, Giles, and doing what you told me. So we just did a recon, patrolled around," Buffy finished. "But we didn't see anything weird."

"Nothing," Angel said.

"Nor I," Giles said, sounding exasperated. "Willow?"

The redhead took a breath. "I did go to the fortune-teller. Her name is Madame Lazabra, and she's actually very young. But it was really warm and stuffy, and when she went to get me some water, I dozed off."

"Ah, *I* fell asleep on the merry-go-round," Xander blurted. "Just a little."

Giles hesitated. Then he said, as if it were some horrible sin, "I got a bit faint in the Chamber of Horrors."

Cordelia raised her chin. "Well, I spent, like, a million dollars with nothing to show for it, but other than that, I stayed on my feet the whole time."

"There's a first," Xander said.

"We need to check this out further. Together. No more splitting up." He nodded at Willow. "We'll go to the fortune-teller first. It's closest."

"But why?" Buffy asked. "We already checked out that stuff."

"And have reached no conclusions," he said, quite crankily. "For once, just listen to me and do as I say." He looked at Willow. "Well?"

Even more dejected and rejected, Willow led the way. She supposed he had a point, going back to investigate together. But she had a feeling that if she had suggested it, it wouldn't have happened.

*People listen to Giles,* she thought. *Even when he's irritable. Me? Not so much. And I'm almost always pleasant.*

"She's in there," she said, pointing at the open tent flap.

Giles led the parade inside.

The area they entered was empty. Giles walked up to the suspended Day-Glo objects and the black curtain. A lettered sign had been attached to the curtain. MADAME LAZABRA HAS CLOSED HER TENT FOR THE EVENING. PLEASE COME ANOTHER DAY.

Angel looked back at the entrance. "There's no one else around."

"Well, let's take a peek behind the curtain," Buffy suggested. "Look around for a demon or something else fun to kill."

"Your cup of blood is always half full," Xander said. "I like that in a slayer."

There was a noise on the other side of the curtain. They all looked at each other.

"No," Giles whispered. "Let's leave well enough alone for the time being."

They trooped back outside.

"Let's go on to the carousel," Giles said.

Buffy thought about mentioning what a time-waster this all was, but she didn't want Giles to bite her head off. What was his deal? Gee.

Xander showed them his spot on the carousel. Giles sat on the chariot bench while Willow, Xander, and Cordelia stood beside the black stallions. Angel hoisted Buffy up onto the unicorn; she felt a little silly but it was still fun as the carousel began to rotate and her unicorn went up and down. Angel was glowing. It was like they were really on a date, all happy, with no death or dismemberment anywhere near them.

"Anyone feel anything?" Giles asked them as the carousel slowed to a stop.

Xander burped and covered his mouth. "Well, I'm not feeling so great. And yet, I'm really hungry."

"God, all you think about is your stomach," Cordelia said.

"Currently, yeah," Xander returned.

"Ferris wheel?" Buffy asked.

"Not fond of heights," Cordelia said.

"We haven't gone to the freak show," Willow ventured, looking at the others.

"We could play some games," Cordelia put in. "The games are fun. They have great prizes."

"You said you lost a ton of money in the midway," Willow argued.

"Are we on Court TV?" Cordelia snapped.

"I just . . ." Willow looked confused. She took a deep breath.

"The freak show it is," Giles announced. "Come. No dallying."

"Not liking freak shows," Willow murmured. "Too freaky."

*You're not wrong,* Buffy thought as she tried to swallow around the lump in her throat.

The group was standing with about fifteen other people in a room painted completely black. Everyone was walking slowly past a row of *things* in bottles of formaldehyde. Two-headed piglets, a calf with six feet . . . they were basically just accidents of nature. But some of them looked human, and they upset the Slayer.

*And I thought I could handle just about anything gross,* she thought. Even the word—"gross"—seemed harsh.

"This is appalling," Giles murmured, echoing her thought. She felt close to him in that moment, and a little sorry for all the times she had kept him out of her world.

*No, wait. That's part of growing up. But I'm not about growing up, so much. I'm about surviving to fight another day.*

"I'll bet they don't have stuff like this in England," Xander ventured. He was green.

"On the contrary, we do, very much," Giles said. "The British fascination with the macabre is well documented. But that makes it no less appalling."

Suddenly calliope music poured from hidden speakers. Strobe lights flashed all over the room, then began to spin. To Buffy's far right, a curtain rose, revealing a small stage hung with red drapes. The silhouette of a tall, caped figure rose from beneath the floor.

"Good evening," said a familiar voice.

A harsh blue light clicked on, revealing Professor Copernicus Caligari.

"Welcome to the House of Freaks!" he cried.

"Not to be confused with the House of Blues!" Xander said sotto voce.

Buffy tugged on Giles's jacket and stood on tiptoe. "Giles, that's him," she whispered loudly in his ear.

Giles nodded to let her know he'd heard.

"Come with me now, to the world of mutations,

aliens, things from another world. Curiosities, monstrosities!"

Thunder rumbled through the speakers, followed by the sound of lightning. Then the calliope music began again—slow, mournful, dirgelike. A few people applauded and a guy in a letter jacket howled like a wolf. The pretty blonde with him giggled.

From another alcove a dark-skinned man in a leather vest, leather pants, and boots appeared with a torch in his right fist. He opened his mouth, leaned his head back, and moved the torch over his lips, then spewed forth a blast of flame.

Willow moved closer to Buffy, and Xander flanked her. Cordelia muttered, "This is so stupid," but her voice was a little wavery.

Professor Caligari waved his hand to the right. "Follow my assistant, if you dare!"

From beneath a red light a hunchbacked figure limped from the shadows. It—he—was dressed like Quasimodo in the Disney movie, and his face . . .

*Are those scars, or fresh wounds?* Buffy thought. It was hard to tell in the bad light. But his features were a ruin, crisscrossed with deep purple lines and red welts. The only part of his face that wasn't hideous was one eye. The other was covered with an eye patch.

Beside Buffy, Willow caught her breath. Buffy shot her a glance as Willow looked away. Her redheaded buddy was so gentle. It took a toll on Willow to see the things being Buffy's friend made visible.

The assistant raised a hand and brought it down,

an awkward gesture that meant "follow me."

He led the laughing, uneasy crowd into a dark tunnel, past a row of little partitioned rooms that reminded Buffy of prison cells. The occupants were separated from the patrons by a wall of glass, and Buffy was glad. Because she needed some distance from what she was seeing.

There was a man whose body ended at his waist and a woman with a full beard and a very hairy back. Also, a guy who was double-jointed and could turn himself into a human pretzel. And a girl who turned into a leopard.

"It's done with mirrors, at least in her case," Giles explained.

Some of the freaks looked very sad. Others, as if they were bored. Maybe daydreaming of Anywhere But Here. Anyone but who they were.

There was a "pinhead," which was a man with a normal-sized body but a very tiny head, and a guy with the beginnings of a third arm growing out of his chest. He looked straight at Buffy and winked.

Buffy pushed against Angel's chest, and he held her, kissing the crown of her head. Then her temple, then her cheek.

Glad of the comfort, she squeezed his hand.

It got worse. It got very gross.

Then, just when Buffy didn't think she could handle any more, the bad went away. The assistant led them into a room called Fairyland. Half a dozen little people—of the human variety—were dressed in ballerina tutus and caps made to look like flower petals.

Holding cheap plastic light-up wands, they swooped around the room on wires. Music box music tinkled in the air.

Seven more little men were dressed like the Seven Dwarves, and they were kneeling before a glass coffin with their heads bowed. Inside the coffin lay the figure of a young girl with brown hair, her arms crossed over her chest. Her face was ashen; her lips, blue.

Buffy knew her dead people, and the woman looked real. As in, real dead.

She looked at Angel, who shook his head and whispered, "Heartbeat."

Buffy gave her one last appraising look before she walked from the room with the others.

"Well, that was disgusting," Xander said, as they trooped through the exit and rejoined the crowds. "Especially that last part."

"That was the good part," Willow argued. "Fairies."

"You are a twisted woman," Xander told her. "Those people were dwarves, Willow. Where does a carnival find twelve dwarves?"

"Little people," Willow corrected him.

Xander said, "Okay. Sorry. Meanwhile, who thinks Snow White was dead?"

"She wasn't dead. She had a heartbeat," Angel said.

"We should pay close attention to what Angel has to say on this subject, because he's had a lot of experience *creating* dead bodies," Xander continued.

Angel did not smile.

"Okay, but she looked awful," Cordelia said. "She needed more blush, at least."

Buffy stopped listening as her senses jogged up to high alert. She knew they weren't alone. Not alone, alone, of course, since they were surrounded by people. But alone in the sense of they weren't the only people interested in the conversation they were having.

Without missing a beat, Buffy whirled around and ran back through the exit. She saw someone in the shadows creeping away. No problem for the Slayer, who put on a burst of speed and threw her arms like a lasso around—

"Principal Snyder!" she cried, instantly releasing him.

"Summers, what are you doing?" he demanded, straightening his tie.

"Oh. I thought . . . um . . ."

"No thinking," Principal Snyder snapped. "Thinking is bad."

He grabbed her arm and marched her through the exit, where Giles and the others all looked extremely busted as Snyder stopped and glared at them.

"What are you people doing here together?" he demanded.

"We're . . . on a field trip," Giles replied, then fell silent.

Willow stepped into the breach. "For the research," she finished helpfully. "Did you know that in the Middle Ages, people watched morality plays, um . . ." She looked back at Giles.

"To learn about being good, moral people," Giles concluded. "We're looking for cross-references in symbols and icons to show the continuity from those days to these . . . days of learning about morality."

"Fascinating," Principal Snyder said, in a voice that added, *so not*. "This is what happens with budget cuts."

"And you're here for? . . ." Giles added. "The fun?"

"I'm here because in the last three days truancy has gone up sixty-eight percent, and I know this carnival is to blame."

Giles looked puzzled as he pushed up his glasses. "But how can that be, seeing as the carnival just arrived?"

Snyder scowled at Giles. "What do you mean? They've been here since last Friday."

There was a beat as everyone took that in.

"No," Cordy said, glancing at the others. "Tonight is opening night."

"Are you on something?" Snyder challenged her.

Giles waded in. "I think what Cordelia is trying to say, is that this is the first time any of us has been to the carnival. So she's surprised by the truancy rate."

"No," Cordelia said again, and Xander grunted through clenched teeth, *"Cor-de . . . lia."*

Willow jumped in. "She's not surprised by the truancy rate," she told their rat-headed principal, "um, because we have discovered during our research that most traveling . . . shows . . . promote truancy and job absenteeism." She stared wide-eyed at Giles, who nodded, urging her to go on. She took a breath. "And it gets worse over time. It's called the Running-Away-to-Join-the-Circus Effect."

She nodded emphatically.

Everyone else nodded too.

Except Snyder.

"You honestly believe that," Snyder said, looking at each of them in turn. They all nodded some more.

"Then I'm going to declare this whole place off-limits to students. Any student caught on these grounds will be personally expelled by me."

"That's a good policy," Giles agreed. "I'm entirely in accord."

*Good thinking, Giles.* Buffy silently congratulated him. If banning the carnival could keep kids away—

"I'm not sure you can enforce that," Cordelia said. She looked at the others as they made silent pleas for her to shut up. *"What?"*

No one said a word, just kept looking strained.

"No carnival on school days, then," Principal Snyder amended. "I'm sure I can enforce *that*." He looked pleased with himself. "So enjoy the carnival tonight. Tomorrow, it's forbidden territory."

"You got it," Xander assured him. "After tonight, we shun the carnival."

Then Buffy heard someone else shuffling away just behind her. She looked at Giles, who was looking at Principal Snyder, and said loudly, "Oh, gee, I think I heard"—she searched for a name—"Jonathan. The other member of our research . . . club. We lost track of him," she explained to the principal. "And so, I must go and find him."

She dashed back into the freak show. It was dimly lit, and a large crowd was coming through, but she thought she saw the heel of a leather shoe disappear around the next corner. It resembled the shoes their Quasimodo guide had worn.

"Coming through!" she cried, but there were too many people. Unless she wanted to create a disturbance, there was no way she could plow through fast enough to catch up with the owner of the shoe.

Frustrated, she turned back and rejoined the group out in the breezeway. Except for Principal Snyder, they were all there, looking bewildered. Except for Giles. Giles was jazzed.

"Find anyone?" Willow asked.

"Thinking maybe our freak show tour guide," Buffy replied.

"I thought for a minute that he might be the guy in the fortune-teller tent," Willow said. "But he was all ewww."

Buffy said to Giles, "Why are you smiling?"

"Because something wicked this way has come," he said. On her look, he elaborated, "Principal Snyder thought this carnival has been here nearly a week. But it opened just tonight as far as we're concerned."

"Yeah, so he doesn't get out much," Buffy said.

"Because, for starters, who would let him out?" Xander asked.

"We can ask people when they think the carnival came to Sunnydale too," Willow suggested.

"Excellent thinking," Giles told her.

She smiled, looking pathetically grateful.

The informal survey got a mix of answers ranging from two weeks ago to one week ago, to tonight.

"And it's weird that it opened on a Wednesday," Willow said. "Don't things open on Friday nights? The beginning of the weekend?"

"Boys and girls, I'd say we have Rising liftoff," Xander said and then burped. "I have to go," he said. "I'm not feeling so well."

"The carnival's due to close soon," Giles said, checking his watch.

"You have a nice watch too," Willow murmured. "Because you have a job."

Giles apparently didn't hear her. He said, "Willow, tomorrow I want you to research anything unusual in the last two weeks—if, as Principal Snyder has insisted, the truancy rate has gone up, and also if there have been any unusual occurrences."

"I'll check the usual places," she told him. "School records, police reports, internal memos."

"Very good."

"I'm thinking Angel and I really should go check out the Alibi," Buffy said. Angel sidled up to her again and laced his fingers through hers.

A sudden crescendo of calliope music blanketed their conversation. The notes were hollow and cold. The tune sent ice-water fingers up Buffy's spine, and she actually felt her heart skip a beat. Cordelia touched her chest as if she were having the same reaction, and Willow wrapped her arms around herself.

"Look," Willow said, pointing.

A spotlight beamed a blue-white circle at the topmost car of the Ferris wheel. A figure in black rose from the seat and spread its arms wide. The figure was wearing a black cape. Long white hair flowed over its shoulders.

"Ladies and gentlemen!" cried a voice Buffy knew. It was Professor Caligari again. By the reverb, she assumed there were loudspeakers scattered throughout the carnival grounds.

"I am Professor Copernicus Caligari!" The figure in the Ferris-wheel chair bowed from the waist. "Thank you so much for coming. The carnival is now closed for the evening. Please come again tomorrow!"

The crowd around them hooted and cheered.

Cordelia muttered, "Talk about your freaks."

Willow said to Buffy, "Do you think he looks like the guy in the woodcut?"

"I don't know. The woodcut is pretty basic," Buffy replied.

"Maybe the one we saw in the freak show was a robot," Cordelia ventured. "Or someone dressed up like him."

As Buffy stared up at him, something passed in front of her eyes. It was like light glinting off something metallic, or a camera flash. She shielded her gaze by raising her arm across her face.

And then it was gone.

She glanced at Angel, who raised his brows and said, "What?"

"Did you just see . . . ," she began, and then she couldn't remember what had just happened.

She thought a minute.

"Yes?" he prodded.

"Nothing." Nothing had happened. "I just felt funny for a minute. I'm okay now."

"Then let's go to the Alibi," he said.

"You got it." Buffy smiled at him. To Giles, "We'll walk with you guys to the exit."

They joined the lazy stampede. Buffy searched the faces of those around her. A couple was arguing. A boy in a stroller was crying. Nothing too out of the ordinary there, when you considered the noise level, the amount of people, and the expense of food and souvenirs. People even argued and cried at Disneyland.

*Of course, I kept my cool all night, even with Angel here,* she thought proudly. *I'm the Slayer. I know how to maintain.*

"Wonder if Willy will be in a talkative mood," Angel said.

"If he isn't, I'll kick his ass until he is," she told him. "I'll kick all their asses." She flexed her biceps. "I'm in great shape."

He laced his fingers through hers and smiled hungrily.

Beside her, Xander slowed and covered his mouth. "It's getting worse."

"Well, if you're going to vomit, for God's sake, do it here," Giles said loudly. "And not in my car."

"Giles, that-that's *mean*," Willow said, rushing to Xander's defense.

"Yeah," Cordelia said. "Cold much?"

Saying nothing, Giles stomped toward the exit.

"God, Giles," Buffy said slowly to his retreating back. She frowned. Then she said to Cordelia, "Maybe you should take Xander home. My watcher has PMS."

"Buffy," Willow murmured.

"What?" Buffy tossed her hair. "Does he think he can treat my friends that way?"

"I guess he does," Xander said weakly.

"Well, he can't," she finished. "I won't put up with it." She raised her chin. "I don't know why I have to have him around anyway. I don't need a babysitter."

"Woof. You go, girl," Xander said.

"Are you okay?" Angel asked her.

She blinked. "Never better."

"Because you seem . . . like you need a good kiss." He smiled at her and held out his arm.

Smiling back at him, Buffy scooted into his embrace and trailed her fingers down his arm, putting her hand in the back pocket of his pants.

Meanwhile, Cordelia looked hard at Xander. "What is wrong with you? *Are* you going to vomit?"

"I don't know," Xander said, gasping.

"Do you need some water?" Willow asked.

Xander shook his head.

Giles huffed all the way to the parking lot, muttering to himself. Buffy scooted up a little so she could hear what he was saying.

". . . lazy girl. *Kendra*, on the other hand, listened to me, performed her duties admirably. But Buffy . . .

she just goes on about it however she pleases. *God*, she's driving me mad . . ."

Buffy froze. Her breath caught.

"Buffy, he doesn't mean it," Willow murmured, drawing close to her friend.

"Who cares?" Buffy shot back, glaring at the back of Giles's head. "Who the hell does he think he is? He has no idea what it's like to be me. Where does he get off judging me?"

"Buffy, um, not so loud," Willow said.

Buffy snickered. "Really, Willow, what could he do to me? Nothing. What is he? Nothing."

She sauntered off with Angel in tow.

Forking off from the others, Xander and Cordy walked through the parking lot toward her car. As he opened the passenger-side door, she caught it and said, "Don't throw up, okay? These seats are leather and *oooh* . . ."

"Gee, Florence Nightingale, I'm loving your concern. Maybe you should just tape my mouth shut," he said irritably.

"Oooh," she said again. She walked on steady feet toward the candy-apple-red classic Porsche 911 in the parking lot. It gleamed like the heart in the Tunnel of Love. It was beautiful. So beautiful.

Silver flashed before her eyes; it was probably the chrome detailing . . .

*"You need beautiful things. There's just not enough to satisfy you, but you have to try,"* said a voice inside Cordelia's head.

She was dizzy from wanting the Porsche. It was

hard to stand there and stare at it without owning it.

"God, I would *kill* for a car like that," she breathed.

"I'll just bet you would," Xander said dryly.

"Yeah," she said, balling her fists. She smiled to herself. "I would."

# Chapter Seven

Tears streamed down Stephanie Hahn's cheeks as she ran for all she was worth. Something was wrong; something was terribly wrong. . . .

"Steph, will you slow down?" David demanded as they burst out of the forest, just a few feet north of the graveyard. "I am breaking into a sweat!"

"Oh my God, I totally ruined my life," she groaned. "How could I say those things to Cordelia Chase? What was I thinking?"

"That you're hotter than she is? Because you are," her twin insisted, coming up beside her. "What is your rush?"

"It's ten," she said. "It closes at ten."

She heard it then, the reedy, sweet call of the calliope, playing up and down her backbone, running along her forehead. Soothing, beckoning, promising . . .

*It will be all right if I can get there in time. It was so stupid that we had to go to that stupid chess-club meeting. Something is wrong, but it will be okay if I can get back to the carnival. It will be okay.*

*He said I was beautiful. He told me I was the fairest in the land . . .*

*. . . the man in the mirror. If he can tell me that again, I'll be all right.*

She didn't know why, but she did know it was true. Down to her bones, she knew that the carnival would make it all right.

And not just the carnival. . . .

She put on a burst of speed, as she had last night when those . . . gang members were chasing them. That girl from school had saved them. It was all a mishmash now. She couldn't remember most of it.

*I was pretty. But I'm not anymore!*

She was in an agony, and it hurt down to her soul. She *used* to be pretty, but her face had melted into what she saw in the mirror now. Hour by hour, she had watched her beauty fade. It had made her shake. Made her sick.

Until she had realized what to do: Come back to the carnival, and it would be all right. It was like a voice whispering: *"Just come back. Come back. You are lovely."*

She dashed through the carnival parking lot, winding her way around the cars, hot tears in her eyes as she mentally willed the calliope to *keep playing, please, keep playing. . . .*

Against the black velvet sky the Ferris wheel was still

lit up. Across the arch the words PROFESSOR CALIGARI'S TRAVELING CARNIVAL swam before Stephanie's eyes.

In front of the arch, one, two, three . . . seven clowns were lined up, shaking the hands of people leaving the carnival. One was squeezing a bike horn. Two were waltzing to the calliope music.

One, dressed all in green, spotted Stephanie and flung both arms up in the air, waving excitedly at her. He began to jump up and down, gesturing for her to hurry, hurry!

The other clowns saw her too. She started crying again; she wasn't sure why, but she raced toward them, her own arms open, crying, "Help me!"

David ran up behind her; then they were both enveloped by the clowns, the dear, wonderful clowns, who hustled them through the crowds—*make way for the Hahns!*—the one in green putting his arm around Stephanie as they dashed onto the carnival grounds.

Uncle Sam, the man on stilts, looked down at them and waved. He said, "Back for a recharge, eh?" Then he laughed jovially and walked on, shouting into a mic, "Closing time, folks! Come back tomorrow! We're here until the full moon!"

Past the merry-go-round and the Octopus and the Tilt-A-Whirl; through the game corridor and around the tents; the calliope music rose and swelled and Stephanie thought her heart would burst from her chest, she was running so hard.

And the clowns gamboled and capered with her into the fun house!

Her pulse was pounding in her ears, almost, but not quite, drowning out the calliope, the dear, wonderful calliope.

And then . . . the clowns were gone.

She and David were in the mirror maze alone.

And they were standing side by side, staring into a mirrored panel together.

Stephanie swayed as a wave of dizziness swept over her. A silver blur obscured her vision—just for a moment, a couple of musical notes—and then she stared at herself and whispered, "Oh, God, I am so beautiful."

David licked his lips. "We both are. We're even hotter than I remembered. Stephanie, we are *incredible*."

They put their arms around each other's waists, touching heads, gazing into the mirror.

A voice whispered: *"Mirror, mirror, on the wall, whose souls are the fairest of them all?"*

"Ours," Stephanie said, reaching forward to touch her image.

Her hand slipped through the surface . . . and then long, skeletal fingers grabbed her on the sides of her face and yanked her forward.

A bicycle horn blatted.

Outside, the carousel started up, drumming and clashing.

David shouted and held on to Stephanie, but she was pulled through the mirror, pulled . . . and he with her.

One scream, just one . . .

And the fun house plunged into blackness as maniacal laughter echoed through the twists and turns.

In the freak show Fairyland the eyes of the girl in the glass coffin flew open. They were completely black.

She pounded her fists on the top and sides of the glass. She kicked.

Vaclav, the Gypsy's helper as well as the assistant in the Quasimodo costume, watched from the curtains, his fists clenched so tightly that blood dribbled from his palms.

Light flashed all around the girl in the glass coffin.

Opening the coffin lid, he reached out a hand to the girl. She blinked as if she had never seen a hand in her life.

Vaclav sobbed once, hard, as his heart broke. The coffin hadn't worked. She was still ruined. And Vaclav knew whose fault it was.

He hated Professor Caligari.

Hated him with a vengeance.

As the carnival devoured the successfully tempted, Professor Caligari leaped off the Ferris wheel and soared through the air. Like a bat on the wing, he glided through the night wind, laughing as he landed on the shoulders of the Seven: his faithful jesters, Messrs. Vanity, Envy, Greed, Lust, Gluttony, Anger, and Sloth. The clowns capered and pranced.

"Have you been playing, Tricksters?" Professor Caligari asked the merry clowns with their painted-on faces and whirligig wigs.

In answer, they carried him to a shiny black dais before his wagon. As one, they fell to their knees, stretched out their arms, and buried their faces in the sawdust, salaaming the Great One.

Through the Employees Only gate the carnies poured in from the carnival grounds. Another day done. A few more souls absorbed. They would gather momentum. It was almost time. And then . . .

Shrouded in darkness, some of Professor Caligari's loyal followers shambled out of their human skins, gathering them up and wadding them into rolls like sleeping bags. Tentacles popped free; faces caved in. Some rolled, some slithered. Some burrowed.

Others, who actually were human but in many cases centuries old, kicked back with cigarettes and popped open beer cans. The fire-eater from the freak show lit a fire.

The carousel creatures detached from their poles, stretching their backs and rolling their heads after long hours of being ridden by humans. The skeletal woman who rode the chariot materialized and took up the reins. Her phantom baby suckled at her desiccated ribs.

Madame Lazabra and Vaclav joined the gathering. Madame Lazabra carried a black velvet box studded with jewels. Vaclav was wearing a pair of jeans and a dark gray sweatshirt. He wore an earring in his left ear and tenderly held the hand of a beautiful young girl, who stumbled forward like a hypnotized maiden in an old-fashioned horror movie.

Her name was Sandra Morehouse, and she had

hung herself last night while Professor Caligari was busy with their intrusive guests. His hold on her had wobbled after she had suddenly remembered that a month ago she had shot a man dead because he wouldn't give her his wallet. Apparently that moment of clarity brought remorse so great that she had tried to end her life. A few hours in the magickal glass coffin in Fairyland had restored her—physically, at least.

Returned as well to his control, she would never remember what she'd done again. Of course, she would also never remember her own name, either.

One had to make trade-offs.

Still, it was a pity. Professor Caligari had thought she might make a fine wife for Vaclav, the Gypsy boy who had joined his retinue in 1856. Without his frightening makeup appliances, Vaclav appeared now as he had when he had joined the carnival, tempted by his lust for the fortune-teller. He had been strong and young, and so, rather than allow the soulcatchers to absorb his soul, Caligari had put him to work.

The secret to keeping him youthful and strong, of course, was annual stays inside the glass coffin. The magickal prism healed diseases and rejuvenated old bones and hearts. Caligari had created it himself after torturing a Middle Eastern mystic for the secret. All the humans took turns lying in it.

That counted him out, of course.

With a special smile for Vaclav, who he knew must be disappointed that Sandra's mind was now gone, Professor Caligari spread out his arms in welcome. His long, thin face flickered in the glow from the fire as the monsters, demons, and human monsters gave him their full attention.

"It's happening," he announced. "Order in Sunnydale is breaking down. Murders and robberies are going up. The souls of the weakest are ripe for the plucking. In fact, as I speak"—he cocked his head—"two more are joining our traveling company."

As Professor Caligari gazed into the faces of those who served him, he thought back through the many guises they had worn—as ancient Romans, Druids, witch finders, necromancers, dance-hall girls, snake charmers, contortionists—and the many places they had visited—the Folies Bergère in Paris, the Las Vegas strip, Renn faires, and county fairs. They had lured the unsuspecting with vaudeville revues, belly dances, magic shows, bear baitings, and witch burnings.

"It's souls I'm after," Professor Caligari reminded everyone. "And a few warm bodies to join our ranks. It takes a lot of manpower to run an operation like this."

He gestured to the new recruit, Carl Palmer. Carl smiled dumbly at him and gave him a thumbs-up. Professor Caligari knew that if the young man's mind were not so clouded, he, Caligari, might have another suicide on his hands. At the urging of Tessa, the girl who ran the coin toss, Carl had murdered his mother for the eight dollars in her purse. Not even enough for another roll of quarters.

But Carl didn't mind anymore. Caligari had seen to that.

"As you know, Sunnydale is a special place. It's on a hellmouth. That means that the mystical energies here are more powerful than other locations in this dimension. Many of the souls we take here will be very, very special."

He took on the tone and rhythm of an itinerant preacher of the Old West, or a man who traveled the plains in his magic wagon and dispensed potions and told fortunes.

"Friends, our business is the collecting of souls. It is our legal tender. It is our life's blood."

To the ignited background music of the carousel, he remembered those traveling days, days of steam locomotives, Comanches, and desperadoes. It had been harder to capture souls back then. There were fewer people, and they lived farther apart. In the pressure cooker of modern life, people cracked faster, too. Folks back then were more suspicious. Also more fragile. A lot of them died before their souls could be collected.

"Humans," the professor said derisively. "They are weak, fragmented, and unclean. They're easily tempted, easily caught in the web of my soulcatchers."

The clowns juggled their spheres higher and higher into the air.

*"Mirror, mirror on the wall, I am filled with lust, anger, vanity, greed, gluttony, sloth, and envy,"* Professor Caligari intoned, in his special, hypnotic voice. *"And when I see it reflected back to me, I seize it!"*

The crowd laughed.

"Others . . . need a little coaxing." He grinned at his worshipful followers.

"Scare them. Throw them off-balance. Kill some, if you wish. But drive them to me. To survive no matter what the cost is their greatest temptation. Humans are so afraid of death that they will barter their own souls to avoid it. And so . . . I want you to stir it up here in Sunnydale. Terrify the inhabitants. Threaten them. Make storms and craziness. Whip them into a frenzy. They'll find that only here do they feel safe. There's something about the carnival . . ."

He snapped his fingers, and at once the carnie clearing wobbled and blurred, and became . . . the keep of a castle.

A church.

A cave.

"Something about being here that makes them feel safe," he concluded. "But, of course, Professor Copernicus Caligari's Traveling Carnival is the most dangerous place in Sunnydale for anyone with a soul."

"And it's about to become a lot more dangerous," came a voice from inside Professor Caligari's wagon.

The owner of the voice stepped from the shadows. Tall, dark-haired, and blue-eyed, an old "friend" of Sunnydale, and of Rupert Giles, the Watcher of the reigning Slayer: Mr. C. Haos.

Also known as Ethan Rayne.

Beside him, a huge puddle of blackness drooped its head, growling at the assembled masses.

"Heel, Malfaiteur," Ethan said to the Rottweiler, yanking at the wickedly spiked chain around its neck. Then to Professor Caligari, "Thank you, Professor. I'm absolutely delighted to be working with you. It's such an honor. I want to let you know that I will do all I can to help you with the downfall of Sunnydale. It holds such a special place in my heart."

• • •

Buffy rammed her fist into the vampire's face again. It was a bloody pulp.

Just like the faces of the three other vampires she had beaten . . . before she dusted them.

"You guys think you can hold out on *me*?" she demanded. "The Slayer?"

"N . . . no," the vampire managed. It was a mess. Fairly new, and not a good fighter.

No challenge here.

She grabbed it by the arms and executed a mind-bendingly vicious knee strike to its groin.

The vampire howled.

"Remember this moment. No, wait. In about five minutes, you won't be remembering anything. Because you'll be a big pile of dust."

She reached out her hand. Angel handed her the stake, running his hand up and down her arm as she got ready for the death blow.

"You have one more chance," she said, showing the vamp the business end of the weapon. "Talk to me about the Rising."

The vampire shook its head. "I just got here," it insisted. "Came to town last night!"

She positioned the stake against its chest. "One more push and you fit in an ashtray," she said.

"I don't kno—"

Dusted!

The vampire exploded.

"God, it excites me to watch you fight," Angel said, kissing her all crazy.

Crazy, crazy, crazy.

Then Angel hissed. He had vamped. He looked up at the sky and pulled Buffy into the alley beside Willy's demon-hangout bar.

"It's getting light out," she realized. "You have to go." She pressed herself against him. "Now."

"We have time." He kissed her again. "Come on, we have time."

Every part of her yearned to say yes. But she also knew it was too risky. In a few minutes Angel would be in grave danger from the sunlight. Willy couldn't be trusted to keep him safe, and Buffy had to make an appearance at . . .

. . . *home,* she thought. *Oh my God, I am so in trouble.*

"Oh my God," she said aloud.

"Is there a problem, ma'am?" came a voice from the other end of the alley. Woman, Southern twang.

Footsteps walked toward her and Angel.

"Hi," Buffy said to the red-haired woman standing behind Angel. "Can I help you?"

Angel turned. "Claire," he said.

The woman smiled. "Oh, hey. Evenin'. Fancy runnin' into you in another dark alley."

Buffy looked from the woman to Angel and back again. Her lip curved. Did this chick actually think Angel was interested in her?

"Let's go," she said, grabbing his hand.

Buffy and Angel reached her home and she climbed through the upstairs window. Angel stayed below, moving under a purple sky to reach his apartment.

Buffy quickly changed into boxers and a baby tee, with no idea if her mother had waited up or what.

She crept downstairs and found her mom in the kitchen, asleep with her head on the table. Her big business checkbook was open. Buffy picked up a piece of paper and inspected it. It was the art gallery's utility bill. It was overdue.

Another bill was for three months of the services of a security company. Unpaid.

A collection notice for shipping.

*And she was going to take me shopping,* Buffy thought. Something in her went *pfffftt* like a balloon. She had been all into herself, all swaggering around and flaunting how cool she was . . . and okay, Slayer. But also daughter.

She ran her fingers through her mother's hair. Joyce Summers bolted awake, then smiled when she saw her daughter.

"I . . . oh, I fell asleep. I thought . . ." She sat up slowly. "When did you get in?"

"I've been upstairs," Buffy hedged. "I didn't realize you were in here."

"Oh. Did you have a nice time? Did you get your homework done?"

The traditional Mom questions. Buffy felt like the worst of daughters, sneaking around and partying while her mom was worrying and scared.

Buffy offered her hand. "Let's go upstairs."

"All right, honey." Joyce glanced down at the field of papers. "I'll clean this up—"

"In the morning," Buffy urged.

She put her arm around her mother's shoulders and slowly they went upstairs together.

They kissed each other good night on the cheek and then Buffy brushed her teeth and climbed in bed.

*If I'm so great, why can't I help my mom?* she thought. *I was so arrogant tonight. Snotty to Giles . . . but what was* his *deal? He was so mean. Oh my God, he dissed me so badly.*

She turned over. Her lips were sore from all the kissage. So nice. Angel was so romantic lately . . . their relationship was moving to a higher level, that was for sure. She had never dreamed a guy could kiss the way he did, be so focused on her. It was almost humbling. But not quite.

*If we keep this up . . . we'll seize the moment. I'm only sixteen.*

*But I'm the Slayer.*

She began to drift. As the metal flashed in the night . . . silver . . .

Now Buffy's car on the Ferris wheel swung jauntily at the very top, and all of Sunnydale lay at her feet.

*"You are the queen of all you survey,"* said the voice. *"No one else has power like you. You are unique."*

"I'm the Chosen One," Buffy said aloud. "Me. The Slayer. Tag, I'm It."

*"Super strength, super healing abilities. It must be difficult to pretend all the time. To be forced to conceal your magnificence."*

"It's kind of a drag," she admitted. "Especially when I get in trouble for it. School, friends, being the Slayer . . . it's hard to juggle it all."

"*It doesn't have to be,*" said the voice. "*I can change all that for you. You can shine like the shooting star you are meant to be.*"

And then the Slayer was staring into something shiny. Her face stared back at her. She gazed into her own eyes.

"*You were meant for greater things,*" the voice insisted. "*To take pride in your nature, not to hide it like something to be ashamed of.*"

"Oh, I'm proud."

"*They don't understand you. They don't really help you. When it comes down to the wire, you always have to handle it yourself, don't you?*"

"They're sweet; they try."

"*But you are the Slayer.*"

"It's a burden," she admitted. "But they do help—"

"*No. They get in the way. They slow you down. You're only being nice. You would do much better without them.*"

Buffy's face looked back at her. It was kind of glowing.

"*Look at you. You have a halo, like a saint. You're a god. You're above them. Don't expect too much out of them. That is so cruel.*"

"I never thought of it that way," Buffy confessed.

"*You need to leave them behind. Handle things yourself. Alone.*"

"Alone," the Slayer whispered, to the sweet cadence of the calliope as it now drifted through her open window.

Because she was not on the Ferris wheel. She was in her bed.

And someone was gazing at her through a frame of curlicues and shining stones; a face, a horrible face, stretching and shifting and glaring and staring. And behind him, David and Stephanie Hahn, strapped down, things with knives moving toward their faces. . . .

Buffy groaned and turned over in her sleep.

Thursday, after school.

Xander had been sick all day, and got to stay home. Cordelia had given him a lift over to Giles's, where they were gathering. Buffy had walked over, but Willow had yet to show.

And there were kittens.

One was gray and white, and one was black, and they weighed as much as a handful of feathers.

"And their names are?" Buffy asked as she nuzzled the black one with her cheek. Xander was lying listlessly on Giles's couch, examining an assortment of little aluminum pouches of cat food. Cordelia was off in a corner, explaining for perhaps the two-dozenth time that she was allergic to cats. Every once in a while she would sneeze very daintily, and someone would think to mutter, "Bless you."

"Names? I don't know yet," Giles said, with a faint hint of pink in his cheeks.

Buffy was glad things were back to better between them. She figured he didn't know that she had overheard . . . what she had overheard. Maybe he'd just been letting off steam. He was under a lot of pressure. After all, he *was* kind of old, and out of his element.

"How about Barnum and Bailey?" Cordelia suggested. "Since we're on a circus theme."

"Carnival," Xander corrected her. "Theme. Not a cruise."

"What*ever*."

"Speaking of the carnival, any new thoughts on what's going on?" Buffy asked.

Giles took a pouch of Little Friskies from Xander and tore it open. "Not so far. I was up half the night with the kittens. They make quite a lot of noise." He picked up their already-brimming dish from beside the couch and started to carry both it and the pouch into the kitchen. "They seem to have no interest in food."

Xander moaned. "I think I have rabies."

"Has either of them bitten you?" Giles asked, alarmed.

Cordelia sneezed.

"Bless you," Buffy said.

"No, but I'm, like, foaming at the mouth," Xander said, licking his lips. "I live in Phlegm Town."

"Yuck. Thank you for sharing," Cordelia said. Then she stared harder at Xander. "Is that a piece of cat food stuck to your cheek? Oh my God, Xander! Have you been scarfing their food?"

Before Xander could answer, he was saved by a sharp knock on Giles's front door.

"That's probably Willow," Giles said. "Here." He handed the dish and the bowl to Buffy, and crossed to the door.

As Buffy gazed down at it and then over to

Xander, Giles opened the door and took a step back as Willow sailed in.

"Guys," Willow said. She was out of breath. "Carl and Mariann Palmer's mom is dead and Principal Snyder is missing!"

"What?" Xander sat up. "That's such great news! Not the mom part," he amended. "That is *horrible* news." He frowned. "How did she die?"

Willow pantomimed hitting something. "Looks like a robbery. In her own house. Carl's fingerprints are all over a flashlight that was lying next to her."

"Good Lord." Giles pushed up his glasses and scratched his forehead. "Are you saying that Carl Palmer killed his own mother?"

"That, or the electricity went out," Xander said.

"Or he was trying to defend her," Buffy pointed out.

"How can you rob your own parents?" Willow asked.

"Ask Cordelia. She's stealing years from hers," Xander said.

"Her purse was open and her wallet was empty," Willow said. "Which doesn't make sense, if Carl did it."

"Yeah, it does, if you're, like, a drug addict or something," Cordelia argued.

"But he *has* money. He has a job," Willow said. "At the library. Or, he did."

"Is he in custody?" Giles asked.

Willow shook her head. "No. He's missing too."

"Oh, God," Cordelia said, covering her mouth. "Maybe Carl killed Principal Snyder!"

"We can hope," Xander muttered, then added, "Just

kidding." Then added, "Not." Then added, "Of course I'm kidding."

"Well, Principal Snyder was last seen at the carnival," Willow said. "And guess what?"

"So was Carl Palmer," Giles ventured.

Her face fell. "You guessed."

"Principal Snyder was going to ban kids from going to the carnival on school days," Buffy said. "And I *swear* that Quasimodo guy was spying on us."

The little gray kitten attacked Giles's shoe. It mewed and batted at the laces. Giles exhaled impatiently.

"Also? Listen to this," Willow said mysteriously. "There is no record of there actually being a carnival in Sunnydale. No news articles, no permits, nothing. It just . . . appeared."

"Out of nowhere, into the here," Giles mused.

"Also? In the last week the crime rate has shot up. There's been a thirty-six-percent increase in robberies, murders, and vandalism."

"I thought I noticed more graffiti in the graveyards," Buffy said as she cuddled the naughty kitten.

"Did you notice any extra graves?" Xander asked.

"Can't say I did," Buffy replied. The kitten batted at her hair, and she laughed.

"Well, we ought to investigate," Giles said. "Go back to the carnival and see what we can find out."

"I can't go," Xander said apologetically. "I can barely move."

"And unfortunately I have cheerleading practice." Cordelia sneezed. "Oh, hey, what a nice letter opener."

She picked up a shiny blade thingie off the bookcase and inspected it, eyes wide with interest. "There's writing on it. 'Ta-mir-o—'"

"Please, put that down immediately," Giles snapped. "It's not a letter opener. It's a sacrificial knife used in the summoning of Astorrith, who is a very powerful demon. If you continue saying those words and simultaneously cut yourself, you might very well summon him."

"Oh, sorry," Cordelia said in a little voice, replacing the knife on the shelf. "You shouldn't just leave things like that lying around in the open. What if it fell into the wrong hands?"

"I don't know, Giles. Until you get these little guys housebroken, you might consider some AstroTurf," Xander said, wrinkling his nose.

"Damn. Did one of them do his business on my rug?"

Xander shook his head, gathering up the fabric of his corduroy pants with a grimace. "No. One of them did *her* business on my pants."

Giles balled his fists. "Those little beasts. They're damned infuriating!"

"Jeez, maybe you shouldn't have pets," Cordelia muttered.

"Okay, that was fun. Going to the carnival," Buffy announced, handing her kitten to Willow. "See you later."

"Very well, you and I will go on ahead." Giles turned to Willow. "Meantime, you check and see if you can glean more information about Mrs. Palmer's death and Principal Snyder's disappearance."

"Oh." Willow looked forlorn as she stroked the kitten's back. It was curled up in her hand like a Tribble on classic *Star Trek*. "I can't go too?"

"You'd do better doing your hacking thing," he said.

Willow took a breath. "But . . ."

Giles scowled at her. "Do you want to help or not?"

Willow looked crushed. The kitten mewed, as if echoing her sentiments exactly.

"Giles," Xander said. "Will's always been a big helper."

The phone rang. With a huff, Giles rushed off to take it in the kitchen. "Yes?" he yelled.

"God, what is his deal?" Cordelia asked. "He's so cranky."

"The watcher gig is a lot of pressure," Buffy suggested, leaning over and giving the kitten a kiss on its small, soft head. "It's hard to keep up with a slayer. Especially me."

The kitten started licking the end of Willow's chin. "Well, at least *you* love me," she murmured.

As if on cue, the cat scrabbled out of Willow's arms and darted under the couch.

"That's cats. Love you and leave you," Xander said. "Oh, say, weren't you a cat for Halloween, Cordelia?"

"Yes, and how lucky for me that I will never love you," she snapped.

Giles bustled back into the room. "Buffy, that was Willy. Two vampires are down at the Alibi, discussing the carnival. I want you to go down there right now and see what you can find out."

Buffy waved her hands back and forth as if she were a traffic cop telling him to put on his brakes. "Giles, I went there last night, remember? By the time I get to the Alibi, those vamps will be long gone. It'll be a total waste of time."

"I disagree." He narrowed his eyes at her.

"Well, congratulations." She folded her arms across her chest.

"Aren't you Miss Thing today," Cordelia said. "And every day," she added under her breath.

"Well, yeah, actually, I am." Buffy squared her shoulders and gave her hair a toss. "The one girl in all my generation, remember?"

"Buffy," Willow said quietly.

"The one girl who is supposed to listen to her watcher, remember?" Giles said. His voice was deadly quiet.

"Well, I *would* listen to you, if what you were telling me to do made any sense."

"Buffy," Willow said again, a little more loudly.

Giles took off his glasses. Xander sat up slowly, staring hard at Buffy as if he couldn't believe what he was hearing.

The tension in the room was rising toward the boiling point.

Giles said, "I beg your pardon?"

"You heard me." The Slayer put her hands on her hips and raised her chin. "Or maybe you didn't.

So I'll say it again. Read my lips. I'm going to the carnival."

"What is wrong with you?" Willow asked her. She looked at Giles. "Something's wrong with her."

"I'm fine, Will. Trust me on this one," Buffy said. "But something is wrong with Giles." She tilted her head. "Because he is way off if he thinks he can tell me what to do."

"He's, um, supposed to tell you what to do," Willow ventured. She slid a glance toward Giles. "Aren't you? I mean, I thought that was what a watcher was for."

"To guide the Slayer," Xander put in.

"Yeah, guide me, not treat me like his German sheepdog or whatever," Buffy flung at him.

"That would be a German shepherd," Cordelia said. "My aunt raises them."

"No one cares," Buffy informed her. She ticked her attention back to Giles. "Now, I'm going to the carnival. Do you want to try to stop me?"

"How dare you," Giles bit off. His eyes were slits. "I have turned my entire life upside down to be your watcher."

"Never asked you to," Buffy said, staring him down.

"Hey, you are way out of line," Xander said.

"This just in," Buffy said to Xander. "What you think doesn't matter."

She headed for the door. Giles took a step toward it, blocking her way.

He said, "If you leave—"

"If you don't get out of my way, I will move you," she said.

They faced each other. Giles took a deep breath and let it out. Then he stepped aside, glaring at her.

"You're right. I can't stop you," he said.

She gave him a sour smile. "You're right."

She swept out of the room, opening the front door, walking through it, and slamming it in Giles's face.

As if on cue, both of Giles's kittens began to mew.

"Oh my God, Giles," Willow said.

"Lock up after yourselves," Giles snapped, staring after the Slayer. "And for God's sake, find a way to shut those things up."

# Chapter Eight

$G$iles blinked.

He was back in the Chamber of Horrors, staring at the false mirror in the Dracula tableau.

But he had had no intention of revisiting the Chamber of Horrors. His plan had been to investigate the games area, because both Carl Palmer and Principal Snyder had been seen there last.

He had not run into Buffy. *I ought to thrash her,* he thought. Only that was absurd, of course. Take on a slayer? Not bloody likely.

Still, his blood was up. He balled his fists as the crowds snaked past the ridiculous scenes of mayhem and violence—*he'd* show them violence, ultra-violence, in fact—and it was only by clenching his jaw that he didn't rail against the girl behind him, who kept snapping her gum. A well-placed palm strike to her jaw, and he could shove her bovine face in.

He found the mirror and stared into it. Waves of dizziness washed over him. Then more anger flooded him, overtaking him.

"Let me out of here," he said, pushing the girl aside.

She stumbled and shouted, "Hey, watch it!" One look from him, and she swallowed hard and looked down.

He pushed, shoved, and got the hell out of there just as someone said, "Call security!"

"Idiots."

He stomped across the grounds, ready to mow down anyone who crossed his path, then out into the parking lot to retrieve his Citroën.

Someone had parked a Toyota Corolla so close that he couldn't get the driver's-side door open.

"Damn it!" he yelled. He pulled back his leg to kick the Corolla as hard as he could, when he suddenly remembered the black flashlight he had in the pocket of his jacket.

He didn't remember how it had gotten there, but no matter.

It would smash the taillight just fine.

The car alarm began to whoop.

He smashed the other taillight for good measure.

Then he climbed into his car on the passenger side and scooted over behind the wheel, dropping the flashlight to the floor.

Hands clenched around the wheel, he scowled as he drove.

He had given up everything he cared about to become a watcher. And for what? An ignorant, rude, arrogant American teenager.

*I could just . . .*

He stared into the rearview mirror. Saw his face. Saw something silver.

He smiled like a damned man.

Yes, he could.


"Wow, sorry, you were really close that time," the white-faced girl in the black hood said to Cordelia. "Want another roll of quarters?"

"What?" Cordelia blinked and looked around. "I'm . . . I'm . . . I was supposed to be going to cheer-leading practice." She looked around. It was dark out. When had it gotten dark?

What was that *smell*?

"Well, you ended up here," the girl informed her.

"And I still didn't win?" Cordelia asked her.

The girl shook her head.

"But I don't remember. I . . ." Cordelia fished inside her purse. She had left her home this morning with a hundred dollars. It was time to make another payment to Haley Schricker, the private coach the cheerleading squad had hired.

It was *gone*.

*"I spent it all here?"* she shrieked. "This is crazy! Is this a dream?"

The girl just looked at her as if she didn't have the slightest idea in the world what Cordelia was talking about.

"It's because I hang out with those people," Cordelia muttered. "Oh, I hate those guys. Something has happened and no one knows it and . . ."

She felt dizzy; saw a blur of silver. She swayed and held on to the wooden post at the corner of the booth.

"I just have to have one of those purple glass baskets," she finished desperately. "I *need* one." She opened her purse and rooted around inside it some more.

"You could go home and get some more money," the girl suggested.

"Yes." Cordelia brightened. "Of course."

The girl leaned forward. "If you hurry, you'll have plenty of time when you get back to win *two* baskets."

"Oh my God," Cordelia said dreamily.

"Do you need a flashlight?" the girl asked. "We have lots of them. They make great bludgeoning tools." She reached in her apron and pulled out a long, black flashlight. She extended her arm, offering it to Cordelia.

"No, I'm good," Cordelia told her.

The girl gave the flashlight a friendly little shake. "Because you might want to kill someone, to get that money."

"Oh. You're right. I might." Cordelia held her hand out for the flashlight. "Thanks."

The girl handed her the flashlight. "You might see something you want on the drive home. You might have to break a window, or hit someone really hard."

Cordelia wrinkled her nose. "You're so clever."

The girl extended her arms. "That's why I make the big bucks."

Cordelia stashed the flashlight in her purse.

She gave it a pat and said, "You don't think you could just give me one of those baskets now, do you? I could pay you for it later."

"You *will* pay for it later," the girl assured her. At Cordelia's perplexed expression, she said, "After you win it." She leaned forward and said conspiratorially, "You know, you have potential. If I put a good word in for you, Professor Caligari might hire you. Let you work with me. Would you like that?"

Cordy was thrilled. "Do you make a lot of money?" she asked her.

"I am rewarded," the girl replied. "I've worked for Professor Caligari for practically ever, and I've never regretted it for a minute."

"It sounds tempting," Cordelia said, raising her brows.

"It's meant to," the girl said.

They chuckled together.

"Well, you should leave now," the girl said. "It's nearly eight and we close at ten on the dot. Midnight on the weekends."

"That's only two hours," Cordelia wailed, turning to leave. She hesitated, staring down at the baskets. "I really have to have a basket." She gazed at the entire revolving display. "I have to have all of it. Just for me. Everything."

The girl gave her an appraising look. "You're very greedy. That's good."

"Does that mean I *can* have it all?"

The girl smiled. "Of course. If you hurry back in time."

"I will."

Cordelia gave her bag a pat and dashed away.

Then she hurried out off the grounds, got in her car, and peeled out of the parking lot. She raced onto the road to head for home.

All of it was going to be hers. Everything. And while she was at it, maybe she'd snag that knife of Giles's, too. He obviously didn't care very much about it, to leave it lying around like that.

She had to go down Main Street, home of Yasumi Pearl, one of her favorite stores in all of Sunnydale. She slowed, attracted to the beautifully displayed necklaces, bracelets, and earrings. She had been hinting for six months that she wanted the triple-strand choker for her birthday.

*But have they bought it? No. How do I know? Because the store only ordered one. And it's still in the window. Right there.*

Only, not. Because it was closing time and the clerk, a woman with platinum blond hair wrapped in a chignon, was in the process of taking the triple-strand choker off its field of black velvet at that very exact moment.

Cordelia pulled to the curb, letting the engine idle as she watched.

*I want that choker.*

The clerk turned away from the window. She was probably carrying the necklace to a safe.

*I deserve that choker.*

She felt dizzy again. Something bright sliced across her eyelids and she jerked back her head.

She stared.

About a quarter of a block past her car, a streetlight was beaming down on a figure. She squinted. It was one of the clowns from the carnival.

It stared back at her. Then it showed her three glass balls in its gloved hands, and tossed them one, two, three into the air. It began to juggle them, tossing them up, catching them, weaving a comet trail of light as Cordelia watched, her lips parted, her eyes unblinking.

*I should have what I want. And I want . . . everything,* she thought.

Without moving her head, Cordelia opened the bag and felt inside for the flashlight. There it was.

She laid it across her lap. The clown swayed as it juggled; she could almost hear music as it danced. Calliope music, drifting on the wind.

She got out of the car.

Holding the flashlight down by her side, she shut the door and walked purposefully toward the jewelry store entrance. She put her hand around the knob. It was locked.

*So* not a problem.

She invented a limp and hobbled to the section of the window where the clerk stood with the choker in her hands. Making a sad face, she gestured to the door.

*Closed,* the clerk mouthed.

Cordelia could tell she recognized her. She should. She was in Yasumi, like, three times a week, lusting after that choker. It was one of the most expensive items in the store, and that was saying a lot because, hey, matched saltwater pearls the size of marbles were very rare.

And very wonderful.

The calliope music caressed her ears.

With an apologetic smile, she pantomimed having to pee.

The clerk debated.

Cordelia pressed her hands together: *Please?*

The woman relented, walking to the front door *with the choker in her left hand.*

Cordelia tried very hard not to let out a whoop of sheer delight.

She glanced around.

The clown had vanished.

The woman opened the door. She was wearing a black sweater and black pants, and she had on a single teardrop black pearl pendant and matching earrings. Cordelia had to restrain herself from tearing them right off her.

"Thanks," Cordelia said brightly.

"Hi. It's Cordelia, isn't it?"

"Uh-huh." Cordelia gestured to the necklace with her right hand as she hid her flashlight behind her back using her left. "Wow, great timing. I was just about to break your window to steal that."

The woman laughed. "You have such excellent taste," she said. "The bathroom's in the back. I'll show you."

"Thanks," Cordelia said again.

The woman led the way. Cordelia followed. The clerk pulled a ring of keys out of her pants pocket and inserted one of the keys into a door with a placard that said EMPLOYEES ONLY.

"Here we go," the woman said as she pushed the door open.

"Yes," Cordelia said. "Here we go."

She transferred the flashlight to her right hand, raised it over her head, and brought it down hard on the back of the clerk's head. The woman grunted and crumpled to the floor.

Cordelia fell to her knees beside the woman and eased the choker from her limp grasp. Nice sweater. She thought about taking it, but she was in too big a hurry. She put the choker in the pocket of her pants.

She grabbed the clerk by the wrists and dragged her into the bathroom. It was functional and nothing more; you'd think a store that charged the prices Yasumi did would have something a little nicer.

There was a skylight of frosted glass; in the moonlight Cordelia caught sight of a roll of silver duct tape on a white wood shelf above the toilet.

She picked it up. There was a box cutter, too. How handy. She retrieved them, then bent down and wound the tape around the woman's head, completely covering her mouth. Then Cordy wrapped her wrists together, and then her ankles.

She remembered from all those cop shows that she should wipe for prints and keep the evidence.

Then she grabbed up her flashlight and wrapped her sweater around the bathroom doorknob, making sure the door locked after her.

As she began to cross the showroom, she glanced at the assortment of black velvet boxes laid on the counter. The clerk had been putting everything away.

*I'll need earrings to go with this,* Cordelia thought as she stopped in front of a mirror on the counter to put the choker on. Boxes were piled up all around it. *And rings. And pins. I'll take it all!*

There were footsteps behind her. Catching her breath, she glanced into the mirror. She saw nothing.

*Oh my God, is it a vampire?*

The footsteps drew closer.

And something growled.

Just before it sprang.

It was nearly eight fifteen at night, and they were making progress.

Willow looked up from the Hans Von Der Sieben Web site and said to Ms. Calendar, "Here's something. His name was actually Caligarius. He was called 'Hans of the Seven' because it was said that he lured people into his cult with 'pleasures of the flesh.' But in reality he was snaring their souls by getting them to give in to temptation."

"Let me see that," Ms. Calendar said.

The two were sitting in the computer lab, each at an Apple. The smart, beautiful dark-haired woman was dressed in one of the long, earth-tone skirts she favored, plus a silky chocolate-brown sweater. And boots. She had such good clothes.

Because of the job, and the money, and of being grown-up and smart.

After the weirdness at Giles's condo, Willow had not gone home as Giles had told her to. She was terribly shaken by what had happened. Buffy and Giles had practically come to blows. If Willow and the others hadn't been there, she wasn't sure if the situation between Slayer and Watcher might have escalated.

So Willow had walked to the school—Giles lived close by—to see if Ms. Calendar was there. Luckily, she was.

Willow had told her everything—including the fact that she was beginning to suspect that all of them were under a spell.

"I just don't know what my spell is," she said. "I'm so clueless. But I figured *you* would be able to figure it out."

"That's sweet, Willow," Ms. Calendar said kindly. "But you're not clueless. You're very bright."

*I'm a nerd,* Willow thought silently. *I would give anything to be like you.*

"Temptation. That's interesting," Ms. Calendar said, coming around Willow's chair to lean over her shoulder.

Willow scrolled down the list, reading aloud. "'The temptations were seven in number: Lust, Envy, Vanity, Greed, Sloth, Anger, and Gluttony.'"

Ms. Calendar nodded, scanning silently as Willow read aloud. "Hmm, mine's gotta be lust," she murmured, then cleared her throat. "Have the others been exhibiting these traits?"

"Well, with Cordelia, it's hard to say because vanity . . . oh, wait." She thought hard. "The Hahn twins went into the fun house and they couldn't stop staring at themselves. That's what Buffy said, and then they thought they were hot."

"Vanity," Ms. Calendar confirmed.

"And Giles keeps losing his temper," Willow continued.

"He does?" she asked. Willow nodded.

"Anger," Ms. Calendar said. "What about Xander?"

"Oh my God, of course! Gluttony." She made a face. "He kept burping and I think he ate some cat food."

Ms. Calendar wrinkled her perfectly shaped nose. "So, that's two for vanity—Cordelia and those twins—and anger, for Rupert."

"Angel's been far more, um, physically affectionate in public," Willow added.

"That would be lust as well." Ms. Calendar tapped the screen. "So that leaves sloth, greed, and envy."

"Mrs. Palmer was robbed for the money in her purse," Willow said. "Oh my God, could it be that Carl got infected by greed?"

"It seems possible."

Ms. Calendar even smelled good. Willow flared. Why did Ms. Calendar get everything? And she got nothing?

"What about Buffy?"

"I think anger, too," Willow said. She clenched her jaw. After all her work, Ms. Calendar was going to put the pieces of the puzzle together. She'd solve it and everyone would think she was a genius as usual, and she was not.

*I hate her,* Willow thought fiercely. She was staring at the face of Hans Von Der Sieben as her fingers clenched like claws. *She has everything, everything, and I—I just—*

"Giles took this other teacher to the carnival," she said. "Really pretty. Very smart. Well employed."

Ms. Calendar's lips parted. "Oh."

"Yeah. I think he really likes her," Willow said savagely. *That'll take her down a notch.*

Ms. Calendar swallowed. She glanced over at the list of temptations. "You know, I think these are also known as the Seven Deadly Sins," she said slowly. "One doesn't just yield to them, one commits them."

She smiled gently at Willow. "Yours must be envy." She put a hand on Willow's shoulder. "I think you *are* under a spell."

Willow was startled. "How-how do you know?"

"Because you are the kindest girl I know," Ms. Calendar said. "You would never intentionally hurt someone. Especially not someone you care about. And you care about me."

Tears welled in Willow's eyes. "But I—I . . . what do you care if I try to hurt you? I'm *nothing*."

"Let me sit down," Ms. Calendar said, putting her hand on Willow's shoulder. "We have a lot of work to do."


The kittens scattered as Giles slammed his front door shut. Sweat rolled down his forehead as he got a bottle of Scotch from the kitchen cabinet and poured himself a drink. His hands were shaking.

He threw it back, drank another.

There was a black book lying open on his table. It was the grimoire he and Ethan had used to summon the demon Eyghon. They had paid a pretty penny for it, and he had carefully packed it away when he'd moved to Sunnydale.

*When did I put it there?* he wondered. *Has someone been in here?*

He looked around and decided he didn't really care.

He carried the bottle with him, drinking from it as he began to turn the thick vellum pages.

He couldn't raise Eyghon again. The demon inside Angel had killed it. But there were other dark gods he could call. And he would, just to show Buffy who was boss. Take her down a notch. Make her more malleable, compliant.

*"Kill her."*

"Yes," he hissed. The letters swam before his eyes as fresh rage overtook him. Why not? She had ruined his life. All that was precious, all that was dear, she sullied it.

He pressed the bottle to his lips and guzzled down the alcohol.

He heard a sound outside his window. Was that a bicycle horn?

As if in fright—or perhaps to be playful—one of the kittens scampered toward him and leaped on top of his shoe.

*"Get off me,"* he said between clenched teeth. *"Or I will kill you, too."*

• • •

Everywhere Buffy went, there she was. And that was so very.

*Loved* the carnival. *Loved* herself. And why not? What was not to love?

She saw her face in a dozen mirrors as she rode the Octopus and the Tilt-A-Whirl. Another dozen in the totally lame Chamber of Horrors.

*Lucky thing I'm so hot,* she thought as she strutted down the midway.

Sensing her power, the other fairgoers glanced at her and hurriedly ducked out of her way. *Make way, make way, Slayer coming through!* No one protested when she cut in line to go on a ride. When she reached her hand into a little kid's popcorn bag, he whimpered and ran away, letting her keep it.

*Mmm, wow, best popcorn I ever had!*

She sauntered up to a game booth. People were throwing coins onto plates and into cute little baskets made of glass. No one was winning anything.

"I'll show you how it's done," Buffy said to a tall guy wearing a UC Sunnydale sweatshirt. She grabbed a quarter out of his hand.

"Hey!" he said.

She ignored him, zeroed in on a purple glass basket, and flipped the coin into the air.

It turned end over end, catching the light, and then it landed with a satisfying *clink* inside the basket.

The white-faced girl working the stall jerked up her head. She looked from the basket to Buffy to the basket again, and the look of complete and utter shock on her face made Buffy laugh aloud.

"What?" she called to the girl. "Haven't you ever seen anyone win a prize before?"

"You . . ." The girl swiveled her head to the left and the right, as if she was looking for someone to tell her what to do next.

"That's mine," Buffy said, pointing to the basket. "And I want it *now*."

"Technically, it's mine," the guy said, his gaze riveted on the basket. "Since you used my quarter."

The girl hadn't moved. So Buffy hopped the counter and sauntered toward the display. Now the girl looked even more freaked.

"Security," she called, but her voice was barely a whisper.

"I'll just take this," Buffy announced. She bent over and plucked the purple glass basket from the tower of prizes. She smiled at the girl. "You're freaking out because no one's supposed to win, right? Because the game is rigged."

She tossed the basket in the air and caught it. She saw that she had the attention of the other players and hopped onto the wooden barrier.

"They're cheating you, people! And you're just too stupid to see it!"

She threw back her head and laughed at them all as she jumped to the ground. Sawdust flew.

She said to Quarter Guy, *"Mine."* Waved it under his nose. "Want to fight for it?"

He took a step away from her.

"You're smarter than you look," she said. "Guess this is your lucky day after all."

With a harsh laugh, she sauntered off. People gave way for her. It was her due.

She reached the end of the line for the Ferris wheel and snickered. Slayers didn't wait in lines. She started to walk around it, planning to cut, when she heard her mother calling her name.

"Buffy?" Joyce *was* standing in line, about six people from the end. That wasn't good enough for the mother of a slayer.

"Hey," Buffy said offhandedly.

"Hi, honey, I didn't expect to see you here," Joyce went on. "Of course, I don't see much of you these days."

"You've been busy," Buffy said generously. She took her mother's hand. "If you want to ride, you really don't need to wait," she said. "We can just go to the head of the line."

Joyce drew back, firmly planted in line. "Buffy, we need to wait our turn just like everyone else." She cocked her head, a quizzical expression on her face. "Are you feeling all right?"

Buffy shrugged. "Never better."

"Good," Joyce Summers said slowly, still giving Buffy the once-over.

*Move along, Mom. Nothing to see here. Nothing going on.*

"This place is fun," Joyce continued. "I was sitting at home working on the bills . . . just some paperwork," she amended. "And I heard the calliope music, and I thought about when you were a little girl. We took you to the circus." She looped Buffy's hair behind her ear.

"We took you everywhere." Her voice grew wistful. "There was more money then. I didn't know how good I had it."

She cleared her throat. "Anyway, I decided to come to the carnival." She wrinkled her nose and added conspiratorially, "I had my palm read in the fortune-teller's tent."

That perked Buffy's interest. As she rearranged her hair from around her ear, she asked, "What was your fortune?"

Joyce laughed softly. "Oh, the usual false optimism they dish out at things like that. Fame, fortune, love." She made a face. "I must have a sign on my forehead that says, 'Needs encouragement.' I envy people who can make themselves believe in horoscopes and crystal balls."

"Well, some people think they're real," Buffy ventured. "The horoscopes and crystal balls."

"That's what I mean. I guess I'm just too grounded in the real world to believe in the occult." Buffy could hear the strain in her voice. "It would be so nice not to be so well-informed."

"We can make our own luck," Buffy insisted. "Or at least *I* can."

"That's my girl," Joyce said warmly.

The line moved quickly—lucky thing, or Buffy would have been tempted to persuade Joyce to change her mind about cutting—and soon they were in one of the little swinging cars, which were painted black. They looked like black coffins, to Buffy's way of thinking. But then, her mind ran to things like coffins.

And falling to her death from the top of the Ferris wheel.

"Ours is number seven," Buffy told her mom as they zoomed backward on the exterior of the massive wheel. Chilly night wind blew in their hair.

"How lucky," Joyce teased, sitting back.

Drunk, in a full fury, Giles had stripped down to his pants. He was bare chested and barefoot, and he meant business.

*Teach her a lesson. Make her sorry. Make them all sorry. Make them pay.*

He was sweating and dizzy, and so drunk he could barely think straight. But he knew what to do.

Surrounded by candles, Giles swayed in the center of the pentagram he had drawn on his carpet with melted wax and blood. He had retraced the pentagram on his chest, with a knife. The letters of the profane name of Astorrith formed from the cuts, and threw glowing black light against the walls of his condo.

Shadows moved over the ancient maps and framed photographs of home, hissing and whispering. The minions of Astorrith had been awakened.

Blood dripped from Giles's hands; he had performed the sacrifices and uttered The Names That Must Not Be Spoken, thrice, thrice, thrice.

"Baal! Cthulhu! Jezebel! Wake your brother Astorrith! Bid him come! I command thee!"

Lightning flashed across the front window, blacked out in part by a shape—a figure wearing a small pointed hat. Giles figured it was a minion, stepping through the veil. A sign that his spell was working.

That meant that the dark god would come to him directly. The time was at hand.

He raised his arms and threw back his head.

"Astorrith, Dark One! Lord of Revenge and Retribution! I have been wronged and I have suffered! I have been insulted and humiliated! See the slights heaped upon thy acolyte and wreak havoc on my enemies! Vanquish all who plague me!"

He bent down—it was a long, shaky road—and plucked up the Blade of Astorrith in his right hand and his grimoire in the other. He began to read.

*"Ta-mir-o,"* he began. *"Dark God of Shadows and Tumult, I summon thee! From the depths of confusion and tumult, rise up! Bring the Wild Ones with you and smite my blood enemy, Buffy Anne Summers! Wreak havoc on her land! Fill her days with storms and monsters!*

*"It is Buffy the Vampire Slayer of whom I speak! Bring doom upon her! Make her long for her own death! Destroy all that makes her smile!"*

He sliced the air with the blade. The veil of reality was diced into chunks, like jagged pieces of a jigsaw puzzle. The edges of the world inside his condo began to bleed, and the first chunk slammed against the floor two yards away from Giles's bare feet.

The floor buckled beneath the oppressive weight. Giles stayed inside the pentagram, riding it like a surfboard as one half of the floor splintered, while the other rippled and broke apart.

The walls cracked like frozen glass dropped into boiling water.

The plumbing burst. Water geysered upward.

The stairs pulled away from the loft. The ceiling bowed downward.

*"Torment her!"* Giles yelled, dropping to his knees.

"Isn't this a lovely view?" Joyce asked Buffy as they dangled at the top of the Ferris wheel.

All of Sunnydale was spread below them. Buffy felt a fierce rush of pride. All those lights, those toy-looking houses, those antlike people. She protected them all, night after night. How many would have died by now, if not for her?

"It's like Paris," Joyce said dreamily. "There's a Ferris wheel near the Eiffel Tower."

"You've been to Paris?" Buffy asked, surprised. She hadn't known that.

Joyce leaned Buffy's head against her shoulder and stroked her hair, the way she had done when Buffy was a little girl.

"No, but I would like to. I wonder if I'll ever get to. But you . . . you have your whole life ahead of you, Buffy. You're so young." She sighed. "I envy you."

"Well, about that," Buffy said. "I've decided to move out."

Joyce's hand stopped in midstroke. "What?"

"Yeah. Listen, I'm . . . really strong and I can . . . ah, become a boxer. Or something like that. Get back into my skating." She smiled at her mother. "I'm ready to live on my own."

Joyce lowered her chin and peered up through her lashes—mom face, the face of dawning suspicion. "When you woke me up in the kitchen, did you look at my papers?"

"Your bills," Buffy confirmed. "Yes, I did. Without me around—"

"Oh, Buffy." Joyce put her arms around her daughter and held her closer. "You are so wonderful. But I'll take care of you, sweetie. You don't need to worry."

"Mom, I'm not worried." Buffy's words were muffled against her mother's shoulder.

"I'm so proud of you," Joyce continued.

*Well, of course you are,* the Slayer thought smugly. *Isn't everybody?*

"You're such a dear." She jerked. "Did someone just take our picture? Oh, I feel a little dizzy."

"Are you all right, Mom?" Buffy asked, turning her head to look at her.

"Yes. I'm fine. I'm just so . . . relaxed." She leaned her head back. "It's nice to just sit and do nothing." She chuckled. "I feel so lazy."

That was when the wind began to blow.

Xander began to blow.

He was sick, sick to death, and that was before he had eaten the candied apple and the four hot dogs.

He didn't remember how he'd dragged himself to the carnival. Last thing he could remember, Giles had dropped him off at the lovely Harris estate, where his parents were "watching TV," which was what they called drinking and arguing.

Retreating from the combat zone, he had hunkered down in the basement, hurling, and figured he would have to skip tonight's further exciting adventures at the carnival.

But he was back, and sicker than sick, staggering down the midway.

And clowns were following him.

An entire pack of them, in your typical clown garb with your typical clown accessories—a horn with a big rubber ball on the business end, a spray bottle, and a terrifying air of menace.

He didn't like those guys.

*Why did I eat that apple? Giles told us not to eat anything here. I couldn't stop myself. It . . . called my name. And I think I mean that literally.*

And he remembered now that the night before, he *had* eaten some cookies. About seven of them. He couldn't stop.

*I didn't ever remember eating them. And the cat food . . . and all the Cheez Doodles I had stashed in my nightstand . . . and the stale Oreos I found in my backpack. . . . I have eaten so much crap in the last twenty-four hours and I can't stop myself. I want more.*

He doubled, clutching his stomach.

Overhead, thunder rumbled. A wind began to blow.

"Buffy," he whispered. "Someone. Help."

He looked back.

One, two, three, four clowns. They strolled toward him with their frozen, terrifying smiles and their flappy feet and their big, gloved hands.

And everything in him told him to keep the hell away from them.

But he was fading. He could hardly walk.

The wind picked up.

*Okay, still in the mood for love . . . so where is she?*

Angel paced around the gravestones and headstones, the monuments and the tombs of Blessed Memories, listening to the calliope as fierce wind whipped at his coat. With a shriek, it snatched the note he was carrying and skipped it away like a stone on a river. The note was from Buffy, on girlie paper decorated with cows; he had found it taped to his door and all it had said was "Meet me near du Lac. B." He recognized her girlish handwriting, the *B* finished with a little swirl.

But Buffy was nowhere to be seen. Maybe he had misunderstood. He had figured this rendezvous was to continue where they had left off—though of course, he would have preferred it to be continued in his apartment. Or someplace equally nice and cozy.

Of course, slayers got detained on business more often than not.

The haunting notes of the calliope whispered on the wind. Sweet and tantalizing . . . like Buffy.

*What was I thinking, denying myself the pleasure of being with her?*

It was great to feel lusty and vigorous. He felt like a man again, not a shadow. Not someone set apart—a vampire, yet more than a vampire. And yet, not just a man, either.

*The things I can do for her, with her. . . .*

Whoever said that the blood was the life, was wrong. It was the flesh.

*Maybe she's at the carnival.*

He turned around and began walking in the direction of the calliope's sound. Giles's condo was nearby. Maybe he'd stop in, see if he had seen Buffy.

Then something changed.

The wind howled, hard; it picked up and became a gale, ripping leaves right off the trees. Yanking branches and flinging them into the air.

Dirt and pebbles pelted Angel as he lowered his head and walked into the wind. It was a full-on storm such as he had never seen in southern California unless . . .

*Unless something is very wrong.*

His coat streamed behind him like wings as he pushed forward. The gale force pushed back at him.

Then from out of the maelstrom, something padded toward him. He smelled it rather than heard it—it reeked of the sulphurs of hell, and of death and decomposition.

It smelled of evil.

And it had no heartbeat.

Squinting, Angel ducked behind a headstone, and braced himself to meet it.

# Chapter Nine

Cordelia's head was throbbing.

She moaned.

Or tried to.

As she slowly came to, she realized that there was tape across her mouth. And her hands were tied behind her back.

The moon had moved, but enough light still streamed through the skylight of the jewelry store bathroom for her to realize the horrible truth: Someone had attacked her, tied her up, and dragged her in there, placing her next to the clerk that she herself had attacked, tied up, and dragged in there.

She pushed her chin against her chest, trying to feel the choker around her neck.

Nada.

*I've been robbed,* she thought, panicking. *Someone took my choker!*

Ignoring for the time being that she had also stolen the choker, Cordelia zoomed into high anxiety. Her cat allergy made her nose stuffy and it was very hard to breathe.

*Oh my God, what if they took my watch, too?*

She blinked and stared hard at the salesclerk. The woman's head was bent to the side, revealing her pearl earring.

She calmed down a little.

*At least I can still have the earrings,* she consoled herself. *Maybe she's still got on her pendant, too.*

Then she frowned as she listened hard to what sounded like a terrible wailing, or shrieking, or . . .

*It's wind,* she realized. *Are we having, like, a tornado?*


Angel peered above the shield of the headstone.

A pack of things crab-walked toward him, scrabbling over the tree roots, headstones, bushes. They flowed like mercury, then snapped back into six compact forms that resembled mastiff-size dogs. Their bodies were covered with dozens of bloodshot eyes surrounded by fangs that blinked and snapped.

Demonic minions.

Then, of all things, two clowns appeared, whooping and dancing in their mufti attire. One carried a seltzer bottle, which it aimed at one of the minions.

The creature shrieked, leaping straight up into the air, and erupted into flames.

The clowns doubled over with laughter. Sniggering, the one with the bottle aimed it at another minion, but its aim went wild and the spray hit a tree. The bark ignited.

The other clown danced a little jig, and then the two slammed their huge bottoms together.

They hadn't noticed Angel. Taking advantage of their distraction, he clambered on top of the du Lac crypt and flattened himself against the roof. Below him, a minion sniffed eagerly, honing in on a new and different scent.

The pack moved on, and the clowns with it.

*That was close,* Angel thought.

Then the roof of the crypt began to rumble, a subsonic vibration Angel felt through his whole body. The trees trembled, shaking off leaves that the wind whisked away.

He looked down the hill as the shaking grew worse. There. In the vicinity of Giles's condo complex, a shadowy figure emerged from the building and rose into the sky like someone hunched over, then straightening up. A massive, dark tube shape, it towered maybe fifty feet into the air. The head was elongated and covered with horns. Its long neck sat on shoulders that were hooked, and arms covered with talons. The rest of the body was snakelike, with tentacles undulating from its long, cylindrical body.

Calliope music and battering winds combined with screams of terror from the humans below as the creature swayed above them.

One of the tentacles unfurled and snapped downward, like the tongue of a frog. When it snapped back, a struggling human being was caught in its grip. The tentacle brought the writhing victim toward the mouth, which opened wide to reveal a huge bonfire and smoking, charred teeth.

The human was tossed in.

The mouth closed.

Smoke emanated from the horns on its head.

*It's Astorrith,* Angel realized. He had never seen the demon before, but Darla, his sire, had. She had described him as a tentacled creature wearing a horned hood . . . fearful to behold, impossible to defeat.

"If you ever see him, Angelus, you must run," she had told him, as together they dined on a fat Spanish grandee. "Never go up against him. It would be insane. And fatal."

Another tentacle reached down. As it moved, the sky around it . . . cracked. Pieces of the ebony sky flared, and then became darker still. It was the weirdest thing Angel had ever seen; he had read about black holes and wondered if that was what the dark places were.

Whipsaw fast, the tentacle wrapped around another human and hoisted it into the air.

He could hear Darla whispering, *"Don't do it."*

Never one to listen, Angel leaped off the tomb and ran toward the creature as fast as he could.

As the Ferris wheel spun crazily in the windstorm, Buffy held on to her mother and stared wide-eyed at the monster looming above Sunnydale. It had appeared out of nowhere, along with the wind. And it was killing people.

*What is that thing?*

Then the wheel zoomed downward; the ground flew up to meet them, and Buffy curled herself protectively around Joyce.

"Brace yourself!" she cried to her mother.

Joyce screamed and clung to her. Then their car zinged back up and around, like a hamster in a wheel. Buffy anchored herself with one hand wrapped around the metal restraining bar across their laps as she held on tightly to her mom.

They reached the top again and began to bullet back down. As they sailed down, Buffy looked over the side of the car.

"Oh my God, Xander is down there!"

He was lying flat on his back on the ground next to Buffy and Angel's make-out bushes. The girl from the coin toss was bending over him, and four clowns bent over to grab his arms and legs.

It was Slayer time. But what to do? Abandon her mother on the Ferris wheel or let the clowns get Xander?

*Mom, Xander, Mom, Xander.*

But there was no choice, really, and Xander would understand. Plus, maybe the clowns were going to help him.

*And if you believe that, you deserve no new suede boots,* she told herself.

She kept hold of Joyce as the Ferris wheel jittered

and scraped, not yet free of its moorings but threatening to be. The vibration set her teeth on edge.

All she could think of to do was wait until their car came unbolted, and then wrap herself around her mother like a human escape pod and eject from the car.

*That might kill us both,* she thought, but she wasn't sure what else to do.

She got ready, and said, "Mom, listen. Here's the plan. When I say go, get ready to jump."

*"What?"* Joyce cried.

"Yes, on the count of one. Two. Thr—"

But at the last possible moment—the double *e*'s—Buffy spotted a red-painted hand brake beside the girders of the supporting base. It was about two feet long and clearly marked: PULL IN CASE OF EMERGENCIES. An arrow pointed in the same direction the wheel was spinning.

Just as they were about to swoop past it, Buffy reached out and grabbed it, preparing herself to lose an arm as she yanked the brake hard . . .

. . . and ripped the brake free.

"Bad design," she muttered, scowling at the red handle in her grip.

But it got the job done: The brake mechanism had engaged; and there was a noticeable drag on the wheel's momentum. It was stopping. Buffy felt confident she could climb down instead of jumping.

And so could her mother.

"Mom," she said, prying Joyce off her.

Her mom's eyes were as big as, well, Ferris wheels.

"Oh my God, Buffy, are you all right?"

"Of course I am." Buffy was mildly piqued. "After all, I'm . . . who I am." She had to remember that her secret was still a secret.

"Mom, we need to get down. We're only about twenty feet above the ground." She pointed over the side of the Ferris wheel. "Can you climb that?"

"I . . . I think so," Joyce said.

"Good. Let's go."

Buffy raised one leg out of the car and put her foot firmly on the thick metal supports that extended from the wheel. The wheel groaned. The car swung wildly.

As she reached for her mother's hand, she glanced down at Xander. He was on his back, flailing his arms and legs like a tipped-over insect, trying to fight off the clowns. But he wasn't going to win.

"Mom," she said. "You need to keep climbing. Do it slowly. I have to go help Xander."

"Buffy!" her mother cried, her eyes widening with fright as she half-stood in the rocking car. Then she took another deep breath and nodded. "I'm okay. Go."

It was quicker to cling to the support and move hand over hand, so the Slayer did so. Once her feet found purchase on the elaborate structure of the wheel proper, she worked her way in toward the center, and then shimmied down until she found another support. It was like playing a life-size version of Chutes and Ladders.

Then she dropped the rest of the way. The wind nearly picked her off her feet; she stood with her face into it to keep her hair out of her face as she gazed up at her mother. Joyce was methodically inching toward the superstructure by the trail Buffy had blazed.

Satisfied that her mother was safe . . . or rather, safe enough, at least for the moment, Buffy ran to rescue Xander.

"It's her!" the white-faced girl shouted as Buffy raced for them.

Alerted, the clowns straightened and assumed battle stance.

Pow! Buffy's foot connected with the chin of Clown number one, the dude with the Rasta braids, and it staggered away from Xander.

A well-aimed punch to Clown number two's jaw, and he was out of commission too.

The other two backed away.

Then the Goth girl attacked, fingers forming claws, and Buffy smashed her fist into her face and . . . *whoa* . . . her skin split apart, revealing purple, leathery stuff beneath.

*Demon,* Buffy translated.

A huge roar wrent the air and a tentacle slammed down on top of the demon girl, crushing her.

*Bigger demon,* Buffy thought as she threw herself out of the way.

The retreating clowns scattered into the wild, panicking crowds.

"Xander," she said, falling to her knees beside him. "Are you okay?"

"That's a negative," he gasped as she raised his head. His eyes were puffy and half-shut. His face was sheened with sweat. "Buffy, I'm so sick."

"It'll be okay. I'll make it all better," she promised him.

She hoisted Xander over her shoulder firefighter style. Last time she had done this, she was in the fun zone with the Hahns. So not having fun now, either.

The Ferris wheel creaked and groaned but did not move. Most of the people in the remaining cars were following Joyce's example and shimmying down the superstructure. Buffy watched a moment longer, her gaze traveling to see if anyone was badly hurt, or somehow incapable of getting down under their own steam. So far, so good.

But there were three guys who were just sitting crammed together in one little car, smiling kind of like they weren't all there. They weren't lifting a finger to save themselves.

"Hey!" Buffy shouted, gesticulating wildly with her left hand as she held on to Xander with the other. "Move it *now*!"

The one in the middle—a guy wearing a UC Sunnydale baseball cap—laughed and waved at her. The other two sat rocking back and forth.

"Hey!" she cried. "You're in danger!"

The one who waved seemed to sort of jerk. He looked around, then down, then shook the guy to his right. He activated too. Then number three got with the program.

"Climb down!" Buffy bellowed.

She didn't know if they could hear her, but they did start evacuation procedures.

*Weirdos.*

Buffy didn't have time to wonder what was wrong with them; her mom had maneuvered her way about ninety percent of the way down when she let go.

"Mom!" Buffy screamed, as her mother plummeted—

—right into the make-out bushes, which cushioned her fall.

Still carrying Xander, Buffy ran to her. Joyce was lying flat on her back on a crisscross of leafy branches; she pushed herself off the canopy of bushes and Buffy spotted her gymnastics-style, with a firm arm absorbing some of her momentum as she landed on the ground.

"Mom, are you okay?" Buffy demanded.

"Buffy, are *you* all right?" Joyce replied, which was a mom's way of saying yes. She looked at her daughter carrying Xander, who was not small, and said, "You must be having an adrenaline rush." She looked around. "We need to get out of here."

"With you on that," Buffy told her, checking to make sure she had a good grip on Xander as mother and daughter took off.

"There she is!" someone shouted.

Buffy glanced over her shoulder to see . . .

. . . *What the heck?*

Several of the freaks from the freak show were barreling after her. Also, a pack of demons that bore no resemblance to humans—gelatinous mounds—and a leathery, lizardlike thing. They all came after the Summers women as they ran toward the exit. Weirdest thing, though: The regular inhabitants of Sunnydale—

the fairgoers—were running toward *them*—*not* toward the exit. Faces rigid with terror, fleeing from the enormous tentacled demon, they were flooding the carnival as if they were drowning and it was their only lifeboat.

"People! No!" Buffy shouted, whirling around in a circle. She jabbed fingers at the bad guys closing in in hot pursuit. "Wicked evil that way too! Come with me!"

No one listened. No one seemed to care demons and monsters were alive and among them.

Buffy grabbed her mother's hand as they made for the exit.

"We're almost there," Buffy assured her. "You're safe with me, Mom. Right, Xander?"

There was no answer.

"Xander?" Buffy tried again.

"Oh my God," her mother panted, as she loped beside the Slayer. "Buffy, I think Xander's *dead*."

Running, Angel could see the bright lights of the Ferris wheel as antlike people climbed down from it. Though it appeared that they were all going to be okay, the scene reminded him of the sinking *Titanic*, how the lights had blazed, then winked out in succession as they hit the frigid water.

He balled his fists and clenched his jaw. If Buffy was at the carnival . . .

Angel was about to enter the other side of the forest when a figure rocketed out of the shadows. He saw Angel and headed right for him.

He was a young guy, about eighteen, dressed in dark cargo pants and a loosely knitted sweater that reminded Angel of chain mail. Angel couldn't place him, but there was something about him that was familiar.

He was carrying something against his chest, and moonlight refracted off of it.

A hundred feet above them both, the demon Astorrith roared. Flames shot from its mouth. And on the ground, the guy put on an impressive burst of speed as he ran straight toward Angel.

Angel met him halfway. He slammed against Angel's chest with something hard, and for a moment Angel thought he had been staked.

Then the guy collapsed, leaving a glass sphere in Angel's grasp.

It looked like a crystal ball.

From the ground the guy shot out a hand and yelled, "Sanctuary!"


Ethan Rayne tried very hard to at least appear contrite as Professor Caligari paced the floor in front of his fantastically infernal calliope. He kept his calm and jerked on the chain of his "pet," Le Malfaiteur, who was growling.

The entire wagon was rocking back and forth in the rough, wild wind, and Ethan half-expected it to rise up into the sky like Dorothy's house in *The Wizard of Oz*.

"I said to terrorize Sunnydale, not destroy it!" the good professor sputtered.

Ethan had to bite his cheek to keep from laughing.

"I assure you, I didn't do this," he told the man . . .

if man he was. Ethan sincerely doubted that Caligari had ever been human.

True, Ethan hadn't done it. However, he *had* instructed one of Caligari's clowns to place Ripper's grimoire out where he would find it.

He had also investigated the break-in at the jewelry store a few short blocks away because he recognized a certain car parked at the curb from his Halloween escapade here in Sunnydale.

As he'd strolled over, Le Malfaiteur had gotten loose and nearly killed that adorable girl, Cordelia Chase. While subduing the enchanted warlock, Ethan had realized she'd been about to rob the store because she was under the influence of the carnival.

He still didn't know why he had knocked her out and tied her up after he stopped Le Malfaiteur from mauling her to death. Obviously to give her a cover story that would exonerate her from her attempted robbery. But why? Because she was an attractive bird? What had caused him such an impetuous moment of Good Samaritanism, if he could be so bold as to coin a phrase?

Ethan was nothing if not bold. But one could never accuse him of being a Good Samaritan.

*Then maybe I did it to mix it up,* he thought. *After all, I did leave her there to potentially die. Tied up and helpless, with an enormous demon stomping about the place. . . . And I left a note for Angel to look for Buffy in a graveyard. Keep the lad busy and out of the way . . .*

He felt better about his predilection for evil. He

would hate to think that he was getting soft in his old age—especially where friends of the Slayer were concerned.

Professor Caligari, of course, was completely unaware of Ethan's internal monologue. He was stomping about . . . and was that *smoke* rising from his skin?

"Sunnydale is running amuck!" Professor Caligari raved.

*Then let's break out the cigarettes,* Ethan thought, watching a curl of smoke lift from the man's scalp. But he said mildly, "At the risk of sounding accusatory, you weren't terribly specific about what degree of terror and mayhem you wanted. Or what sort, either."

"On the streets, friend. The clowns marauding, causing mischief, that sort of thing," Professor Caligari said, tapping his forehead with his finger, as if to indicate that Ethan was remarkably thick.

And as he bellowed and gesticulated, the strangest thing happened: The dead center of the calliope began to glow with a faint green, pulsating light. Ethan watched it out of the corner of his eye because he wasn't certain Caligari was aware that Ethan could see it.

It beat like a heart. Surreptitiously Ethan laid his hand over his own heart, to see if the rhythms matched. They didn't. The one in the calliope was much, much slower.

"Do you at least know who—or what—that demon is?" Professor Caligari demanded. Ethan figured that any second now, Caligari's minions would be pounding on the door and demanding to be let in.

Ah, there they were now. Sounded as if they had a battering ram.

Caligari swore in a language Ethan didn't know and threw open the door.

A clown burst inside, carrying a young white-faced girl, whose human skin actually covered just the left half of her face. The other flat ovoid eye was smoking.

*Fascinating.*

"Tessa!" Professor Caligari cried. "That thing killed her!" He burst into a rage, stomping, whirling around. Little flares of flames flickered over his face and scalp.

Le Malfaiteur rose and stretched.

Ethan gestured. "Can't you put her in that glass coffin thingie?"

"It's only for humans," Caligari said, his voice laden with sorrow. "She's been with me for centuries. Damn it."

The clown tenderly picked up Tessa and went back outside. Pushed by the wind, the door smacked back open. An uprooted oleander bush tumbled past. It was followed by several vampires.

*And I was told they couldn't fly,* Ethan thought merrily, wondering what precisely they were doing there.

Pulling on Le Malfaiteur's chain, he crossed to the space and peered out.

"I'll go see what I can do about the demon," he said. "But that means my price will go up."

The professor narrowed his eyes. "You *did* do this," he said. "You're shaking me down!"

*He's smarter than he looks,* Ethan thought, for of course that had been his plan. One of several Ethan had set in motion. The clowns weren't the only ones who could juggle several things at once.

"You wound me, Professor Caligari," he said mournfully. "Come, Malfaiteur."

Sorcerer and enchanted warlock stepped into the storm.

"Where are you going?" Professor Caligari shouted after the pair.

*To see a man about a demon,* Ethan thought silently.

Angel stood in front of the refugee from the carnival. His name was Vaclav, and he was trembling with terror. Apparently the sight of Astorrith and the death of his girlfriend had pushed him over the edge. He told Angel that he'd been the one to eavesdrop on the Scoobies at the freak-show exit, and he had been searching for them ever since. But when Astorrith had approached, he had run as far away from the carnival as he could, with no thought of where he was going.

"It was destiny that brought me to you," he told Angel, in a thick Eastern European accent.

Angel wasn't so sure.

Now the two surveyed the wreckage that had once been Giles's condo complex. Fires raged; a hydrant shot water straight into the air. A woman with blood in her blond hair lurched toward them, waving her arms. Dogs barked.

Angel headed for Giles's condo.

On the second story of what had been the Watcher's home, a purple-haired clown was dancing in the firelight. It was rooting through a pile of notebooks—the Watcher Diaries, Angel realized.

*Getting information on the Slayer?*

Embers dervished around the clown, igniting its clothing until the wind extinguished it again. It looked as though it were dressed in old-fashioned flash paper, the kind Victorian magicians used to make dramatic mini-explosions during their tricks.

"Please, we must run," Vaclav begged. "I have Madame Lazabra's crystal ball. I stole it. If they find it on me, my punishment will be hideous."

Angel patted his coat pocket. "*I* have her crystal ball," he reminded him. "And they *won't* find it on me."

As if on cue, the clown stopped dancing and stared down at the pair. Then it opened its mouth, threw back its head, and let out an ungodly shriek.

"No," Vaclav moaned, whipping Angel around.

Five more clowns faced them, spreading out. Then one flickered out of sight. It reappeared. Then another.

Then the one that had stood on the second story of the condo tapped Angel on the shoulder and said, "Boo!"

Angel didn't hesitate. He went into heavy action mode, hitting and kicking, leaping, smashing. He fanned in a circle and took on all comers, while Vaclav raced away, shrieking, without trying to help.

The clowns ringed around Angel, tiptoeing, prancing, giggling, and laughing. One raised a seltzer bottle and aimed it at Angel's face; he shielded his eyes with his hands. Acid hit his palms and he grunted from the searing pain as the skin dissolved.

Ignoring his wounds, he rushed forward toward his attacker, catching it by surprise. He kept running, knocking it over, and took off after Vaclav.

Down the block around the corner and across—

—*Giles?*

The half-naked, soot-drenched librarian was staggering across the street, waving a Scotch bottle at the cars squealing their brakes to avoid hitting him. He was carrying a large book, which the wind kept trying to yank away from him.

Angel easily caught up with him, pushing him out of the way of an oncoming car and to the curb. Giles fell into the gutter on his knees. He reeked of alcohol.

"Astorrith," Giles slurred, "wrath upon my enemies."

"*You* summoned Astorrith?" Angel asked incredulously.

Giles's eyelids fluttered. "Spoiled girl."

Angel pulled him to his feet. "Come on," he said. "We have to find Buffy."

Giles wagged his head from side to side. "*Kill* Buffy." He narrowed his eyes. "Angel," he slurred. "Kill you, too."

With the clumsiness of a drunk, he tried to hit Angel with his bottle. He missed, and his book tumbled from his grasp.

Angel caught it. It was a grimoire. With his free hand, he grabbed the bottle from Giles and threw it down. It crashed against the sidewalk.

"Come on," he ordered Giles.

"Not going wiz you," Giles informed him petulantly.

"Yes. You are." Angel made a fist and hit Giles squarely on the jaw.

As he anticipated, Giles's knees buckled. Angel hoisted Giles over his shoulders and took off.

Angel found Vaclav two blocks away, flagging down an olive green truck. "USMC" was painted in black on the passenger-side door. United States Marine Corps.

And none other than Claire Nierman was driving.

Angel raced toward the truck. Vaclav looked over his shoulder, and he brightened when he saw Angel.

"Oh my God!" Claire cried. "This is so crazy!"

"Yeah. It is," Angel replied.

"I'm sorry I deserted you," Vaclav said.

"It's okay," Angel told him. He looked back expectantly at Claire. "We need to get out of here," Angel told her.

"Of course," she said. She ticked an uneasy gaze toward Vaclav and Giles. "Who are these guys?"

Angel regarded Vaclav. "I'm not sure about him, but this one's a friend."

"I am seeking sanctuary. I . . . I know things," Vaclav said. He looked anxiously at Angel as though he were begging him not to say anything to betray him.

Angel said, "Hold on." He carried Giles around to the truck bed and carefully laid him down. Giles had cut sigils and signs into his own chest. Was he drunk *and* possessed?

Angel lingered a moment, then hurried back to the passenger door while Vaclav waited for him. Angel nodded at him, then at Claire, and said, "Get inside."

"Perhaps I should ride in the back with . . . that man," Vaclav said.

"I'm not sure about his condition," Angel said. "Better stay in here with us."

Claire frowned. "I thought you said he was a friend."

Angel nodded. "He is."

When he said nothing further, Claire shrugged and said to Vaclav, "Come in and scoot over. Make room."

There were only two seats, so Vaclav wedged himself between them, half-squatting and half-kneeling, as Angel got in and slammed the door.

Claire peeled out.

"What the hell is going on?" she said.

"End of days," Angel tried, "or something close." He tried to think of where to go. Buffy's?

Vaclav said, "Please, I beg of you. Get us as far away from here as you can." He glanced at the book on Angel's lap. "A grimoire? Are you a sorcerer?"

Angel didn't reply.

"I'll take you three to headquarters," Claire suggested. "We've got a detail going out after that thing. My boss has some special weapons." She looked excited. "Real experimental stuff."

*Wait a minute,* Angel thought. *She said she was here on R&R.*

*And she's not freaked out enough, considering what's going on. . . . And people in the armed services don't refer to their commanding officers as their "bosses."*

"Headquarters," Angel said nonchalantly. "Do you mean the armory?"

"No," she said, after a beat. "I mean, yes."

Claire took her right hand off the wheel and reached down to her left side. She came back up with a wicked-looking pistol and pressed it against Vaclav's temple.

"Let me guess," Angel said. "You're not with the military."

"No, sir." She smiled grimly at him. Then to Vaclav, "We saw you give the crystal ball to Angel," she continued. "You hand it over, Angel, or I'll blow his brains out."

*She knows who I am. That whole vampire attack in the alley was a setup.*

"She's with the professor," Vaclav said, panicking.

"No, I'm not. Give it to me, Angel," Claire said firmly.

"Please," Vaclav rasped. Angel could smell the fear on him, hear his fluttering heartbeat.

"Okay," Angel said.

He reached in his pocket and pulled out the crystal ball. He held it up where she could see it.

Claire's pupils dilated. She smiled.

Angel threw it at her. Not as hard as he could—there was no sense in killing her—but it clocked her. As she slumped forward, Angel pushed her against the side of the cab. Then he grabbed the wheel and steered while Vaclav bent over and retrieved the crystal ball from the floor.

"I can't believe you did that!"

Angel glanced from the road to the ball. It was intact. Inside, dozens of faces writhed and stretched—some of whom he recognized—the principal of Buffy's school, the waitress at the Lucky Pint. They were all in terrible agony.

Angel knew what was going on: They had been trapped in a hell dimension, where they were being tortured. The ball was a window to their suffering.

The truck swerved to the left as a blast of wind buffeted it. Angel tried to straighten it out.

"Look out!" Vaclav shouted.

The wind hit it from the other direction. The truck jumped onto a curb and roared up the grassy knoll directly in front of Buffy's school.

His right hand on the wheel, Angel knocked Claire's foot off the gas pedal. Then he pushed down on the brake pedal.

The truck lurched to a stop and slid back down the hill.

Lights were on in the school's main building. Angel hoped that meant someone was there.

The wind blew hard against the driver's-side door as Angel forced it open. He grabbed the unconscious Claire to keep her from falling out.

Vaclav clutched the crystal ball and the grimoire.

Angel carried Claire over one shoulder, then laid her down on the dewy grass while he collected Giles. The wind slapped his face and clawed at his coat.

In the back of the truck Buffy's watcher was coming to, raising himself up on his elbows and groaning. The sound was lost in the wind, but Angel could hear it.

"Giles, can you walk?" Angel asked him.

"How dare you!" Giles sputtered, his head lolling. "You kidnapped me!"

Angel picked Giles up by his shoulders and put him on his feet. Giles could barely stand.

Then Angel flung Claire over his shoulder and half-dragged, half-carried Giles toward the front door, where Vaclav stood diffidently by.

Vaclav said, "Is this sanctuary?"

"For no one else but you," Angel said, "to hear Buffy tell it."

He pushed on the door—it whipped open hard, propelled by the wind—and pulled Vaclav inside.

"Angel!" It was Willow, followed close behind by Ms. Calendar.

"Rupert!" she cried.

"Damn you," Giles bit off. "All of you."

Ms. Calendar drew back. Then she said, "He must be under the influence of an anger spell. Like you said, Willow."

"Where's Buffy?" Willow said anxiously. "And Xander and . . ." She gestured to Vaclav. "Hey, that's the guy from the fortune-teller's."

"I am Vaclav," he said. "I seek sanctuary."

"You can have it, if you help us," Angel said.

"Who's that woman?" Ms. Calendar asked Angel.

"Claire Nierman. Working for someone," he replied. "She said she was military, but she's not."

Ms. Calendar paled. "If the military ever heard about the Slayer, then . . ."

She trailed off as Angel gazed at her. "You have

the most beautiful voice," he said. "You're incredible. Has anyone told you what pretty hair you have?"

"Lust spell, definitely," Ms. Calendar murmured.

"And your eyes . . . they're like doe eyes." Angel was mesmerized.

"Yes, well, gaze on them quickly. Astorrith will rip them from their sockets," Giles proclaimed.

"Oh my God, Giles," Willow blurted. "That's awful!"

"They're bewitched," Vaclav told Willow. "It's the carnival. My master tempts mortals to weakness, and then he tears their souls from them! He destroyed the woman I love!"

"We were right," Ms. Calendar said, nodding at Willow. She said to Vaclav, "It's okay. We've created a spell that restores victims to their original states."

"Yes," Willow said. "I'm no longer envious." She flushed. "Well, no longer acting on my envy. It's good and suppressed."

"We'll do the same for you and Giles," Ms. Calendar told Angel. "Let's get to it, shall we?"

"I'm sorry about your woman," Willow told Vaclav as they began to walk. "Maybe we can help with that, too."

"I'm not going anywhere with you lot," Giles proclaimed, crossing his hands over his chest.

"I stole this," Vaclav said, holding out the crystal ball.

"An Orb of Thessulah?" Ms. Calendar asked, growing pale.

Angel had no idea what she was talking about. He didn't care. Her mouth was incredible.

"It's the Gypsy's crystal ball," Willow filled in.

She turned to Vaclav. "Tell us what to do with it."

"I will," he promised her.

"That's my grimoire!" Giles said, lurching at Vaclav. "You stole my book!"

Ms. Calendar seized it from Vaclav. "Then come and get it," she said, turning and hurrying down the hall to the computer lab.

Like an angry two-year-old, the drunken Giles followed.

# Chapter Ten

Joyce looked at Buffy in the rearview mirror. "We need to get some help."

They had found Joyce's SUV in the carnival parking lot. Her purse long gone, Buffy's mom retrieved the extra key she kept in the magnetized box in the wheel well, and they were off.

"Mom, no one can protect you like I can," Buffy assured her. "I can handle this."

Joyce glanced from Xander to her daughter and back again.

"Buffy, if he's not already dead, then he is dying. We have to get him to the medical center. He needs immediate attention."

"No, Mom," Buffy insisted. "They won't be able to help him."

"How do you know?" Joyce's voice was shrill. She

was scared. "You're a sixteen-year-old girl, not a medical doctor."

"Mom, just drive," Buffy snapped. "I know what I'm doing. I . . ." She trailed off.

The huge demon creature stood dead ahead.

An enormous tentacle rose up into the air, curling and undulating, then whipped downward, aiming at the vehicle.

"Back up!" Buffy yelled. *"Now!"*

Joyce obeyed. Their vehicle screamed backward one hundred, two hundred, three hundred feet. But the thing rolled toward them, tentacles flapping, curving up into the sky, then coming down hard, smashing trees, crushing a bus stop.

"Okay, stop!" Buffy ordered.

Joyce looked at her daughter. *"Stop?"*

Buffy nodded. "Yeah. I'm going to take that loser down."

Joyce's mouth fell open. "Buffy, you can't possibly do anything to that-that monster! You're just a girl!"

Buffy looked at her coolly. "Oh, Mom, I *so* am not."

She reached for the door handle.

Cordelia thought she heard movement beside her. A shifting. A rustling.

"Dear heart?" a man called from the doorway of the jewelry store bathroom. Something told Cordelia to keep her eyes closed and pretend to be unconscious.

"Miss Chase, is it not? I'm wondering if you've seen my old friend Ripper. It seems his condo is gone."

*Oh my God, it's that Ethan Rayne guy,* Cordelia thought. *No one else would call Giles "Ripper." And Ethan Rayne is completely evil.*

*Is he the guy who knocked me out and tied me up? Why would he do that? Is he that into pearls?*

Then she heard the same growl she had heard just before everything went black. Adrenaline flushed through her and she began to panic.

*Stay calm. Stay . . .*

He bent over her. She could feel his shadow move across her.

"It's all right. I know you're awake," he said. "You may as well open your eyes."

She debated.

"Come on," he urged her.

She opened them.

"Oh!" He smiled down at her. "I didn't think you were awake. But nice to see you, all the same."

*Damn it!*

He reached a hand toward her mouth. "Now, if I tear this off, will you scream?"

She shook her head.

"Because if you scream, I shall be very cross with you. And you don't want to see me cross, do you?"

She shook her head again.

"Very well, then."

He gathered up a corner between his thumb and forefinger, and pulled.

*Yow!* It hurt!

She screamed.

• • •

Still filthy but much calmer, Giles sat at Jenny Calendar's desk with a cold pack against the lump on his forehead while she set down a fizzy glass of Alka-Seltzer beside his grimoire. He was bare-chested, and he had redrawn the symbols he had inflicted upon himself for the summoning of Astorrith with blood she had fetched from the science lab. Angel informed them both that it was pig's blood, which, to Jenny's way of thinking, was too much information.

Himself again, Giles was preparing to send Astorrith back into his—its—own dimension.

"And the spell you used is called a Weakening Spell, you say." Rupert's voice was calm. His horrible fury had dissipated.

Jenny was very relieved by the change in him. He had been like a man possessed; she knew of what she spoke. She hoped never again to see Rupert act like he had today.

"Yes," she told him. "Willow and I prepared it."

"I was her guinea pig," Willow confirmed shyly, looking up from her job of drawing the pentagram on the floor.

Jenny could tell that the spell had worked on Angel, too. He'd said nothing about his lusty behavior, but it was obvious he was embarrassed.

Claire Nierman was still unconscious. They had yet to learn who her real superiors were. But Rupert had advanced the theory that she was working with Ethan. Vaclav had told them about Ethan's alliance with Professor Caligari, which had surprised Giles not in the least. Nor Jenny. Leave it to Ethan Rayne to work so many angles that they collided with each other.

Jenny hated him. He was once responsible for her own demonic possession. She was not a violent person, but she did believe in justice. And if she ever had the chance to deal some justice in Ethan Rayne's direction . . .

"I'm ready," Giles said. He drank down his Alka-Seltzer and rose, bringing the grimoire with him. He had to clear his head before beginning the ritual to send Astorrith out of their dimension.

Vaclav moved from the student desk where he'd been sitting and flanked Jenny as she stood outside one of the points on the pentagram. Willow got up from the floor and stood on her other side.

Rupert cleared his throat, walked to the center of the five-pointed star. He opened his grimoire and began.

*"Baal! Cthulhu! Jezebel! I call upon thee!"*

"Will this work?" Vaclav whispered to Jenny.

She nodded. "I hope so."

He hesitated, and then he said, "Pardon me, but are you by chance of Gypsy blood?"

She blinked. Swallowed. Ticked her glance toward Willow and Angel, to see if either of them had heard.

"No," she said firmly.

"Ah. My mistake." Vaclav turned his attention to the ritual.

Rupert was shouting.

*"Minions of Astorrith! I summon thee!"*

• • •

"Buffy, get back in this car!" Joyce shrieked at her daughter through the open driver's-side window of her SUV. Had Buffy lost her mind?

Seemingly oblivious to the horrible danger, Buffy was swaggering—that was the only word for it— toward the creature that had nearly smashed in the top of the SUV more than once.

The monster zeroed in on her child like a huge cat spying a mouse. Bizarre, horrible noises emanated from it.

Standing in the whipping wind, girl and nightmare regarded each other.

Joyce was so terrified she could barely think. Somehow she managed to put the car in drive and drove it forward, toward Buffy. It was a miracle; she was so numb she couldn't feel her foot on the gas pedal.

Buffy flung wide her arms. "You want me?" she cried. "Come and get me!"

The monster squealed again as it began to bend forward, tentacles flapping. From the center of its head, its mouth opened, revealing a raging fire.

"Buffy!" Joyce screamed. She pushed back the door latch and prepared to leap out.

Except that she couldn't. The wind was blowing directly against the car. It pushed hard; the SUV rocked; it began to tip on two wheels. The wind threw her out of her seat. As she lay sprawled on her side, she hit the button on Buffy's armrest to close the windows.

The monster lurched forward, its tentacles undulating. It flapped two of the tentacles toward her daughter, who moved into a prizefighter's stance.

Joyce sat back up and laid on the horn.

Buffy waved her off as if to say, *Don't bother. I can handle it.*

Sobbing, Joyce floored it, burning rubber, zero to sixty in—

The monster's tentacles were *smoking*. Its mouth was boiling flame. And all of that came crashing down on her baby, who didn't move a muscle as it rushed toward her.

She screamed again as Buffy was engulfed and—

—the creature vanished.

*Vanished.*

And the wind died with it.

Joyce braked, flung herself out of the car, and ran to Buffy, who lowered her arms, straightened her knees, turned, and strutted toward her.

As Joyce threw her arms around her and began to sob, Buffy said proudly, "See? Piece of cake."

"I didn't mean to scream," Cordelia told Ethan as they sat with their backs against the door to the bathroom. His bizarre dog-thing, Manufacturer, really liked her. It was laying its creepy head on her thighs, and she was letting it, because Cordelia Chase had a plan. Her hands were taped together, yes, but she could still move her fingers. While she was pretending to pet the dog, she began slipping her fingers into her front pants pocket . . .

. . . where the box cutter was located.

"It was like getting a free lip wax," she continued, "but still . . ."

She wondered if he realized that she had managed to gather up the dog's chain, too. And that Manufacturer couldn't raise his head from her thighs even if he wanted to.

"Hush," he said, cocking his head. "Listen."

"What?" Pet, pet, pet, inch, inch, inch.

"*Listen*. The wind is gone."

But there was something else:

The calliope. She heard its eerie . . . no, scratch that . . . its beautiful, haunting melody.

It was calling to her.

She said to Ethan, "I have to get back there. All my prizes are waiting for me. I can give her pearls for rolls of quarters."

He regarded her with a quirky grin.

"Well, I've never been one to turn a hostage away," he said.


Astorrith was gone, sent back to the dimension from whence it came. Giles quickly washed all trace of acarna from his body, found a light gray Sunnydale High T-shirt in the lost-and-found, and rejoined the others in Jenny's computer lab. Jenny herself was studying the crystal ball of Madame Lazabra.

Giles wondered if she would forgive him for this one.

Willow was standing at a whiteboard. She had made some headings in blue marker:

*CALIGARIUS.*

*ETHAN RAYNE.*

*VACLAV/SANDRA.*

*SPELLS.*

*SOULCATCHERS.*

*HELL DIMENSION.*

*BUFFY?*

*XANDER?*

*CORDELIA?*

*CLAIRE/MILITARY?*

When Willow saw Giles, she smiled hopefully at him. They were all looking to him for answers, even Angel, who stood silent and apart from the others. Giles just hoped he could provide some. His head hurt and he was deeply worried about Buffy, but he had to focus.

Walking to the whiteboard, he took the dry-erase marker from Willow. Everyone settled in for a strategy session; he, in turn, looked at Vaclav.

"Tell us everything you know," Giles said. "Leave anything out, and we will deny you sanctuary. Are we clear?"

"Yes," Vaclav said anxiously.

Willow raised her hand. "First of all, our friend Xander Harris has been really sick ever since he went to the carnival."

"Does he like to eat?" Vaclav asked. "My master may have tempted him with food. Gluttony. The Tricksters often poison it." He looked down, ashamed. "They enjoy inflicting harm on others. It's what nourishes them."

"I . . . He said he didn't eat anything," Willow said. "But we've all been under these terrible spells."

"If he has been poisoned, what can be done to make him well?" Giles asked intently.

"He is human, yes?" Vaclav asked.

Willow blinked. "Yes."

"Then he must be put in the glass coffin in the freak show," Vaclav said. "It is ancient, as are many of us. Well, I'm just two centuries. The coffin is what keeps us all alive. Heals us, if we are injured."

"So that's why that woman was in the coffin?" Willow asked. "To make her stay young?"

"Or to heal her?" Giles asked quietly.

Vaclav's lower lip trembled. "She was brought back from near death. But not completely."

"What do you mean?" Giles said, tapping the end of the marker against his finger.

There was a long pause. Then Vaclav said hoarsely, "Her mind was gone. It happens. They can still be useful." His chest heaved and the stillness in the room stretched into what Giles surmised was a moment of silence to acknowledge the girl's suffering. And Vaclav's own.

*He loves her,* Giles realized. And if that was why Vaclav had decided to betray Caligari, Giles was glad of his suffering. No, that was wrong. Glad that he had a reason to help.

Then Vaclav cleared his throat and said, "For most of us, it works. It will probably work on your friend."

"Probably?" Willow looked from Vaclav to Giles, and wondered if he had the ability to explain that probability away.

"What keeps your master alive?" Ms. Calendar asked.

"Souls," Vaclav replied. "He collects them. You can see them in the crystal ball. He preys upon your weakness, and then once he rips your soul from you, you go there. To be tormented." He shivered. "You cannot let him capture me! He'll send me there!"

"We'll do everything in our power to keep you safe," Giles said.

"How are we going to get Xander into the glass coffin?" Willow fretted.

"We'll have to find him first," Giles said gently.

Angel pushed away from the wall. He still thought it was awfully convenient that Vaclav had "just happened" to run into him.

"I'll do that. I'll look for him and Buffy. And Cordelia." Angel gestured with his head to the unconscious Claire Nierman. "I'll take her truck."

Giles nodded. "Yes. Good idea. Willow will tell you how to perform the Weakening Spell. Perhaps it will cure Xander's sickness as well."

Quickly, Willow gathered up the ingredients for the spell—several kinds of herbs, a white candle, and a handful of the half-dozen talismans Ms. Calendar had created from a book she had found in Giles's vast collection in the library. They looked like tiny people made out of cloth. She put everything in a plastic grocery store bag.

Meanwhile, Ms. Calendar typed out the ritual on her Apple and printed it for Angel. She went over it with him, making sure he understood every word. Angel folded the paper and put it in the grocery bag.

After she was done, Ms. Calendar hesitated. "Maybe one of us should go with you. What if . . . what if something happened to you and they took *your* soul?"

Angel hadn't stopped to consider that. Take away his soul, and he was a monster.

But there was no time for that now.

"You're all needed here," he insisted.

Then he left.

He went outside, got in the truck, and drove away. He'd go to Buffy's first. Maybe she had—

*Calliope music.*

Angel unrolled his window.

Sweet and beckoning, tempting, whispering, insinuating. *"Come to me and I will give you pleasures. Your greatest weakness will be your greatest delight.*

*"Come to me."*

Angel's scalp prickled. He could almost taste the music. It played inside him. Inside his bones and his mind and his unbeating heart.

*"Come to me."*

And then he saw them, emptying out of late-night bars and convenience stores, houses, and apartments: the citizens of Sunnydale, in long pants and jackets, bathrobes and slippers, shuffling down the dark streets. They reminded him of zombies.

*"Come."*

*Oompapa.*

*"Come now."*

*Deedle-deedle-dee.*

*"Step right up and feed me your soul."*

Angel shook his head to clear it.

*"Come."*

He got the paper out of the grocery bag and read it aloud to himself. He pinched the herbs between his fingers. He used the cigarette lighter to light the white candle's wick, and let it burn until he felt more centered.

The calliope's tune was no longer a siren song.

But it would be for anyone else who hadn't yet been on the receiving end of the Weakening Spell. For them, it would be a sweet call . . . to their doom.

Angel floored it. Buffy would likely be headed for the carnival, just like everyone else.

He hung a left onto Main Street. The sidewalks were crammed with people trudging past the Sun Cinema and the Espresso Pump. Neon signs painted their slack faces with bright pink and lime green.

He cruised past the alley where just two nights ago, he had first run into Claire Nierman. Things happened fast in a dangerous world.

He drove carefully. The wind had caused a lot of damage. Tree limbs had smashed car hoods. Trash cans, benches, and newspaper containers were tipped over. The crowds walked over them, around them, as the calliope beckoned them with whispered promises, delicious temptations.

The Seven Deadly Sins.

From the corner just beyond Yasumi jewelry store, someone waved at him.

It was Ethan Rayne. Cordelia was with him. Also, a strange black dog.

Then Ethan froze, turned, and ran; it was a quick and easy thing for Angel to stop, leap out of the truck in hot pursuit, tackle Ethan, and throw him to the ground.

The dog-creature began to growl and show its teeth.

"Hullo. It's Angel," Ethan managed, huffing as Angel turned him over on his back. "Fancy meeting you in the center of mayhem and destruction."

"I could say the same," Angel replied.

"Angel!" Cordelia cried, sounding far happier to see him. "You have wheels!"

"Where's Buffy? What's going on?" Angel demanded.

"Haven't the slightest," Ethan said.

Angel shot out his arm, grabbed the animal by the neck, and vamped. "Tell me *now*."

"You wouldn't dare bite Le Malfaiteur," Ethan said. Then, sighing, "I thought you were Claire. You're driving her truck."

"Angel, we have to get to the carnival right away," Cordelia said. "All my stuff is there! My glass basket! It's all mine! She's promised them to me."

So Cordelia's weakness was greed. He was surprised. He had expected it to be vanity.

"We'll go," Angel told her. He said to Ethan, "You're going to help me stop this."

"Not bloody likely," Ethan said, smirking.

"I'll kill you if you don't," Angel threatened. "And your big dog, too."

"Oh," Ethan said, startled. "In that case . . . kill my dog." He chuckled. "You know I'm nothing if not practical, Angel. While I would love to trust that your highly developed sense of morality would kick in before you made my heart stop, I'll help you."

Grimly satisfied, Angel kept hold of him and the dog as they walked to the truck. He said, "Cordelia, there's a plastic grocery bag on the seat. Get it."

"No, we have to go to the carnival *now*," she insisted.

"If you get it for me, I'll take you there."

"Okay," she said, hurrying to retrieve it for him.

"Got it," she reported, showing it to him.

Making sure the keys were not in the ignition, he threw Ethan and his dog into the cab.

Cordelia handed him the bag. Angel took out the herbs, the talismans, and the page of instructions. He laid everything on the hood of the car and quickly performed the ritual, down to lighting the candle again with some matches he found in the street beside his right front tire.

"Oh," Cordelia said, rubbing her hands over her face. "Angel. Oh, my God. I-I'm better." Her eyes grew enormous. "I knocked out the Yasumi salesclerk. Oh my God!"

"It's okay," Angel said.

"It is *not*!" she cried. "They'll never let me shop in there again!"

"We've all been under a spell." Maybe she was still under it, if the foremost thing on her mind was the future of her relationship with a jewelry store. On the other hand, she *was* Cordelia.

"Buffy, too," she told him. "She's been under a spell."

"Of lust?" he asked, wondering just how obvious the two of them had been. When they'd been bewitched, it hadn't mattered.

"Lust?" she echoed, sounding confused. "Buffy?"

He tried another tack. "What's she been like? Angry? Greedy?"

Cordelia shook her head. "She has been totally stuck-up. Well, she's always stuck-up, but she's been arguing with Giles, telling him to leave her alone because she can do everything herself. Miss Thing to the max!"

Angel listened hard, running down the list of the Seven Deadly Sins: Lust, Envy, Anger, Sloth, Gluttony, Vanity, and Greed. Which was Buffy's?

"Pride," he said slowly, answering his own question. "Vanity is another word for pride. Buffy's proud."

"Well, if you want to call it that. I would say 'stubborn' or maybe even 'stupid,' but whatever it is, she nearly took Giles out for telling her what to do."

"That's not good," Angel muttered.

"Hel-*lo*? Haven't I been saying that?" Cordelia raised her eyebrows and pursed her lips.

"She might not listen if I try to do the spell," Angel continued, parsing out what to do.

"And that would be *so* new for her, the rascal," Cordelia grumped. "Are *you* listening to *me*?"

From inside the truck, Ethan Rayne laid on the horn; Cordelia screamed and hopped into Angel's arms.

"Oh, I'm just so overstressed," she murmured. "I'll probably break out. This is all Buffy's fault."

Easing Cordelia down, Angel glared at Ethan through the side window. Wide-eyed, Ethan jabbed a finger straight ahead through the windshield.

As a flood of vampires and demons raced toward them.

"I feel like dancing," Joyce announced as she and Buffy skipped the parking lot and drove straight up to the entrance of the carnival. They got out of the car and walked onto the enchanted ground of the carnival.

Joyce sighed and smiled pensively. Then she yawned. "The music is so beautiful. Oh, I want to just sit and listen to this music forever. I never want to move another muscle as long as I live."

Buffy was barely listening. The voice inside her head was the one worth listening to.

*"Slayer, this is your kingdom. Come to me. Come and receive the crown you so richly deserve."*

"I am," Buffy said.

A large, shimmery rectangle appeared directly in front of her. It was silver, gleaming. A mirror, or a door?

*"Come,"* the voice urged her.

Buffy stepped forward, into the rectangle. She was bathed in silver light. Her skin gleamed as if it were metallic.

*I am so beautiful,* she thought.

*"Yes, you are,"* a voice replied. It was Professor Caligari, with his white hair and his long face and his extremely yucky hands.

He was sitting on an ivory—bone?—bench in front of a pipe organ made of bones. Skulls, both human and demon, grinned at her. Spinal columns rose to the ceiling of a dark room.

Not a pipe organ. A calliope.

A noise behind her startled her. She turned.

There were seven clowns, each dressed differently. She had seen some or all of them before. One wore a little pointed hat; another had Rasta braids. A third, purple hair.

As she gazed at each in turn, it began to wipe off its makeup with a piece of cloth—a red bandanna for one, a lacy handkerchief for the more elegant one in the pointed hat. Yet as they swiped the bright white, red, and blue, she couldn't see their faces. She wasn't sure they had any.

Next came their costumes. Beneath them, they wore black robes decorated with random red sevens. Their hands were hidden inside their sleeves, and their hoods hid their faces.

And now Buffy stood in the center as they encircled her, the dark room blurring into a silver horizon.

"I told you that there are exceptional souls to be savored here in Sunnydale," Professor Caligari said to the seven men. He extended his hand toward Buffy. "This is a slayer. The reigning Slayer. Can you imagine what her soul will taste like?"

"Wait a sec," Buffy said.

Then Professor Caligari began to play the calliope. The notes danced over her skin, whispering at her, making her forget what she was going to say. Oddly, that didn't bother her.

The men began to move, swaying, dancing. Buffy joined them, stepping in a smaller circle inside their larger one. All her cares and fears evaporated. There was nothing she could not handle, here inside the protective ring of music and magicks. The men, the calliope music, the world were silvery and beautiful.

> *"Mirror, mirror on the wall,*
> *Who's the strongest of them all?*
> *Who's brave and true?*
> *Who's the queen of the carni-val?*
> *You, Buffy Summers, you."*

Then she saw herself on the cliff again, as she had long ago in a dream . . . or had it really happened? Watching the leapers through the bonfires. Druids, on Samhain.

She smelled the wood smoke, and the burns . . .

. . . the burning of the witches as the eager villagers screamed for their deaths . . .

. . . the lions roaring in the Colosseum as the hapless Christians flung themselves against the barred exits . . .

. . . Professor Copernicus Caligari, Doctor Emeritus, surrounded by glass jars labeled MEDICINALS as he stood in front of his black wagon, thumbs hooked around the lapels of his goin'-to-meetin' suit. He had a handlebar mustache and thick sideburns; his hair was short and he had a bit of a paunch from all the dinners widows in calico fixed for him as he made his way across the prairies and the badlands.

"Step right up, folks, step right up! We've got it all! Wild West show! Indians! A trained bear! And a mermaid!"

The crowd pressed forward eagerly.

"Forget your troubles! Forget the drought! Sit a spell and partake of our marvelous entertainments!"

Then her vision shifted back, and the seven men in robes surrounded the Slayer as Professor Caligari played his calliope.

She wore a crown of roses and a white dress, and she was perfectly, wonderfully unique.

"You are the one girl in all your generation," Professor Caligari reminded her as the calliope music slid across her skin like a lover's caress.

The seven men bowed low.

"Let me introduce you, Slayer, to Greed, Lust, Anger, Sloth, Gluttony, Envy, and of course, your favorite: Pride."

The men straightened. They were dressed as clowns again—

—Buffy blinked—

—who pulled spheres of glass from their colorful sleeves and began to juggle them.

*"Round and round and round she goes,"* the calliope sang. Up, down, around, up and down . . .

*". . . like your life, your oddly mixed life of boredom*

*and death-defying adventures that does not do justice
to the specialness of you. But we here, we understand."*

The glass spheres glittered and twinkled. The calliope played.

And Buffy stood radiant and alone, chin raised.

Proud.

The clowns winked in and out of existence, grinning and flirting. She grinned back, reaching for the
glass spheres. But they appeared and disappeared like
soap bubbles.

Then they were the men in deep-hooded cloaks
again; seven ringed around her. They pulled their
hands from their sleeves and she saw hooks and barbs
and talons, but no fingers—

She froze.

"No, it's all right," said Professor Caligari. Only
that wasn't his name. It wasn't even Hans Von Der
Sieben. It was Caligarius. She knew that now. And
these were his first acolytes, the men who made the
sacrifices of their souls that gave him his first taste of
power. They were ancient beings, devoid of souls, or
pity, or any bit of goodness.

"These are not for you," Caligarius assured her.
"You will reign beside me, lovely queen. All you must
do is vanquish our enemies. They have never respected
you, never admired you. That must anger you."

Buffy was terribly confused. Because she *was*
angry. Very angry. Furious. But . . .

"They will come, and they will try to stop us. You
can't let that happen."

"Of course not," she said slowly. "But what did

you say about my soul?" She couldn't remember.

His features softened. "Don't worry about that. I would never harm you. Why should I harm you?" Caligarius asked softly.

The calliope played on. Only it wasn't a calliope anymore; it was flutes and drums . . . the clashing of cymbals as the hunters searched the forests and hills not for rabbits or deer, but for human sacrifices . . .

*This is wrong,* she thought.

"*Shh,*" Caligarius whispered. "*It's all right.*"

The silvery notes enfolded her, soothed her, eased her back into the good place she had found.

Where she was special.

"*Yes.*"

"Wait," she said, fighting against it, fighting . . . why was she fighting?

*Because I am a fighter. That's what I am.*

Because something here was not right.

Buffy blinked at the silver door.

But it wasn't a door. She was standing in the mirror maze, staring at herself in one of the panels. Alone. Her reflection stared back at her.

"Mom?" she called.

The calliope music played.

"*A-hunting we will go, a-hunting we will go . . .*

"*Come to me. Be with me. Your pride will be your greatest pleasure. And you should be proud. You are one of a kind. The only one in all your generation.*"

"Come to you," Buffy said, reaching out a hand toward the mirror.

Something reached back.

And grabbed hold.

Hard.

"Oh my God, Angel!" Cordelia cried as demons and vampires swarmed over the people in the streets. It was like a monster stampede, and as they approached, the sleepwalking people woke up and started screaming and trying to get away.

Two demons with corkscrew horns roared and leaped on their closest prey; a shambling corpse in a grave cloth bit into the shoulder of a man in an Emeril sweatshirt and a pair of sweatpants. A couple of trolls grabbed the shins of a heavyset woman in a flannel nightgown. A pack of Sunkist-orange, slithery snake-things with enormous rows of teeth sprang at two teenage boys in Sunnydale High School letter jackets.

It was a madhouse!

Angel opened the cab and yanked Ethan Rayne out. He flung Cordelia inside, tossing in the sack of stuff he had used in his magick spell on her. He slammed the door hard behind her.

As she grabbed the sack, she fell on top of Ethan's dog-thing. It stank like matches being lighted. And it growled!

With a shriek she turned back to the door.

Mere feet beyond it, three vampires and something purple and gooey were dragging Angel off. And Ethan Rayne was cheering them on—until a pack of trolls and two big gray blobs converged on him.

"Angel!" she cried, cracking open the window just the teeniest little unsafe bit.

"Get to the carnival!" he yelled over his shoulder as he whomped the purple gooey thing with a totally solid roundhouse kick. "Follow the directions for the ritual!"

"Keys!" she cried, batting at the window. Then something clinked; she looked inside the grocery bag and found them. She jammed them into the ignition and started the motor as a vampire in a black leather jacket flung itself onto the hood of the truck.

She screamed, shifting into reverse as fast as she could. She was crying and shaking. Monsters were coming. Monsters were everywhere!

All glowing eyes and big, sharp fangs, the vampire was clinging to the windshield and grinning at her in anticipation. Ha! She hit the brakes.

The vampire's face rammed into the windshield, which held. Then it ricocheted off the hood. Another one leaped at the truck. Some kind of round, glowing thing rolled up beside her door and started flinging itself against it.

Cordelia backed up as fast as she could go, gaze ticking from the glowing thing to the crowds of demons and monsters to the zombie-people and back again.

"Carnival, carnival," she said, forcing herself to stay calm. After all, she was good at maintaining, even when the pressure was intense. Look at how well she handled the terrible burden of her popularity.

"I'll get to the carnival. I'll follow the directions on

the paper." She stuck her hand in the sack. "Oh my *God*, where's the paper? It's not here! The paper's not here!"

Her fingers brushed the folded edge. "Oh, wait, here it is. All I have to do is follow the directions. I can do that."

"And ah will 'elp you," Ethan Rayne's dog-thing told her in a French accent.

Cordelia started shrieking.

# Chapter Eleven

Xander heard the voice of an angel.

"Xander, Xander, oh my God, he's dead! Look at how pasty he looks. Well, he always looks pasty. You can carry him, right?"

Or rather, the voice of Cordelia.

He tried to open his eyes. Every part of him was nauseated. He was so sick. He couldn't imagine being sicker. He wanted to die. Really. In case anyone was listening.

There was a lot of jostling.

"Your spell is working, right? No one can see us? They don't know we're here?"

"It should 'old." It was a guy's voice, deep and French. No one Xander knew. He didn't care, except for the knee-jerk jealousy. He hated the jostling. The jostling was evil. If it didn't quit, he'd . . . he'd . . .

*Calliope music.*

*Yes. Gentle and beckoning and reassuring and . . .
food.*

He was soothed. And hungry.

"Okay, Xander, listen, um, if you aren't dead, I'm
doing a spell on you, with the help of this warlock
named Le Malfaiteur. That's right, right?"

*"Oui,"* said the guyful voice.

"Anyway, he is really *hot,* I mean, ha, he was
Ethan Rayne's imprisoned dog, only he got free of the
spell while Ethan was distracted fighting for his life
from all those demons and vampires and things and so
now he's helping me. He wasn't even attacking me in
the store, just trying to warn me about Ethan! You got
that?"

Xander had not a clue, but it didn't matter. The
music filled him.

He was so hungry for more.

"Okay, I'm ready. I've got the herbs and everything.
Wait! Le Malfaiteur, do you have any matches? Oh,
that's so *amazing*! What do your other fingers do?

"Xander? Can you hear me? It's called a Weakening Spell. It should help you. If you're not dead. Hey,
Le Malfaiteur, can you move it along? Maybe they
can't see us, but I can see them. And Xander may be on
the brink . . ." She let out a little sob.

The calliope whispered to Xander. It sang. It said,
*"Eat of the fruit of good and evil. Eat more. Consume.
Devour. You are ravenous."*

The music crept into his gut. Xander floated on the
notes, listening to the crescendo. He drifted and dozed.

"'. . . and so I demand his unbinding!'" Cordelia recited.

Xander heard the rustling of a paper near his ear. "Okay, I hope that helped." Fingers snapping. "Hello? Hello, do you hear me?"

He couldn't open his eyes, but he knew he was lying on a very hard surface. It was very cold.

"You're sure the wards will hold?" Cordelia asked.

"For now. I can't make any guarantees."

"Okay, listen. We're going into the freak show, but no one else will be able to go in. They'll think it's locked. Except maybe if the bad guys are snooping around, they might figure out that it's bewitched."

"My wards are very strong," the guy said, sounding a bit offended. "And we have the amulets your sorcerer made for you."

"My . . . oh! Giles! He's not a sorcerer!"

"If you say so, *ma belle*."

"Okay, you're creeping me out."

"It would be best to hurry," the guy prodded.

"Okay, all right. Xander, we're putting you in something that will help you get well. It's that glass coffin in the freak show, but don't freak out. It'll heal you. I hope. Angel said so. That girl we saw in it? They were using it to heal her. That didn't go perfect, but it was better than nothing. Anyway, don't be scared. We're going to close the lid now. We don't know if we're supposed to, but here goes nothing!"

*Whump!*

*Knock-knock-knock.*

"Xander? *Xander?* Oh my God, he's not breathing!"

"They're overrunning the town," Willow announced as she looked up from her screen. She had hacked into the dispatcher's computer system at the Sunnydale Police Department. They're saying 'gangs,' but you know that's what they always say."

"Vampires and demons everywhere," Ms. Calendar murmured as she moved to the window and peered through the venetian blinds at the night. "According to those dispatches, it's worse than when the Master tried to open the Hellmouth. And we have hours until it's light. They're sure to come here."

"My master . . . tried to open the Hellmouth?" Vaclav asked in a frightened, hushed voice.

"Different master," Willow explained. "But same hellmouth. Which, well, we're pretty much sitting on top of it." She made a little face. "Sorry."

"We prevailed that time," Giles reminded them. "And we'll prevail again."

Ms. Calendar moved from the window and picked up the crystal ball. "Rupert," she said, "there are more people in here. In the hell dimension. I recognize some of my students. Larry. And there's Chris Vardeman."

"Damn. One assumes they're being absorbed via Caligari's dread machinery," Giles said. He crossed to Vaclav. "Explain it to me again."

"The professor has soulcatchers on the grounds,"

Vaclav said. "They hypnotize you, make your temptations rise to the surface."

Giles nodded. "Those would be the clowns. With their juggling balls."

"No. But they help the process." He shook his head impatiently. "The Tricksters are his minions. From the First Days. The soulcatchers all have shiny surfaces." He pointed to the crystal ball. "The word escapes me. Mirrors, only more focused. Normal ones make rainbows. But these make a . . . rainbow of the vices. The Seven Deadly Sins."

"A rainbow. You mean a spectrum," Giles considered.

"Yes," he said in his Bela Lugosi voice.

"Prisms," Willow offered.

Vaclav looked excited. "Yes, that's the word. They are prisms. They focus your weakness, and then you are lost in it. In lust, or greed . . . and we lure you in. We promise you what you want most."

"But why set out my grimoire for me to find?" Giles asked. "Why tempt me to summon a horrible demon that can just as easily destroy the carnival itself?"

Vaclav shook his head. "That I cannot tell you. It makes no sense to me, either."

"Ethan Rayne," Jenny Calendar said coldly. "He loves chaos. Worships it. He wouldn't pass up a chance like this to pump up the volume."

Giles exhaled. "When I get my hands on him . . ."

"The soulcatchers," Willow said, keeping the grown-ups on task. "Shiny surfaces. Prisms that focus our bad impulses. What and where are they?"

"I'd be willing to guess that one of them is located inside the Chamber of Horrors," Giles said. "In the vampire scene." He looked at Vaclav. "Yes?"

Vaclav hesitated, fingers kneading the edge of his sweater. "I don't know where they are."

"What about the moon ball on the carousel?" Willow said.

"Perhaps," Vaclav said, lowering his gaze.

Willow pushed back from her computer. "We should go to the carnival now and see what we can find."

"First we should try to figure this out," Giles asserted.

"But the others don't know about the . . . soul catchers," Willow argued. "We need to help them."

"You can't help them now," said Claire Nierman as she awkwardly sat up, her hands bound behind her back. "It's too late."

Everyone turned. Giles walked toward her, squatting down beside her. "Why do you say that?"

She looked away. "I only have to give you my name, rank, and serial number."

"We know you're not with the Marine Corps," Giles said with deadly calm. "You're with Ethan Rayne, aren't you?" he said. "He's been working both sides of this, just like Jenny said."

At the name, Claire's eyes flickered, and Willow knew that Giles was right. Maybe she was even Ethan's lover.

"And you probably know who I am. I'm Ethan's old mate Ripper. And I'm willing to bet he told you why I was called that."

Claire frowned and bit her lower lip.

"So tell me," Giles suggested. "Why do you say that it's too late to help them?"

A little bit of her fear faded with her bravado. "Tonight's the Rising. Caligari's strength is at its peak. He'll take out everyone in Sunnydale before this night is over."

*"Tonight?"* Giles stared at her. "But the Rising was two nights ago."

"You had it wrong, honey," she said disparagingly. "You got fed misinformation. It's now."

"Well, I don't see why you're smiling about it," Willow piped up, protectively crossing her arms over her chest. "I mean, you're here with us and not Ethan."

"He'll find me. He'll come for me," she said, crossing her legs at the ankles as she got more comfortable.

"Oh my God, look!" Ms. Calendar shouted. She nearly dropped the crystal ball; then as she caught it, she thrust it toward Giles and Willow.

Willow ran over and peered into it.

Her blood turned to ice. Her face was a flash fire.

Xander's face swirled in the glass.

Mottled, bruised, and screaming.


Angel was no quitter, but two hundred and forty years of living made a man realistic.

Even if that man was a vampire with a soul.

Far be it for him to say that Sunnydale was beyond redemption, but it wasn't looking good.

Everything in him wanted to abandon this fight

and get himself to the carnival, where he might be able to do something that would tip the odds toward a better outcome than this one. If Buffy was there, she was probably in trouble. Unless Cordelia had been able to cast the Weakening Spell on her, she would still be in thrall to Caligari's magicks.

Up to his neck in assailants—at last count, three lizard-green Shrieker demons, a Lindwurm, and an albino poison-spitter—he was worried about Cordelia's chances of getting to the carnival, much less casting a spell on a prideful, bewitched slayer. He wondered what she had done about the dog.

He raced down an alley with his attackers in close pursuit. Ethan Rayne had disappeared from his radar. If he wasn't dead, then he had probably headed for the city limits. That was Ethan's way—wreak havoc and leave.

He got around a corner and leaned against the brick exterior, regrouping as he waited for the mob that was after him to arrive. It was nice to have a second to rest. But it would be two seconds at most. He knew that.

He pushed away, preparing for a fight.

As a clutch of axe-wielding ogres dropped down from the roof above him.

The merry-go-round of the damned:

The threshers in the center of the carousel diorama finished beating Xander with their drumsticks and their cymbals. The falcons soared back onto the gauntlets of the hunters, their prey dangling from their claws and

beaks: half-eaten hot dogs; pieces of popcorn; chocolate chip cookies soggy with soda; cold, congealed
onion rings; and kettle cirb mixed with gum.

Carnival carrion.

Holding Xander down, the men in gauntlets force-
fed it to him as he choked, struggled, and gagged. They
laughed. They sang, *"A-hunting we will go!"*

They laughed harder when he vomited.

They fed him more.

In his terrible new world the hunters and their
threshers were real people. Xander was trying to figure
out how many there were. He thought maybe eight. He
was so sick it was hard to pay attention.

Then one of thc sadists carried him back onto the
carousel floor and plopped him on his fiery black
carousel horse. *"Behold the wages of the sin of gluttony!"* he bellowed, and he rechained Xander's wrists
to the pommel on the saddle. The horse reared,
chuffing smoke and fire. Its hide sizzled, and Xander
gasped.

He could no longer scream.

Then the now-familiar sizzling erupted deep inside
his chest and head, and he shuddered as the golden
carousel pole rose. He knew the rhythm now: up when
it sucked the life out of him, down for a moment of
release. In tune with his heartbeat.

Each time it went up, the carousel rotated one
increment. Of what kind of measurement, he had no
idea.

He was not alone. Hundreds, if not thousands, of
tortured people sat on creatures all around him, beside

him, behind him, and in front of him. The carousel was a vast machine, and the bruised and beaten people on the carousel animals were like galley slaves, only instead of sitting at long oars and rowing, they were powering the rising movements of the poles.

And each time the poles went up, a calliope note sounded. Their energy was making the calliope play.

In this dimension or the other one or both, Xander had no idea.

*"Food, glorious food!"* the calliope played. And God help him, Xander was hungry.

Then two of the hunters were unchaining him again; he moaned because he knew what was coming.

They held him down and force-fed him again.

Then he was on his horse, his insides crackling, and the carousel rotated again.

He was losing consciousness when he heard a familiar voice.

"You people are in so much trouble. I have friends in high places, you know, and once they hear about this, you are going to have more than the school board to answer to!"

It was Principal Snyder, one creature ahead of him. The man sat astride a half-horse, half-fish creature. Xander stared at his bald head, drinking in the sound of his voice over the discordant notes of the calliope. How bad was Xander's world, that he was happy to see him?

"Hey," Xander called to him. "Principal Snyder."

Snyder looked over his shoulder with a horribly bruised face and two black eyes. His lip was split.

"Harris!" He glared at him. "I should have known you were behind all this."

Xander huffed. "Do I *look* like I'm behind all this?"

Then the person riding beside Xander turned to him. Despite the bruises on his face, he looked vaguely familiar. He was a guy from school. Xander suddenly realized that he was surrounded by Sunnydale High students.

Whoa, gluttony was big in the California public school system.

The guy said, "Why are you different from us?"

"Different?" Xander asked.

"Yeah. Look at me."

Xander really looked. The guy was kind of half-there, like a ghost, or a hologram. Xander could see the black stallion he rode right through him. And it looked like a regular carousel horse, not a frothing nightmare.

Xander hadn't noticed that before. He was too busy getting tortured or something.

"Look at yourself," the guy said.

Xander was nearly solid. Still a little blurry, but not like the other guy.

"How did you get here?" the guy asked him. "What ride were you on?"

"Ride?" Xander considered. "I wasn't on a ride. I was sick, and I got put in something. I think it was a coffin."

The guy said, "Well, I was riding this carousel. Only it wasn't like this."

"So was I," said the girl on the other side of Xander. Her face was black-and-blue.

He realized he was beginning to see them more clearly. He was able to think, where before he had just plodded along.

Something was happening to him. Something that he thought might be good.

*I'm getting better.*

He yanked on the chain tied around his wrist.

It broke with a clank.

In the center of the carousel one of the falcons on an outstretched arm jingled its bells and cocked its head. The hunter who held it frowned and swept his gaze out at the riders.

Xander swallowed hard.

The hunter moved back into position in a jerky, automaton motion. His face grew hard, and he looked like a statue.

*I think that's good.*

Xander freed his other hand, grabbing the chain so it wouldn't make a sound. As the girl and the guy watched in astonished silence, he reached across and pulled the girl's left hand free of her chain. Her right was still tethered.

"Try it yourself," Xander whispered.

She tried, but nothing happened. Same with the guy.

Xander leaned over and wrenched the guy's right hand free. Then the guy's left.

Others saw and moved their hands, straining against their chains. But they were held in place.

"How did you do that?" Snyder hissed, struggling against his own chains. Xander tried not to take satisfaction in that. It had to have something to do with the coffin, or the spells Cordelia had been talking about. Now he wished he'd been able to pay better attention.

"There was something about a warlock," Xander told him in a low voice.

"Warlock? Are you insane?" Synder shot back. Xander waited to see if it occurred to Snyder that believing in warlocks was, at the moment, nowhere near the craziest aspect of their existence.

"Not so loud," Xander cautioned him.

"Are you telling me what to do?" Snyder asked. His bloodshot eyes were so huge Xander half-expected them to fall out of his head. "You are a student!"

"Shut up," Xander told him.

*"What?"*

Ignoring Snyder, Xander broke the chain around the girl's right wrist, and she covered her mouth with both hands as if to keep herself from crying out. Xander motioned for her to put them down. There was no telling when an evil-statue-guy might notice.

"Oh, God, can you get us out of here?" the guy to Xander's right whispered excitedly.

Then their attention was taken up when the threshers banged their drums and crashed their cymbals. The noise rang in Xander's ears, until louder screams masked it. Something—someone?—appeared in the diorama. It was another Sunnydale High School student, a beefy guy in a letter jacket who, yeah, could very well have gluttony issues. He was on his hands and knees, looking around as he screamed, and Xander didn't blame him because it was extremely terrifying simply watching the figures in the diorama as they lost their robotlike stiffness and began wailing on the guy with their drumsticks and cymbals.

"What's going on? Who *are* you people?" the guy was shrieking.

*"Behold the wages of the sin of gluttony!"* one of the hunters proclaimed, lifting the hood from the falcon on his arm.

"Oh my God! Someone help me!" the guy screamed. "Please!"

Xander hated not being able to help, but he did the next best thing he could: He took advantage of the distraction to slither off the black stallion and creep to the trio of riders ahead of him. He yanked hard on the chain of the guy beside Principal Snyder. The chains broke immediately.

"Me, next, me!" Snyder demanded.

"Shut up," Xander said again, and he got to work.

"You can't just leave me here," Claire said to Giles from the door of the computer lab.

Willow's forehead wrinkled. Giles commiserated; the police dispatches indicated that the riots were heading this way. It was quite possible they would overrun the school. At least they had untied her hands. That would give her a better chance at survival. But not much of one.

"She was going to shoot me," Vaclav reminded Giles. "Angel stopped her."

"Don't be silly," she said quickly. "I was just pretending. I would never hurt anyone."

"I'm sorry," Giles said. "Lock the door behind us."

Then they raced down the hall and into the library, where Giles began grabbing holy water and stakes while Jenny Calendar threw together some protective amulets.

Willow said, "What should I do? Tell me what to do!"

And then the phone rang.

Startled, they all glanced at it, and then Willow raced to grab it.

"Hello?" she said, and then, "Cordelia!"

"I'll take it," Giles said, dashing across the library. "Yes, Cordelia?"

"Giles," she whispered, the signal fuzzy and faint. "We need you. You have to come now. Le Malfaiteur knows what to do and you have to come and Xander's messed up and . . . oh my God!"

"Stay calm," he urged her.

"Hel-*lo*?" she blurted. "I am in the middle of total evil here!"

"Yes. Who is Le Malfaiteur?"

"He's this warlock. He is, like, French or African or something, and Ethan Rayne cursed him because he cheated in cards, hold on, he says he only cheated because . . . *Listen, we don't care why you cheated!* Where was I?"

"The warlock."

"Yes! He used this invisible spell on us to get Xander into the coffin, only now I think Xander is dying."

"We believe he's in another dimension," Giles said.

"Really." There was a beat. "Well, that's good! They don't think Xander is dying," she said away from the phone.

"Okay, listen, I have all this stuff to tell you," she continued.

"I, as well," Giles said. "Are you—"

"Me, first," Cordelia cut in. "This phone wasn't even worth stealing. It is a piece of junk! It weighs a ton and the signal sucks and *oh my God, I am being greedy! The Weakening Spell is wearing off!*"

"No, no, it's not. You're always greedy, remember? You're fine. Stay with me, Cordelia," Giles urged. "Have you seen Buffy?"

Ms. Calendar and Willow listened as they finished putting together the supplies. Vaclav chimed in on Giles's side of the conversation, and Willow started putting the puzzle pieces together. It was as Vaclav had told them: The carnival used magickal prisms to find people's weak spots. Then Vaclav broke down and spilled. He had been too afraid to tell them everything, but now that Cordelia and the French warlock were on the grounds, he obviously felt more confident about sharing.

There were seven prisms, each attuned to one of the Seven Deadly Sins. Bewitched by the mirror ball on the carousel, Xander's gluttony had gotten the better of him. The crystal ball was the focal point for envy.

Willow wondered what she, Willow, might have done if she had more fully succumbed to her envy. She was deeply ashamed that she had tried to hurt

Ms. Calendar's feelings, even if the computer teacher understood and forgave her.

What might Angel have done if he got too lusty?

Giles's anger had raised a demon that had nearly destroyed Sunnydale.

Vaclav said that next the carnival sucked the souls right out of people. But where did the people go?

"But what are we to do with the prisms?" Giles asked Vaclav. "Yes, hold on Cordelia. Vaclav is going to explain things to us."

Vaclav hesitated again, and Willow was about to encourage him to speak up when he exhaled and said, "I'm not sure. I do know that they are somehow connected to the calliope. There have been times when one of them would be damaged, and the calliope would sound . . . sour."

"So maybe what we should do is find them and destroy them," Willow suggested.

Vaclav considered. "When the calliope sounded wrong, Professor Caligari would touch his chest. The way a person does when there is something wrong with his heart."

"So you're saying his heart is connected in some way to these prisms?" Jenny asked. She looked at Giles. "There's a lot of literature online about symbolic magicks. These prisms could represent the chambers of his heart. If the chambers are completely destroyed, his heart will fail."

"Are you hearing this, Cordelia?" Giles asked.

"So . . . we find and destroy the prisms," Willow ventured again.

"The thing is," Jenny cut in, "in cases like these, you usually have to inflict a lot of damage very quickly or the being can stop you. It's a little complicated, but . . . "

Giles took up the threat. "What you're saying is if we don't destroy all the prisms . . . wait." He nodded. "Yes, Cordelia. I'm listening."

Everyone was quiet. Then Giles said, "Oh, of course. Why didn't I think of that? Thank you, Le Malfaiteur."

After a few more minutes, Giles said, "Yes, good, all right, we'll try to meet you at the freak show. Yes, Jenny has a cell phone."

Ms. Calendar nodded.

"Yes, it's a lovely cell phone. Very good," Giles went on. "No, I don't think you'd be allowed to keep it once this is all over."

Giles hung up and faced the others.

"We have a plan," he said. "I'll explain it on the way."

He, Ms. Calendar, Willow, and Vaclav took off, racing through the student lounge to the faculty parking lot. Jenny unlocked her car and everyone slid in, Giles in the front seat with her, Willow and Vaclav in the back.

Willow stared into the crystal ball, watching Xander's face. He was still beaten, but he was looking around at something they couldn't see, and talking, although they couldn't hear him.

*I wonder if he's where the people go when their souls are stolen,* Willow thought anxiously. She was so scared to go back to the carnival. Scared it would happen to her. But she would go to hell and back to save Xander. Or Giles. Or even Cordelia.

*And especially Buffy. Where* is *she?*

Jenny peeled out like a teenage boy and they headed for the carnival.

Demons and people were racing all over the streets. Buildings blazed. Smoke choked the moon and screams pierced Willow's eardrums.

"Can you summon Godzilla?" Willow asked Giles.

A man spotted them and waved both his arms as he ran toward them, calling for help.

"Drive on," Giles said quietly. "Get around them."

*Not needing to go to hell to help,* Willow thought. *Hell has come to us.*

"This is what my master brings," Vaclav yelled. "This chaos and mayhem. And then the people come to us like lambs to the slaughter. We devour their souls." He buried his face in his hands.

"It's not your fault," Willow said, patting his shoulder. "Um, not that much, anyway."

Vaclav dropped his hands into his lap. "I was his collaborator for two centuries. And then, when Sandra's mind was taken . . . only then did I rebel."

"But you did rebel," Willow said. "You're trying to help us stop him now. That's good."

"But my soul . . . he'll take my soul," Vaclav said.

"Only if he defeats us," Willow said.

They shared a look.

"He'll take my soul," Vaclav said brokenly.

"Right, then," Giles said. "On that triumphant note of optimism, let's go through our plan one last time."

Willow listened carefully.

"Le Malfaiteur has corroborated Vaclav's opinion that the prisms, the calliope, and Caligarius are connected. We need to collect all the prisms and put them together so that they're touching," Giles said. "Once that is done, then we perform a Tobaic Ritual of Destruction. It's a very ancient rite said to have been used against a number of the last pure demons who walked the Earth before humankind banished them."

"So, we think he's that kind of demon, a . . . tobacco demon?" Willow asked.

"It's a sort of all-purpose destruction ritual," Ms. Calendar said. "It works in a lot of cases." She nodded at Giles. "That's a very elegant solution."

"Thank you," Giles said.

"A lot of cases, but not all?" Vaclav asked worriedly.

"There is a chance it won't work," Giles said. "In which case, we may simply try to smash the prisms."

"Then why not try smashing them first, in the rides?" Vaclav demanded.

"Because they're prisms," Giles began patiently, but Ms. Calendar turned around from the front seat and said, "Believe me, we want him stopped as much as you do. Rupert's right. The method that has the best chance of working is to gather them together first."

Vaclav nodded, still looking pretty worried.

And then . . .

"Wow," Willow whispered.

The calliope played over the landscape, and the people who had survived the gauntlet of monsters had become hypnotized again . . . or zombified, or whatever one wanted to call it.

Although it was three in the morning by Giles's watch, the carnival was in full swing. The Ferris wheel was completely restored, and shone brightly. The other attractions—rides—sparkled and whirled. The carousel creatures bobbed up and down.

From Giles's distant vantage point, he could see riders, and people pouring into the entrance like cows placidly walking into the slaughterhouse.

Jenny stopped short of the parking lot, which was full of cars. People had driven here in a fog, gotten out, and were trudging slowly toward the carnival.

As the group got out of Jenny's car, Giles said, "Everyone, do you have the wards I made for you?"

They were protective amulets he had cobbled together from things Jenny and he had on hand, guided by Le Malfaiteur's instructions over the library phone.

They all nodded. Then he said, "Jenny, your phone?"

She took it out of a bag clanking with weapons and supplies and handed it to him. He fished into his pocket for the number of the phone that Cordelia had "appropriated" from a person or persons unknown, and dialed the number.

It was answered on the first ring. It was Le Malfaiteur. He said, "*Alors,* Monsieur Giles. You are ready?"

Giles said, "Yes," and gestured to the others to crowd in.

As they did so, the warlock invoked the magick spell that would cloak them in invisibility.

They faded from sight, and then Giles was staring at trees, and streets, and other people shuffling past them.

Quietly the four crept toward the carnival.

"Okay, now what?" Cordelia whispered to Le Malfaiteur as she peered at Xander through the top of the coffin. He didn't look any better.

"I don't know why the coffin's not working," Le Malfaiteur said beside her. Since they were both invisible, she couldn't see him. But she hadn't lied on the phone: He was tall, dark, and probably twenty-four; he had worn perfectly tailored gray wool pants and a navy blue silk shirt. And a thin silver chain, and a matching, tiny hoop in his left ear. Stylish, but with a little bit of flair.

The warlock went on. "Maybe he had to be part of Caligari's evil family or something. Maybe there was a spell to perform first. Ah don't know."

*"You don't know? We stuck him in there and you don't know?"*

"Shh. Someone's coming."

Cordelia held her breath. Along with utilizing the wards, they had put up a closed sign in front of the freak show entrance, but some people just didn't pay any attention or assume that rules and regulations applied to them personally.

She looked fearfully, waiting, watching. And seeing no one.

*Hey, seeing no one!*

"You guys?" she whispered.

"Yes. We're here," Giles replied.

• • •

In the mirror maze Buffy yanked back through the mirror, equally hard.

And whatever had hold of her, released her at once.

"Okay, then," she said.

Then she saw the reflections of the seven robed men.

She whirled around.

They were nowhere to be seen.

And the fun house went dark.

"I am getting really tired of this place," the Slayer muttered.


"Okay, you know your jobs," Giles said. They were standing around Xander's coffin. Or so Giles hoped. They were still invisible. "Each of us has a prism to collect. I'll go to the Chamber of Horrors and get the mirror."

"I will get the one in the Tunnel of Love," Vaclav said. "That's lust. Lust is what brought me under Caligari's thrall."

"Lust can be cool," Cordelia said. She cleared her throat. "I'll get the purple basket in the coin toss."

"The mirror ball in the carousel," Ms. Calendar said. "I'll get that since lust . . . is taken. That's gluttony, right? Seriously, I'm on a diet every other week."

"You would never guess that," Willow murmured. "The crystal ball is the sixth, for envy. And we already have that."

"So you're going to the fun house," Giles reminded her. "To get the mirror in the maze."

"For vanity, right."

"That leaves sloth, for me," Le Malfaiteur said.

"Yes," Vaclav said. "It's on the Ferris wheel. There is a little mirror at the top. Not all people notice it. Only those for whom sloth might be tempting."

"All you did was cheat at cards," Cordelia said.

"Ah, but when one is a warlock, it is so tempting to use magicks instead of stirring oneself to perform physical labor."

"Oh, I'll bet your performance is just . . ." Cordelia trailed off. "How much longer will the invisibility spell last?"

"It's hard to say," Le Malfaiteur confessed. "This is a magickal field. I can sense it growing stronger and stronger. Soon it will negate my magick. Your talismans will only prolong it a little while."

"Then we need to hurry," Willow said anxiously. "Okay, once we've taken the prisms, we bring them back here."

"If you can," Giles replied. "Otherwise smash them where they are."

Buffy ran through the dark, feet flying, Slayer senses fully ratcheted past stun to kill. She remembered the twists and turns of the maze before she got to them, ducked down, around, zooming for all she was worth.

Then it was time to get the heck out of there.

*No problem,* she thought, racing down a corridor as the crazy laughter followed her.

Except there was a problem:

The floor gave way and Buffy tumbled down, down, down, like Alice in the rabbit hole.

She landed on her feet and whirled around. She was in a pit about two stories high and a football field wide. It was carved out of the earth. She could smell the mud, and something else—the distinct odors of evil—sulfur, ash, smoke, and the stench of death. The ground vibrated rhythmically; steam rose from vents in the ground and the sides of the pit. A strange, red glow revealed Caligarius; he was standing approximately a hundred feet away from her.

Only, he wasn't Caligarius any longer.

He was a wicked-tall demon, maybe not as tall as that other guy who had appeared with the wind, but far more terrifying. He was a brilliant red, with horns on his head, and he looked exactly like the sort of bad guy to be tempting people with sins.

*Brrrr.*

He reached down and plucked Buffy up as if she were featherlight and raised her to his face, which was, like, ten feet across.

His laugh rumbled and echoed like a genie laugh in a cartoon.

Wind whipped at her hair. And she heard the calliope music.

It was coming from his chest.

"Slayer," he said, in deep reverb. "I am humbled by your greatness. I have tried numerous times to defeat you."

"Well, you get an F in defeatation," she said. "Don't feel bad. French is the subject that stumps me."

As he laughed again, she ticked her eyes left, right, trying to come up with a strategy. She didn't have enough clues. But she was willing to bet what she smelled was the Hellmouth, and Big Demon Guy was using its energy. Power user, power source.

Except she didn't think she could shut the Hellmouth down.

"This town has been so good for me," he said as if he were reading her mind. "It's so evil here. The Hellmouth has nourished us. The souls here are so ripe."

"That's because we put ourselves in paper bags and sit on the counter for a couple of days."

More reverb laughter. "I like you. I don't want to kill you."

She wrinkled her nose. "Gee, I wish I could say the same. But my mom taught me never to lie." *And speaking of my mom, where is she?*

She wanted to scan her surroundings some more, but as the veteran of many fights against many demons, she knew she'd better stay focused on her adversary.

"All these people will feed me soon enough," he said. "And I'll grow stronger, and I'll move on to the next town. And the next." His eyes narrowed. "I understand there's another hellmouth in Cleveland."

"I'll stop you," Buffy promised him.

"I've been stopped before," he replied easily.

"I will end you."

"So proud." He smiled, revealing more fangs than one demon decently ought to have. "You're one of the proudest human beings I've ever met. You like to go it alone, don't you?"

*I have to go it alone,* Buffy thought silently. *I'm the Slayer.*

But even as she thought the words, she knew that they weren't true. She had friends.

"I'm like you," she said. "I'm so proud it's sinful."

"Your soul will be nectar on my tongue," he said.

And then he picked her up, dangled her above his mouth, and tossed her in.

*Yes!* Vaclav exulted as he traced the mesmerized gazes of the people in the swan boats at the large, ruby heart above his head. They began to activate, as if someone had thrown a switch, falling into each other's arms and kissing.

*I'll climb up the balcony,* he thought, *and . . .*

. . . and then he saw Sandra, sitting in a boat by herself. She was staring at the heart. And she was *smiling*. There was life in her eyes again.

"Sandra?" he whispered, hurrying toward her.

She opened her mouth and extended her hand.

"There he is!" she screamed.

Faces tightened. The shuffling crowd staring at Van Helsing's mirror began to grumble about pushing; about it being too hot; about how lame the Chamber of Horrors was.

When the mirror disappeared, they began to howl with disapproval.

And the rooms filled up with a strange, purplish glow. It cast them in silhouette.

*The jig's certain to be up now, if it wasn't already,* Giles thought as he slipped the mirror under his arm and raced out of the tent.

On the revolving floor of the carousel, Jenny looked from the chariot bench to the mirror ball. She had taken gymnastics in high school, but she doubted she'd be able to vault to so great a height. And if she fell . . .

Then she studied the three black stallions in front of the bench. If she climbed the pole and shimmied over . . .

Yes. A much better solution.

The Ferris wheel turned slowly as Le Malfaiteur, still invisible, watched for a chance to sneak onto one of the carriages.

But none of the passengers wanted to get off. Too tired, they said. Too relaxed.

*Too lazy,* Le Malfaiteur thought.

The people in line began to grumble.

Then he thought he heard a scream, thin and strangled, from the topmost carriage.

When it came back down, no one was sitting in it.

*They 'ave been taken,* he thought.

He felt his magickal field shift. As he had explained to the others, the power of the carnival was increasing.

He considered what he was doing. Perhaps it was too complicated. The girl—Cordelia—was beautiful, and she was attracted to him. She had inadvertently freed him by reciting her Weakening Spell while Ethan Rayne was distracted. But she loved the boy who lay in the coffin, whether she knew it or not. So it was doubtful that she would willingly step into the embrace of Le Malfaiteur. And he was tired of séducing women with magicks.

These people were not wealthy. They would offer him no financial reward if he helped them further.

And if Professor Caligari's minions caught him, he was certain to be sorry.

He wasn't sure why he should bother.

He looked up at the top of the wheel. It was a long way up.

A lot of effort.


Buffy was suffocating. She lay on the floor of the room where she'd seen the calliope while the clowns pranced around her, doubled over with hooting laughter.

Caligarius turned and smiled at her from over his shoulder as he put his hands on the calliope keyboard. He played a dirgelike funeral march she had heard before, then stopped and shook his head.

"'Pavane for a Dead Princess' is far more appropriate," he said.

He played on as Buffy clutched her neck, fighting for air.

Then the calliope notes went sour, and faint, and she figured she was dying.

But the clowns stopped laughing and looked at Caligarius. He frowned and squinted, staring hard at

Buffy; then he cleared his throat, and resumed.

The calliope screeched. The sound was fainter still.

"What are you doing?" he blurted.

And although Buffy knew that what she was doing was nothing, she smiled.

That flustered him. He rose from the calliope and advanced on her, his image doubling and blurring. Buffy was on the verge of passing out and trying hard not to show it. Something was going wrong, and Caligarius was freaking out. From her point of view, that could only be good.

The room flickered.

Two of the clowns disappeared.

Then the side of the room vanished.

The clowns came back. The side of room reappeared, but a part of the ceiling winked out. There was blackness above it, and twinkling stars.

"What's going on?" he said, grabbing her arm.

Big mistake. Maybe this was an illusion, maybe she was really in the demon's stomach, but it seemed to hurt Caligarius when she grabbed his throat and squeezed as hard as she could.

He gagged and tried to pull away.

But Buffy held on.


The evil carousel of doom flickered. Lights on, lights off, lights on again. Drums banging, drums . . . silent. The hunters were people . . . they were animated figures. The fiery steeds rose up.

Froze.

Descended.

Xander traded glances with the girl beside him. They both looked at the guy on the other black horse. He swallowed hard and nodded at them. They had a plan: When Xander gave the word, they would flank him as they broke the chains of as many riders as they could. Then they would fight their jailers. Xander didn't have much of a plan past that, but at least it was better than waiting for another round of torture.

The guy licked his lips and said to Xander, "Your call, man."

The carousel slowed down. Principal Snyder looked over his shoulder and said, "If I'm not the first person you free, you are having detention for the rest of eternity."

*Maybe he's just plain nuts,* Xander thought. *That would explain a lot.*

"Okay, this is it," Xander announced. To the girl, "Get ready. On my count."

But before he could even say "one," the carousel went completely dark. His horse bucked, and then it stiffened.

Cheers and screams mingled in the darkness.

"Three!" he shouted.

The carousel vanished, and he tumbled to the ground.

He began to run.


Le Malfaiteur shifted his weight and yawned.

*I'm being affected,* he realized. *I just don't have the energy for this. We have the perfect word in French: ennui.*

*This is not my battle. I wish them well, all of them.*

He ambled away from the Ferris wheel, preparing to leave. He had no idea where Ethan and his little girl-friend had gone. He didn't care, as long as their paths never crossed. Revenge was too much work to even ponder.

He looked down and saw that he could see the vague outline of his hand. His spell of invisibility was wearing off.

He hurried his pace. It was easier to leave quickly than it would be to fight his way out of the carnival.

"Adieu," he said, thinking of Cordelia. He kissed his fingers and blew her a kiss.

Xander landed in the midway, or what passed for it in hell, the food stalls and games all lit up. But there was no one playing. There were no customers. Except two: Carl Palmer was flinging coins at stacks and stacks of glassware. He was chained to the booth, and he had been severely beaten.

And was that . . . *Cordelia?*

Xander ducked around a concession stand to stare at her. He caught his reflection in the shiny surface of a glass platter, and he was stunned. He looked worse than Carl.

Then everything flickered, as it had on the carousel.

Cordelia cried out and Xander ran to her, throwing his arms around her; they passed through her but she turned around and screamed, "Xander!'

"Cordelia!" He lunged for her again.

Missed again.

"It's a prism!" She darted forward and grabbed a purple basket made of glass.

Then she disappeared. And like the carousel, the midway went dark.

"Cordy!" Xander shouted. "Carl!"

"Who's that?" Carl shouted back through the darkness. "Where are you?"

Xander ran to his voice.

Willow stood in front of the fun house, which was glowing with a silvery light. She did not want to go inside. But she mustered up her courage and took one step in; then another, twisting and turning in the metallic glow.

*I hope I'm not being exposed to radiation,* she thought anxiously.

She thought she felt someone behind her. She cried out and whirled around.

Above her head, a skull wearing a pirate hat shouted, "Arr!" Laughter echoed down the corridor.

Willow stumbled left, right; she got twisted around more times than she could count.

She was trembling from head to toe. She was so scared that tears began streaming down her face.

But she kept on going.

*Buffy told us the layout, pretty much. Shouldn't I be coming to the mirror maze soon?*

As she turned another corner, she caught her breath.

A clown statue smiled from the end of the corridor. She raised a hand, wondering if it could see her.

Waved back and forth to see if it reacted. It didn't move, didn't blink.

Didn't try to kill her.

*Maybe I'm still invisible. If I could find the mirrors, I'd know.*

She crept forward.

The clown remained motionless.

She tiptoed along the left wall, trying to keep as much distance between herself and the clown.

She dodged around it.

And around the next corner, she reached her destination: the mirror maze.

Willow stared in amazement. Every single mirror was smashed. Every one.

*Is this really bad, or kind of bad?* she wondered. *Or was Giles wrong?* She didn't know what to do now. He had said for each of them to bring the prism back if they could.

She went past panel after panel, shattered into pieces that were strewn across the floor.

Where they had stood, silvery rectangles glowed and vibrated; and she heard faint shouting emanating from them. It sounded like human voices, like a big, intense, angry crowd.

*Is it the souls being tortured in the hell dimension?*

She tried to make herself call Xander's name. But her throat was dry as dust.

Then she looked down, and saw a blur of her hand.

*The spell is losing power,* she thought. *I'd better get back to the others.*

Sparing one more look at the glowing rectangles,

she gathered up as many fragments of the mirrors as she could and made her way back out of the fun house.

"Anyone here?" Giles asked as he carried the mirror into the freak show and laid it beside the crystal ball, alongside Xander's coffin, as had been agreed. Once he let go of it, it was visible again.

Then he saw his hands, and his shoes. He was visible again.

At that moment Willow ran into the room with large jagged pieces of mirrors in her hands. He saw her clearly.

"Giles, oh my God!" she cried. "I went into the maze and all the mirrors were broken!"

"Let me help you," he said. "You're about to cut yourself." He rushed to her and carefully took the shards, putting them beside the crystal ball. What happened?"

"I don't know."

"Did you notice anyone about? Did you see Buffy?"

She shook her head. "No. A clown, but it didn't move. Maybe it broke the mirrors."

"Perhaps Buffy broke them."

"I don't know," she said. "The entire fun house was glowing, Giles. Everything was silver. And on the way here, I saw the carousel. It was glowing all yellow!"

"The Chamber of Horrors was bathed in a sort of black light," Giles said. "Perhaps when we remove the prisms, their absence causes some kind of refraction of light." He looked down at the fragments. "I don't know what this means. But we'll proceed on our course and see where it leads, yes?"

"Yes," Willow murmured. She felt somehow responsible for the broken mirror, although she'd done nothing to cause it. She was becoming more afraid. Things weren't going as planned.

*We've always pulled it off before,* she reminded herself. *But Buffy's the Slayer because some other girl didn't pull it off.*

*Buffy won't fail. But we might.*

At that moment the room they stood in seemed to . . . flicker. Fairyland lost its distinct edges; then it returned.

"What's happening?" Willow asked, moving in a circle.

"I don't know. Perhaps more of the same effect." Giles examined the mirror he had brought, experimentally shining it against the walls.

There were footsteps, light and quick.

It was Ms. Calendar, also fully materialized, carrying the mirror ball. "Rupert, the carousel is giving off this golden light! And the Tunnel of Love is shimmering with some kind of scarlet energy."

"Then perhaps Vaclav managed to steal the red heart," Giles said. "Did you see him?"

"No," Ms. Calendar replied, looking worried.

"I hope nothing happened to him," Willow murmured.

The freak show winked out again, longer this time.

"What's that?" Ms. Calendar cried, her dark eyes flashing. "What's happening?"

"I think the carnival is beginning to break apart," Giles told them.

"That's great!" Willow said. "Right?"

"Yes, if it happens fast enough, and if it's a complete job," Giles replied. "However, they'll certainly trace the source here. We have to think about leaving."

"What about the destruction spell?" Willow asked. "Should we do it now?"

Giles considered. "Perhaps we can wait a little while longer for Cordelia and Le Malfaiteur. But if they don't show soon, it might be prudent to go ahead and try to do as much damage as we can."

"We're missing two prisms," Willow said. "All the mirrors in the fun house were broken, which was probably a good thing. I'm not sure I would have been able to break the glass."

"Buffy didn't mention anything about that when she told us about the fun house." Giles picked up a shard. "I wonder if she did this."

"Or someone or some*thing* else," Ms. Calendar ventured.

"Gulp," Willow said.

Ms. Calendar nodded. "Yes. Bringing the pieces of the mirror was good, Willow." She took a breath. "I have the printout of the incantation," she said, reaching in the pocket of her skirt and unfolding it.

"We'll start arranging the objects in a circle." Giles gestured for Willow to help him.

They were almost finished making the circle when Cordelia rushed in. The purple basket was cradled in her arms. "It was so weird! I got, like, stuck, and I thought I saw Xander, but . . . I'm so confused. I think I was hypnotized again and *ooh*, this basket is pretty."

She held it in her outstretched hands, smiling with a dazed expression on her face.

"Put it down in our circle," Giles told her. "It's tempting you."

She groaned.

"*Cordelia.*"

She set it next to the mirror.

"All right. I guess this is it," Ms. Calendar said.

"Help me!" It was Vaclav. "Help!"

He came barreling toward them with the ruby heart against his chest. In close pursuit, horned demons and humans raced after him. The girl who had been in the coffin was one of them, a bright smile stretched across her face, although her eyes were vacant and unfocused.

"We need to erect a barrier!" Ms. Calendar spread her arms and began to chant. Giles recognized the structure, if not the precise vocabulary, of a Sumerian warding spell. He joined in, striving to reinforce it as best he could.

The warding spell worked. The horde of attackers smashed into the invisible barrier Giles and Ms. Calendar had erected. Their monstrous faces contorted with rage; they balled their fists, claws, and talons and pummeled at the perimeter, roaring with fury.

"Run out the back! We'll try to hold them!" Giles said to Willow, standing with his legs wide apart and extending his arms. "*Ta-mir-o! Baal! Cthulhu! Jezebel!*"

"Not him again!" Cordelia protested.

"You don't have the blade!" Ms. Calendar reminded him.

"Yes, I do," Giles said, yanking it out of his pocket.

"Don't call that Astorrith guy," Cordelia begged him. "He'll take out half of Sunnydale."

"Cordelia's right, Rupert," Ms. Calendar said. "It won't help."

Giles thought a moment, then nodded his agreement; Ms. Calendar turned to Willow and said, "All right, then. Let's proceed with the spell of destruction as fast as we can. Willow, you need to help us with this, good?"

"Okay." Willow licked her lips and took a deep breath as she looked anxiously at the horde of monsters pushing at the barrier. "I'm ready."

"We only have six prisms!" Vaclav protested.

"We can't wait any longer," Giles replied. "Jenny, please, begin."

Ms. Calendar took a slow, cleansing breath. Then she began to speak in a low, authoritative voice, *"In the name of the Goddess of Destruction, I order the beating heart of this demon to shatter!"*

She went on, and Vaclav held his breath as the young red-haired Willow joined in when Ms. Calendar invited her. Also Mr. Giles.

*"These chambers must sunder! Hear me, dark Lady, and break his heart, break it, make it shatter!"*

Vaclav's mouth filled with bile as he pressed his fists against his mouth to keep from screaming.

"Nothing's happening!" Cordelia cried.

The five looked at one another. Vaclav saw frustration on their faces. Also despair. And terror, and he knew they were mirrored on his own face.

But he also saw a fine resolve settle over them. They were noble people, these friends of Angel's. He could not be one of them—he had done too much evil—but he could help them.

"So . . . we need all of them, right?" Cordelia said shrilly. "The prisms? And we're missing the Ferris wheel one?"

Just then, the barrier they had created . . . wobbled. Vaclav had no other word for it. It was weakening. He knew why.

"The magicks are building," he told them. "It is the Rising. The power of my master is at its zenith tonight! The dark forces gather. We are lost!"

"Great," Cordelia bit off. "So let's get the hell out of here."

"I'm afraid we may no longer have that choice," Giles said as he and Ms. Calendar moved toward the barrier. "Let's try to keep it going," he told her. "For as long as we can."

She nodded.

"If we can't leave, then someone needs to get the prism and bring it back here," Willow said.

Vaclav raised his hand. "Me. I'll do it." He was moved by their courage; he had been a part of evil for so long, he hadn't thought there was any good left inside him. His love for Sandra and his admiration of these people—and Angel—had brought it forth. "I will do it," Vaclav vowed, laying his hand over his heart. "Or die trying."

Giles hesitated.

Cordelia huffed. "*You* can't go," Cordelia said to Giles. "You have to stay here and help with the ward. Same with Ms. Calendar. And Willow is your, like, magickal backup plus, *please*, she'd get, like, two feet before they slaughtered her. And *I* have a fear of heights. So. He's our only hope." She smiled grimly at him. "Since my guy bailed."

"We don't know that," Willow said. "He might have been killed." She looked stricken. "I mean, he might be delayed."

"I can do it," Vaclav insisted. "They haven't come through the back way. If I go now, I might be able to get out."

"Go then," Giles said softly. "And thank you."

Vaclav inclined his head. "I will not fail."

Then he raced out the exit.

Ms. Calendar looked over her shoulder at Willow. "Willow, help me erect another ward at the exit. I'll teach you the words." She looked at her earnestly. "Can you do that?"

Willow swallowed hard. "Um, yes, yes, I can."


Buffy kept squeezing Caligarius around the neck as the room flickered and shifted and changed and rearranged—from room to enormous, viscous internal body parts to room again. And as she squeezed, Caligarius grew; he was becoming the demon once more. She couldn't let that happen; she didn't understand what exactly was going on, but she knew she had to kill him as he was or . . .

He shrank back down. Fighting to pull her off him, his gaze ticked anxiously from her to the calliope behind him.

*To the calliope behind him.*

She looked.

The center of it was glowing a brilliant emerald green. It was pulsing rhythmically.

Green steam was shooting from the pipes.

No, not steam . . . green demon blood.

*It's his heart,* she thought.

But it didn't matter. She had no more oxygen; she was beginning to faint. She wouldn't be able to do anything about it.

She was going to fail.

And he knew it. An evil, triumphant smile spread across his face. His eyes glittered.

*"What now, proud one?"* he taunted her.

*Now I'm going to die,* Buffy the Vampire Slayer thought, beginning to let go. *Mom, I'm so sorry. Willow, Xander, Giles . . .*

Vaclav flew like the wind blowing across the steppes of his native Bulgaria. The carnival had disintegrated into pandemonium; the patrons had awakened from the mesmerizing effect of the soulcatchers and the calliope. Now they were screaming hysterically and running in panic from Caligari's minions. Vampires had joined the fray.

Vaclav had to stop the carnage, end this here, now. He had lost Sandra—she was still one of *them*—but he could save Angel's friends.

He ran so fast he almost fell over his own feet. The carousel was glowing; the Tunnel of Love as well. Mr. Giles was right; when the prisms were taken, the rides that concealed them glowed with color.

Since the Ferris wheel did not throw off any unusual hue, he could assume that Le Malfaiteur had failed in his duty.

There was no longer a line of people waiting to get on, and no attendants overseeing the ride. All the carriages were empty, and still the wheel turned.

With a mad dash, he hopped into a carriage as the wheel swooped downward. As it arced back up into the air, someone cried, "Vaclav!"

Terrified, he looked back down at the ground. It was Madame Lazabra, surrounded by the freaks of the freak show. He had wondered where they had been. All he knew was that somehow Le Malfaiteur had been detained. Vaclav had dared to hope that that meant he had destroyed them.

Otto, the man with three legs, was aiming a crossbow at him while the twelve dwarves of Fairyland raced to the Ferris wheel ramp and piled into the next approaching carriage.

Their carriage was three below his; as he looked down on them, they shook their fists at him. Six of them scrabbled out of the carriage and began to climb up the superstructure. They moved much more quickly than Vaclav would have thought them able.

From the ground Otto let a crossbow bolt fly.

It hurtled through the air, and missed.

But the next one might not.

He crouched inside the carriage, gazing fearfully over the edge at the ground below as he was swept aloft. The members of Caligari's dread family were massing. Beyond, he saw domes of ethereal color surrounding some of the other rides—the Tunnel of Love, the fun house, the Chamber of Horrors, the carousel.

Demons and humans were beginning to climb into other carriages in pursuit of him, he knew; others crowded around the console at the base, pushing buttons, then pulling on the emergency brake.

With a terrible groan, the Ferris wheel slowed, then ground to a halt.

*They will get me,* he thought sickly. *They will stop me.* Then he saw a flash of movement on the superstructure of the wheel itself. He squinted, seeing nothing . . . or was there a hand gripping a metal strut?

Then he heard a voice.

"What the 'ell, *merde*!" the voice shouted. "Vaclav?"

It was the voice that had cast the spell of invisibility over them on the cell phone. It was Le Malfaiteur.

"How do you know me?" Vaclav shouted back.

"I was Ethan Rayne's dog. I saw you at the encampment."

The hand flickered back into Vaclav's range of vision, and then the man's head.

"I can see you!" Vaclav told him.

Le Malfaiteur intoned the words of the invisibility spell; then he vanished.

"Where have you been?" Vaclav said. "They waited and waited!"

"I was . . . I'm 'elping now," he said. "I thought of Cordelia, so lovely. Too pretty to die." He chuckled. "Ethan and I both have an eye for the ladies."

"Well, she may be dead by now!" Vaclav told him. "You have to get the prism. They need it to complete their spell!"

He heard shouting; voices getting louder. One of his "friends," Max, who was wearing his true visage—he was a purple chitenous demon with claw-like legs—was scrambling toward them like a man-sized crab; he was being followed by Bettina, the Lindwurm, who was inching up the metal girders. Heading for him.

He added, "You need to stay invisible. If they see you, they'll go after you."

"I can't 'old it very long," Le Malfaiteur said. "The magickal field is too strong."

"Hurry!" Vaclav implored him.

Le Malfaiteur did not reply. Vaclav waited, then called out, "Where are you?"

And then he realized that he shouldn't talk to him any longer. Their enemies—once his only family!—were getting closer. He could see their eyes, which seemed so foreign to him now.

"Vaclav, damn you, what are you doing?" Max shouted at him.

Vaclav took a breath. He ticked a glance where he had last seen Le Malfaiteur. He could see the barest outline of his body. He had moved an astonishing distance; of course, he was a warlock!

But he was becoming more solid.

*I have to do something,* Vaclav thought.

He looked at Max, and at all the others. At the glowing domes surrounding the rides. He thought of the centuries he had traveled with the carnival; he could hear the chuffing of the horses and the jingling of the bells on the Gypsy's wagon.

*Maybe it's not too late. Maybe they will take me back,* he thought desperately. *I'm so terrified.*

But he knew what Caligari would do to him. He would take his mind, and make him like Sandra, and that new one, Carl.

He peered over at Le Malfaiteur. He was almost there. But he was nearly fully visible.

He stood in the carriage. "What we're doing is evil!" he shouted at Max. At Bettina, whose underbelly was beginning to glow as she moved into position to shoot her heat at him, wrapping herself around a girder. "The carnival must be stopped!"

"*You* must be stopped!" Max shouted back.

*Yes,* Vaclav thought, shaking with fear. They were focusing on him.

Rushing at him.

Getting ready to kill him.


"You are dying, Slayer," Caligarius crowed as the world grew dimmer around Buffy. She couldn't breathe. She wasn't sure her lungs were even working anymore.

Things were flickering around them, and she could tell he was freaking out.

But he was still standing, and she was not.

"You are dying," he said again, maybe to rub it in. "And Sunnydale will die with you. Even better, it will go to hell. And it will be your fault."

*My fault?*

Those were fighting words.

*My fault?*

Better than any magick spell on earth, they galvanized her.

Blindly she pushed past him, flinging herself at the calliope. She reached out both her hands and grabbed at it.

*If this is his heart, I'm going to squeeze the life out of it.*

It was not pretty, but death rarely was.

Vaclav's self-sacrifice had bought Le Malfaiteur the time he needed to get to the prism. It was a simple little mirror secured to a metal rod, and angled such that as one passed, one might take a glance into it . . . and feel so incredibly lazy.

He chuckled and reached out a hand. He still didn't know why he had bothered to come back. On the one hand, he had nursed a niggling little fear that perhaps if Caligari won the day, Ethan would return to claim a reward. Ethan Rayne on his own was a formidable foe, but allied with one such as this . . . Ethan might do more than turn him into an animal next time their paths crossed.

Was it self-preservation, then? Or . . . was it because of that pretty *jeune fille*, Cordelia? Hard to say. At any rate, *bien*, here he was, like some ridiculous musketeer in a novel by Dumas.

But he plucked the prism like a ripe piece of fruit—a tempting apple, perhaps—and recast his invisibility spell.

They were still tearing Vaclav's body to shreds.
*Requiescat in pace.*

In the freak show, the monsters slammed against the wards that Giles, Ms. Calendar, and Willow had erected and strengthened numerous times.

"The barriers are weakening," Giles said.

*Oh my God,* Cordelia thought, *we're gonna die!*

And then, like some kind of hero, Le Malfaiteur appeared beside her. Poof! Just like that! He was holding a small mirror in his hand, and Cordelia cried, "Wow, am I glad to see you!"

"And I you," he said, laughing, as he grabbed her around the waist and gave her the best, juiciest kiss. It was an earth-shaking, mind-blowing—

"Ritual," she said breathlessly. "Now."

"Now," Giles agreed.

While Le Malfaiteur strengthened the wards, Cordelia placed the mirror with the other prisms. Then Giles, Ms. Calendar, Willow, and Le Malfaiteur spread out their hands.

*"By the dark Goddess of Destruction, by the power of entropy, we call upon the ending! The ruination! Break this heart!"*

Willow was crying, afraid of the strange, shadowy sensation that was pouring through her as they chanted; and she was grieving for Vaclav. Le Malfaiteur had told them of his sacrifice.

But they had to press on. They had to try to destroy this thing, now—

*"Make the heart of the demon end, make it stop!"*

*"We call upon the Goddess, the Dark Lady, stop it now!"*

"Oh my God, something is happening!" Willow screamed.

Blinding white light filled the room.

The carnival was strangling. Withering.

And though Caligari knew it, he was not willing to go down without a fight; he reappeared as his huge, demonic self, clutching his heart as Buffy, trapped inside it, did all the damage she possibly could.

"I would have made you my queen," he thundered.

She didn't know how she could hear him. How she could understand the words he spoke. She was blind from lack of oxygen. She couldn't feel. She could only . . . slay.

So she ripped and clawed and tore. She swam in green demon blood, drowned in it, as his heart began to pound too fast, too hard, trapping her, pulling her inside the chambers and flinging her from one side to another.

*I'm dying,* she thought. *But so is he.*

"I will not die. The souls will feed me," he gasped. "They will feed me and I will rise again! I always have. And I will now!"

The carnival glowed with lights, refracting and shimmering against the black velvet night. Seven attractions blazed with light—the six that had housed prisms, and the freak show—and then they all became white, crystalline, and pure.

In the fun house, figures burst out of the glowing rectangles: Carl Palmer, the Hahn twins, Principal Snyder and the carousel riders; and leading the charge—Xander Lavelle Harris.

They were the souls Caligari had trapped and fed on for millennia. Following Xander, they flooded the fun house as the lights flashed and the laughter echoed down the corridors for the last time  thousands of shimmering ovals poured out after them, having no form other than light.

But having an agenda nevertheless: escape.

"No!" Caligari shouted. "No, stop them! Stop *him*!"

Then he fell to the earth in an enormous, ground-shaking collapse.

Buffy yanked and pulled her way out of his chest cavity, swimming in foul demon blood as it gushed out of the exit wound she created.

She panted, sucking in breath after breath. Her lungs felt seared; her mind began to clear.

She turned and stared at the demon. He was beginning to disintegrate already.

She slipped and slid on the viscous liquid as she cried, "Mom! Where are you?"

The carnival shifted and shimmered, a kaleidoscope of the disguises it had worn: burlesque houses and opium dens and the Grand Guignol of France; public executions and cockfights and medieval jousts.

Witch burnings and Druid festivals; raves and concerts and gladiatorial combats.

Images crisscrossed one another as they winked in and out of existence, as the people in the images lost definition, some to decay into skeletons, others to dissolve into light.

And then Caligari's body came apart in huge, decaying chunks. Maggots wriggled in the flesh. It quickly liquefied and sank into the ground in rivulets, soaking the earth with its foulness.

Buffy staggered backward, covering her mouth. The need to inhale was stronger than her revulsion, but she hated drawing the terrible stench into her body.

From out of the ground a black mist rose on geysers of steam. It was pure, distilled evil. It was the heart of darkness.

It was what was left of Caligari, and if she could have flung herself into the air to destroy it, she would have.

The steam and the foulness formed the shape of a horned death's head, which hovered high into the air and glared down at Buffy.

"It is the Rising," it told her. "It is not too late to join me. We can start anew."

She realized it was trying to appeal to her pride. She was amazed.

"No, you can lose, *loser*," Buffy said, heaving with exhaustion. "You can end."

It glared down at her one more time. Then it began

to dissipate, fading out against the starry, moonlit sky.

Buffy staggered forward, calling for her mother.

The freak show was gone. Giles, Ms. Calendar, Cordelia, and Willow stared in wonderment at one another. They were standing in the clearing by Blessed Memories Cemetery.

Then they looked down at Xander, who was lying on the grass at Cordelia's feet, bathed in moonlight and in the strange lights filling the sky.

He opened his eyes.

And Willow and Cordelia both burst into tears.

"Buffy!"

Joyce Summers ran to her daughter in the dark clearing in the forest.

They embraced, hard. Buffy closed her eyes, wincing because she was covering her mother with demon blood.

Only she wasn't.

There was no demon blood.

Buffy looked around. All trace of the carnival was gone. No rides, no lights, no people, no demons.

She listened.

No calliope.

She looked toward Sunnydale. There was a hazy glow of flames on the horizon.

There was still work to be done, then.

"What's going on?" Joyce asked, bewildered.

"It's all right, Mom," Buffy said.

The two held each other.

Then Xander, Cordelia, Giles, and Ms. Calendar ran toward them.

She looked at Giles.

"Where's Angel?" she asked.


*It's not a bad way to go,* Angel thought, as he beheaded another Shrieker with a sword he had taken from an orc. He was covered with green demon blood, and plenty of wounds of his own.

*But I would have liked to say good-bye to Buffy.*

The ground shook and he thought, *What now?*

He wasn't ready for what he saw: a glowing swarm of oval lights, rising into the sky and arcing across the face of the moon like a phalanx of comets. Darting and shimmering. Dancing and rejoicing.

Souls. Liberated.

*Buffy did it.*

Angel did something he very rarely did: He smiled.

Around him, his attackers stopped and stared. A trio of albino poisoners spat venom on the sidewalk; as it sizzled, they slunk away, casting anxious glances over their shoulders at Angel, who let them go.

Weapons dropped. Vampires darted back into the shadows.

The fight was over.

There might be some mop-up, but the good guys had won.

*She did it,* Angel thought again.

*But did she survive it?*

His answer walked out of the smoke, slowly at

first; and then, as Buffy Summers the Vampire Slayer saw him, she ran to him. She whispered, "Angel," and put her arms around him.

And his soul soared.

# Epilogue

It was really over. Giles, Ms. Calendar, and Le Malfaiteur had cast runes, searched for portents. The carnival was gone. The nightmare, ended.

"It's so weird how no one, like, notices," Cordelia said, as she admired her new choker. And her pendant. And her earrings. "I mean, saltwater pearls this big are so *rare*."

The Yasumi company had richly rewarded Cordelia for foiling a robbery and saving the life of the salesclerk, whom Cordelia had gone back to and untied. She had her picture in the paper, which caused her no end of grief, because she had a scratch on her cheek. Giles told her to wear it proudly, because it was a symbol of her bravery in battle.

"Oh, *please*," she had sneered.

"It is remarkable," Giles said, of the oblivious after-state of the little town still swimming in denial. "I think we are able to remember what happened because of the magicks we used."

"Or we're just lucky that way," Buffy said with a sigh.

He, Buffy, Willow, Cordelia, Xander, and Ms. Calendar were standing in the clearing where the carnival had stood. It was gone now, all trace . . . and all memory of it. Not a single person beyond their small company had any recollection that Professor Copernicus Caligari's Traveling Carnival had come to town. As there had never been any permits or articles about it in the paper, there was no proof that it had ever been there.

No one remembered the crazed swath of destruction caused by Astorrith. Giles's condo was said to have burned down because of a gas leak. While it was being rebuilt, he was staying at a nearby hotel, and Ms. Calendar was helping him shop for new clothes and kitchen things.

Buffy thought he looked great in his new Dockers and loose-fitting sweater. But it was obvious he felt like he wasn't decently clothed. He kept tugging at everything and muttering under his breath.

But of the carnival of souls: All anyone remembered was a terrible storm, and some deaths. One of them had been the bludgeoning of Anita Palmer, Carl and Mariann Palmer's mother.

Carl was in custody for the homicide, and under

suspicion about his sister's disappearance.

Giles had promised Buffy he would try to help him get out of it. But she wasn't sure Carl wanted out. He didn't recall why he had killed his mother, but he knew that he had.

She felt so sorry for him.

*If I can explain it to him, I will,* she decided.

Joyce Summers's memory was also blank. Which made things ever so much easier for the Slayer.

Witness the brand-new kick dress she was wearing!

As for Vaclav . . . they didn't know what had happened to him, but they were glad he had helped. They had a moment of silence for him. And then they moved on, just as Sunnydale had.

As for the chaos . . . no one remembered much of that, either. The dead were buried with reasonable explanations for their passing. Car accidents, mostly. There really weren't very many—by Sunnydale standards.

Life was back to normal . . . by Sunnydale standards as well.

"Well, we'd better go to school," Buffy said to the others.

Giles drove them back. They trooped into the auditorium where they had once died a thousand deaths in a talent show. Giles, almost literally.

They found seats, and settled in. Jenny Calendar sat next to Giles, and they smiled at each other.

The Hahns were there, too, in amazingly nerdy sweaters with moose faces on them. They sat beside each other in the center of an otherwise empty row, the outcasts they had always been . . . or nearly always.

Principal Snyder came out to a mixed chorus of boos and cheers. Like the others, his face was undamaged. Well, except for its natural appearance.

"How can he not remember that I saved his immortal soul?" Xander kvetched. "That is so unfair."

Snyder held out his hands for silence. The students all settled down.

"I'm happy to announce the results of our student council fund-raising survey," he relayed, with an expression that was anything but happy. He actually looked like he was chewing glass.

"We're going to have a blood drive." He huffed. Then he threw down the clipboard. "This is idiotic. We'll have a carnival, just like all the other schools."

"This is so inappropriate," Cordelia said. "He has no clue." Then she brightened. "Ooh, carnival! I'll be the queen!"

Buffy exchanged weary glances with the others.

Willow said quietly, "You know, even with the lust spell, Angel was never attracted to Cordelia."

Buffy blushed. "Wow. That's true."

"Score one for Dead Guy," Xander said grumpily.

"Participation will be mandatory," Snyder went on.

*It always is,* Buffy thought.

She whispered to Willow, "Anywhere But Here."

Willow thought. "Tuscany, John Cusack, riding mopeds."

"Good," Buffy complimented her.

"Your turn," Willow said.

Buffy cocked her head. "Graveyard, Angel, smoochies."

Willow frowned slightly. "That's not Anywhere But Here, Buffy. That's *here*."

Buffy smiled. "Yeah. It is."

# ABOUT THE AUTHOR

Bestselling author **Nancy Holder** has published more than sixty books and more than two hundred short stories. She has received four Bram Stoker Awards for fiction from the Horror Writers Association, and her books have been translated into more than two dozen languages. A graduate of the University of California at San Diego, Nancy is currently a writing teacher at the school. She lives in San Diego with her daughter, Belle, and their growing assortment of pets. Please visit her at www.nancyholder.com.

"I'm the Slayer. Slay-er. Chosen One? She who hangs out a lot in cemeteries? Ask around. Look it up: 'Slayer *comma* The.'"

—Buffy, "Doomed"

INTO EVERY GENERATION,

A SLAYER IS BORN

Seven years, 144 episodes, three Slayers, two networks, two vampires with souls(!), two Watchers, three principals, two pigs, one Master, one Mayor, countless potentials: It all adds up to one hit show.

The Watcher's Guides, Volumes 1–3, are the *complete* collection of authorized companions to the hit show *Buffy the Vampire Slayer*. Don't be caught dead without them!

# Buffy the Vampire Slayer™

## Into every generation,
### a Slayer is born . .

Before there was Buffy, there were other Slayers—called to protect the world from the undead. Led by their Watchers, they have served as our defense—across the globe and throughout history.

In these collections of short stories written by best-selling authors, travel through time to these other Slayers. From France in the fourteenth century to Iowa in the 1980s, the young women have protected the world. Their stories—and legacies—are unforgettable.

You've waited long enough.
Find out what happened to
Buffy *after* the Hellmouth
ate Sunnydale, in this
exciting new book!

SUNNYDALE WAS ONLY THE WARM UP

QUEEN of the
SLAYERS

NANCY HOLDER

*Picking up just after the series
finale,* Queen of the Slayers *is an exclusive
look into the much-missed characters' lives.*

With the closing of the Hellmouth and the "awakening" of
hundreds of potential Slayers, Buffy Summers thought she had
overturned the Slayer's self-sacrifice and earned herself a
much-deserved break of normalcy. But the thrill of victory is
short-lived. The Forces of Darkness are not ones to graciously
accept defeat.

Willow's magickal distribution of the Slayer essence left girls
across the world discovering their latent power. But soon Buffy
hears word that a number of the fresh Slayers are being
coerced to join an army of Slayers—governed by the mysterious
"Queen of the Slayers," an awesome evil determined to claim
the intoxicating Slayer essence for herself. The deciding
apocalypse is drawing near. Alliances are formed and loyalties
betrayed as it comes down to Slayer versus Slayer, leading to an
ultimate battle of champions—from Buffy's past and present.